"Did you know you were pregnant when we slept together?

"I don't sleep around with married women, lady, especially pregnant ones. You've made me something I really did not want to be."

Never much good at lying, Becca realized her mouth was still hanging open when Aiden stopped his tirade.

"You thought I was married?"

He scowled. "Not then. But when I saw you here—pregnant as a house—what was I supposed to think?"

"Uh…" It finally registered in Becca's tired, stressed-out brain. He thought she'd been cheating on her husband. He didn't know she didn't have a husband. He didn't suspect the baby was his.

A nervous, relieved laugh escaped before she could stop herself.

"Wait a minute." Aiden peered at her in the gathering darkness. Then he snatched up her left hand. "You're not wearing a ring."

Becca pulled her fingers back. "I'm not married." It was too late for that.

"If you're not married, whose baby is that?" He pointed at her belly as if it were repugnant to him.

"It's mine."

Dear Reader,

Have you ever held on to a belief until some life-changing event forced you to rethink things?
Such is the attitude of Aiden Rodas. Kids in his future? Bite your tongue! After the way his father abandoned him as a young child, Aiden is determined the Rodas line will end with him.

But Aiden didn't count on Becca Thomas, an older career woman who's let life pass her by and is now playing catch-up by having a baby of her own, on her own. When Aiden discovers that the baby Becca is carrying is his—holy moly!—he becomes determined to always be there for his child. And that means acknowledging to the world that he had a lot to do with Becca's pregnancy.

Aiden doesn't fit into Becca's plans at all, but this expectant dad won't leave her alone, and soon Becca's not sure she wants him to.

I hope you enjoy my twist on a May-December romance. I love hearing from readers through my Web site at www.MelindaCurtis.com or at P.O. Box 150, Denair, CA 95316.

Melinda Curtis

EXPECTANT FATHER
Melinda Curtis

HARLEQUIN®

TORONTO • NEW YORK • LONDON
AMSTERDAM • PARIS • SYDNEY • HAMBURG
STOCKHOLM • ATHENS • TOKYO • MILAN • MADRID
PRAGUE • WARSAW • BUDAPEST • AUCKLAND

ISBN 0-373-71301-0

EXPECTANT FATHER

Copyright © 2005 by Melinda Wooten.

Printed in U.S.A.

Don't miss any of our special offers. Write to us at the
following address for information on our newest releases.

Harlequin Reader Service
U.S.: 3010 Walden Ave., P.O. Box 1325, Buffalo, NY 14269
Canadian: P.O. Box 609, Fort Erie, Ont. L2A 5X3

To all the fathers out there who never cease to be surprised
when they're told they're going to be a dad
(this is how babies are made, guys).

Special love to the dads in my life—John, Paul, CR, Jeff, Jim,
Sam, Pop, my own Dad and my husband. You all turned
out okay when the babies arrived!

CHAPTER ONE

"MOVE! MOVE! MOVE!" Spider shouted as he sprinted after nineteen men and women through a tunnel of flame.

No one heard him above the roar of the fire.

The Silver Bend Hot Shots were in a race for their lives down a mountainside they'd been trying to save. A few minutes ago, they'd been scraping away brush with shovels and Pulaskis, clearing a firebreak below a tame flank of the Flathead, Montana, fire and joking about how there'd be no overtime because this one would soon be out.

Then the wind changed, no longer a gentle breeze drifting up the slope from the creek. Instead it came from above, injecting life-giving oxygen into the smoldering embers until it was a ten-foot-tall wall of menacing flame. The new fire toyed with the Hot Shots for only a moment before bending across their six-foot-wide break and igniting a fresh blaze on the opposite side with a heated kiss. Tools scattered and packs were abandoned as the group began a desperate run for the ribbon of water they'd started at this morning.

As one of the two assistant superintendents of the crew, it was Spider's job to make sure everyone made it out ahead of him. One misstep by someone and they'd go down like dominoes, more food for the fiery dragon on their heels.

How much farther?

Ahead of Spider, the fire seemed to be closing ranks around them. The heat and smoke made it difficult to fill his lungs with air. His heart pounded wildly from exertion, adrenaline and fear.

Someone stumbled. Swerving to the side, running perilously close to the tongue of flame on his right, Spider dragged Victoria back onto her feet.

"We're not going to make it," she cried, barely audible above the angry roar of the fire.

Even as some part of Spider agreed, he rejected defeat. At thirty, he still had things to accomplish, places to see and women to meet. He was single, with few responsibilities and few regrets, with only his dad to mourn him. The world was his oyster.

Too bad he was about to be fried.

Tap-tap-tap.

Inside the Fire Behavior tent at base camp, Becca Thomas smiled and tried to ignore the little one trying to get her attention. She focused instead on the most recent satellite photo of the Flathead fire taken that morning and compared it to the latest computer simulation she'd run on the computer provided by NIFC, the National Interagency Fire Center.

Tap-tap-tap.

"Give me a minute," Becca murmured, rubbing her stomach, hoping her baby would be patient. She was happy to be pregnant, even if she was thirty-eight and single. She'd thought it all through, had planned down to the last penny. She and the baby were going to be all right on their own.

Her attention returned to the papers on the table that was her desk in this portable camp. There was something about this simulation she didn't like. As one of NIFC's senior Fire

Behavior Analysts, Becca had learned to trust her instincts. She prided herself on finding the chaos factor in the weather, terrain and fuels, along with a dozen other things she considered when making predictions about a fire's behavior. Still, there were things she couldn't control—the way fires created their own wind and weather, and the decisions made by those in the field as to the risks they were willing to take, sometimes against her advice.

Tap-tap-TA-A-AP.

Sitting hunched over her makeshift desk at the Flathead fire was not her baby's favorite position. Becca would have to get up soon. Until then...

What was it about the simulation that troubled her? She ran her finger over the inputs—the fire's point of origin, wind speed, types of fuel, degree of slope, humidity readings. She returned her attention to the map of the area. The locations where lightning had struck and started the fire were marked, as was the perimeter of the fire as of eight hours ago.

The fire had spread from three strike points down three sides of a tall peak within the Flathead National Park, a remote, rugged mountain range lacking paved roads. It was bound to the east by the almost vertical, rocky cliffs of the Continental Divide. Everywhere else, the fire was moving hungrily through two generations of forest—giant pines and spruce towering sixty to eighty feet in the air, and younger trees twenty to forty feet high, interspersed with small, steep meadows that hadn't yet given way to the forest. This area had not seen fire or been thinned by logging in years. Add to that two years of drought and you had one heck of a fuel source. If they didn't stop it, the fire could easily work its way down to civilization in as little as a week.

Becca's finger ringed the area around the fire once, twice,

trying to pinpoint what was bothering her. And then she saw it—a small, thin creek twisting its way through ridges and rises. It wasn't much, but in a craggy place like this the wind could ride along the creek bed and push to the top of a ridge, where it could dance with the wind cresting over the top of the mountain, creating a whirling dervish that would wreak havoc on an otherwise tame bed of fire. Making it unpredictable. Making it treacherous.

Tap-tap. The baby continued its protest. Becca pushed herself up out of the chair and began an ungainly pacing. At seven-and-a-half-months pregnant, she had the grace of an elephant.

Ignoring the sweat trickling between her breasts, she paused, squinting down at the map. The creek was mostly in Sector Three. Before dawn they'd sent a team in that area to build a fire line. The crew would have looked for an anchor to their line, something that would offer a safe-retreat zone or a natural barrier to the fire. A creek?

"Is something bothering you? Can I get you anything?" Julia, Becca's assistant, offered, starting to rise from her seat in front of their computer. "Maybe NIFC shouldn't have sent you out here." Julia pronounced the federal agency *nif-see.*

"No, I'm fine." Becca straightened, stretching her aching back. Maybe she was overthinking this one. Maybe she was looking for pitfalls and challenges where there were none because this was her last fire before the baby came, her last fire in the field if her career plans worked out right. And her plans had to work out right. She'd bet everything on them, had even put an offer on a little house outside of Boise a few weeks ago.

Someone shouted outside, an urgent command Becca couldn't make out.

The stuffy, cramped tent that served as the office for the two women on the Fire Behavior Team barely sheltered them from the sun's rays and did little to keep out the constant noise of base camp. Over the last three days, NIFC had created a small tent city to organize the fight against the Flathead fire in the middle of nowhere, complete with command tents filled with computers and phones, shower and kitchen trailers, and generators large enough to power it all. Not that NIFC expected this fire to last long. The plan was to contain it with as few resources as possible, leave a skeleton crew to mop up and move on.

The unusual sound of booted feet racing past filtered through the tent's canvas walls, accompanied by more urgent voices.

"Did you hear what they said?" Becca swung around in the direction of Julia. In the process, Becca bumped her tummy against the desk, spilling water from her open water bottle all over the fire maps spread across the worn surface. As quickly as she could, Becca shook out the maps, then mopped up with the paper towels she kept below her table because she'd become such a klutz.

When she looked up, Julia was already moving to the door wiping at the makeup under her eyes. The unusual-for-late August heat and mountain humidity melted makeup right off one's face, but Julia kept on trying. "I think someone said the fire overran a crew."

Becca froze, unable to move as fear raced through her veins. Her brother had died in a wildland fire when she was in college. She knew how devastating such a loss was on a family. Since then, she'd worked on fires where lives had been lost, and each time, she'd asked herself what more she could have done to prevent the tragedies.

Only when her hands started to shake did Becca snap out

of her shock, running them down the sides of her belly in an attempt to regain some measure of calm. "We need to get to the Incident Command tent ASAP."

"How could this happen? The computer didn't predict anything that dangerous." Julia looked at Becca with wide eyes. She was still new enough to place complete faith in computers.

"We won't know until we talk to the Hot Shots. Let's go see what the IC team knows." Although Becca tried to keep her words light, she left the tent dreading what they might discover. Had she let someone else down?

Minutes later, they joined the rest of the Incident Command team in the main tent.

"We've got a bunch of Hot Shots heading into camp with singed whiskers and eyebrows." Not one to waste time, Sirus—Socrates to the firefighters—the Flathead Incident Commander, had a map spread out on the old, scarred meeting table. "They were lucky. They all made it out alive and relatively unscathed. I want the IC team to meet them in Medical and find out exactly what happened. I want a complete report on my desk by morning." For a moment, Becca was relieved, until Sirus gave her a stern look. He was no happier than she was with the situation.

Becca operated almost exclusively in California, and was only filling in on this fire. Because she'd never worked with Sirus before, Becca still had to prove to him she was capable. Erratic fire behavior when she'd predicted none wasn't going to help Becca's credibility. She couldn't afford to show her new boss any weakness.

Not now. Becca passed a hand over her belly. Not when so much rested on Sirus's recommending her for another position.

"We'll understand what happened before the evening briefing," Carl, the team meteorologist, assured Sirus, setting his baseball cap more firmly on his bald head. "It won't happen again."

In his first year with NIFC, Carl, like Julia, needed to become more familiar with the unpredictable nature of fire before he made such confident statements. Becca often found herself patiently explaining things to Carl, a tricky situation due to his unaccountable ego. Rumor had it he'd been a TV weatherman until his hair had fallen out. Carl didn't like Becca counseling him, but that hadn't stopped him from hitting on her.

Puh-lease. Her belly was so large she couldn't even see her toes when she looked down. What kind of guy hit on a pregnant woman? Only the most desperate, as far as Becca was concerned.

"We may want to consider that we've got too much fire for the number of crew we've got working," Becca said as she pulled her T-shirt lower over her belly, only to have it rise back up. Becca forced her lips into something she hoped resembled a smile for the team, a hodgepodge of men and women from different disciplines, including communications, supply and personnel. She didn't know what had happened out on the fire line, but she was already blaming herself for not thinking about that narrow creek sooner. "Maybe we've even got a sleeper."

One of the trickier fires, sleepers tended to be underestimated and take firefighters by surprise, sometimes with deadly consequences.

"Let's not go jumping to conclusions." Carl laughed and gave Sirus a look as if to say "Let's not panic over what the little woman got in her little head."

Not wanting to see IC's reaction, Becca turned to go wait in the Medical tent, her mind already full of questions. Where had the fire crew been? Had the wind changed suddenly? What was the fire like before they realized they were in danger?

"No need to rush." Bobby, the supply officer, pulled her aside and lowered his voice. "Unfortunately, we've run out of gas and they're hiking down from the drop point." The drop point, or DP, was five miles up the mountain trail, ten miles on a narrow, winding dirt road.

Fire crews were comprised of men and women of action. The Hot Shots would chafe at having to cool their jets while they waited for transport.

But Becca was willing to bet they wouldn't wait. They'd hike to the camp. And when they arrived, the adrenaline of survival would have worn off and they'd be in no mood to talk to an official IC representative, much less a tent full of them. More than likely, they'd want a hot meal, a cold drink and an audience of their peers. By the time she talked to them, they'd have woven the truth into something that was several steps removed from reality. She wouldn't get the detailed information she needed to identify where her fire prediction had gone wrong.

Unless she met them along the way and got the story first.

Becca stepped into the doorway, looking for Julia.

Her assistant had hung back to talk to Sirus. She was trying to be his next Fire Behavior Analyst and, with a bit of hard work, Becca thought she might just make it. "Sir? Which Hot Shot team should we expect?"

"The Silver Bend crew," he answered, stone-faced. His stepson, Jackson Garrett, led that team.

Becca's fingers clenched the doorframe. Working in California, she'd effectively avoided the Silver Bend, Idaho, crew for more than seven months. She'd hoped their paths wouldn't cross on this one special assignment.

For just a moment, Becca considered waiting in the Medical tent with the rest of IC, hiding at the back of the crowd when the fire crew reached camp.

She blinked, coming out of her panicked stupor. No. She would not compromise her duties, even if it put her plans for the future at risk. If she didn't get to know this fire intimately, other firefighters might face unnecessary danger.

Becca knew only one Hot Shot from Silver Bend, although one was more than enough. Aiden Rodas was a wiry, good-looking, risk-loving playboy. He was younger then Becca, with a really immature nickname—Spider—and a really immature attitude. Not that most Hot Shots didn't have nicknames, Aiden's just seemed to stick out more than others.

She'd seen him the other night at a briefing. He'd stood at the rear of the tent, his eyes skimming over her as if she were chopped liver while she explained what the fire would do during the next twelve hours. He didn't seem to remember that he'd slept with her, which meant he didn't know he'd helped create the baby she carried.

And she wasn't about to tell him.

"THEY'RE QUIET," Cole Hudson said, half under his breath.

"Yeah, too quiet." Spider considered the somber team of men and women walking the wooded trail behind them. "Chainsaw, you don't suppose they're all meditating as we hike, do you?"

"Nope." Cole hefted his namesake, a thirty-six-inch chainsaw, across his broad shoulders and grinned at Spider before continuing to hike down to base camp. He'd abandoned his chainsaw and day pack containing gasoline when the fire belched this morning, but had been lucky enough to pick up new equipment at the DP.

Spider followed his friend down the steep, winding mountain path. "You think they're thinking about the fire?"

"Yep."

The crew, including Spider, had talked excitedly about their hair-singeing escape on the hike back. Spirits still up, they'd recounted their tale to the staffers at the DP while Jackson, better known as Golden, had radioed their situation back to base camp and received instructions to return and debrief IC. And then they'd received the news that they had to hike down the mountain because of some supply snafu, and the team had gotten quiet.

Surviving a run-in with the fire had left Spider feeling like a superhero. That was what he loved about being a Hot Shot—going head-to-head with Mother Nature. Having to walk back to base camp cut him down to size. Admittedly, reality tended to suck after an adrenaline rush like he'd experienced today, leaving him shuffling his booted feet like an old man. Spider imagined the rest of the team felt the same.

He was ready to fill his belly with a hot meal and grab as much sleep as he could before their next shift. But first the group would have to be checked out by the medics, file some reports and obtain more equipment.

"We can't exactly come down out of the woods looking whipped," Spider observed. Other crews would give them grief. The Silver Bend Hot Shots were a proud bunch, unused to defeat.

"Nope."

"I suppose you think we should do something about it."

"Yep." Chainsaw swung around to grin at Spider again, nearly taking off Spider's head with his chainsaw.

Spider ducked and wove to the left. "Couldn't agree more."

They were a tight-knit group that watched out for each other. Spider had a bad feeling about this fire. It was hungry, and not just for timber and grass. It looked tame, but there were signs that said otherwise.

If Spider saw Socrates he'd tell him what it was like up on the slopes. He'd tell him about the timber as dry and parched as kindling, just waiting for a spark to set it aflame. He'd point out that the seventy-degree slopes were just waiting to trap a fire team and overtake them as they tried to scramble up to safety.

He may consider himself some kind of superhero, but his grandmother hadn't raised no fool. There were adrenaline-pounding risks, and then there were fool's errands. Spider hoped this fire wouldn't turn into the latter.

"It's not going to look good, us coming into base camp with our tails between our legs." Logan McCall, the crew's other assistant superintendent, commented, catching up to them along with Golden.

"Agreed. Any ideas?" Golden asked, looking at each of the three men as he spun his gold wedding band around his ring finger with his thumb.

Spider tilted his head from shoulder to shoulder in an attempt to loosen up. "Yeah, let's head back to the front line and forget all this political BS."

Golden looked heavenward. "Sure, let's head out without Pulaskis." The combination ax and hoe used to dig out brush as they cleared fuel from a fire's path was an essential fire-fighting tool. "Or shovels."

"Or gas," Chainsaw added.

"Otherwise, I'd have no problem heading back out to a hungry fire," Golden concluded.

A hungry fire... Spider couldn't stop the ominous thought. What was wrong with him? It must be the downside of adrenaline. He had to lighten up. He tried to smile, but only one corner of his mouth seemed to work.

"They'll be serving dinner soon," Chainsaw groused, swinging his chainsaw to the ground. "I can't believe they didn't have a transport for us down from the DP."

"I can," Spider mumbled. Not only had the fire teased them today, but the normally anal, almost military-like structure of NIFC hadn't yet kicked in full force. Case in point: vehicles without gas. Maybe NIFC thought the fire would burn itself out or be contained in a day or two.

Logan slapped his hand on Spider's shoulder. "So what are we gonna do about it?"

"I'm schlepping my tired, filthy butt down the mountain, aren't I?" Spider made a halfhearted protest. He was sweaty from the oppressive heat beneath the fire resistant Nomex pants and long-sleeved shirt that had protected his skin mere hours ago. What he wouldn't give for a mountain lake or stream to swim in.

"Look at all the gloomy faces." Chainsaw gestured toward the rest of the group, who started to cluster around them, looking just as hot, tired and beaten as Spider felt.

Normally, he loved being where the action was, making wisecracks to lighten the tension. His Hot Shot lifestyle provided lots of fodder for excitement and amusement, which he gladly spread to keep up team morale.

So why couldn't he shake the grim feeling that clung to him? Because, he suddenly realized, the crew wasn't hanging together well. A few were underperforming. Didn't anyone else see it?

Spider knew a weakened crew could be dangerous—even deadly. He'd been on fires where others had lost their lives, been on fires where the dragon's breath had singed him, all because the crew members had been distracted, tired or simply fed up with fighting.

Something was going to have to change. First off, the one woman on the team, Victoria, was going to have to either shape up or realize she had no place on his, or any other, Hot Shot crew. He'd have to tell Golden. Thank heavens she was in his unit.

Earlier today, she'd rolled down the cuffs of her protective gloves because it was too hot. And then she'd gotten burned when a smoldering stump she'd been trying to yank out of the ground had flared into flame. It was a rookie mistake, unexpected in a second-year Hot Shot. Spider didn't know where her mind was, but it wasn't on her safety or that of the crew's. Golden liked to nurture and protect his firefighters, but Spider had no patience for underachievers.

Then there was the fact that his father was working on this fire on another crew. Even though his dad had more than twenty years experience, the guy had no legs. You could see the pain on his face with each deliberate step he took. If things got ugly and his crew had to race to safety as Spider's had, his dad wouldn't make it. He didn't know who had let the old man pass his physical last spring, but someone should make him retire.

"This situation isn't hopeless, just pretty damn depressing," Golden said with a shake of his head. "Let's move."

Hopeless? It didn't matter that Spider couldn't find a happy thought at the moment. Nothing was supposed to be that bad.

Spider forced a grin on his face. "Wait. I've got an idea."

"COME ON, BABY," Becca spoke under her breath. "Move your butt so I can feel my leg." The baby had shifted and was rest-ing on something that cut off the circulation in her right leg, which now felt as if it were sandbagged as she forced her way uphill.

Sometimes being pregnant was sucky, but it would all be worth it in the end.

Becca didn't usually let anything slow her down or get in the way of her goals. A planner by nature, she was working toward a fire behavior management position at NIFC's headquarters in Boise. She'd do just about anything NIFC wanted her to do to be given the job, because there was no way she could chase fires from one forest to another all summer long and raise this baby.

The Boise position meant giving up being in the trenches, crafting attack strategies to make firefighters' lives safer, but it was a trade-off Becca was willing to make in order to have a child of her own. She'd focused too long on her career, letting the chance for romance, marriage and babies pass her by. To get the job, she had to appear tough and in control for just a few more weeks, in spite of her pregnancy, which slowed her down in ways she hadn't expected.

The baby sure hadn't shown any signs of wanting to slow down. It considered her bladder a trampoline and her rib cage a punching bag. Her baby was go-go-go, just like Aiden Rodas.

Becca groaned.

She did not want to think about Aiden—not his smile, not his enthusiasm, not his unique observations on life. He'd actually told her that nothing in life should be harder than checkers. He didn't realize life required complicated planning.

"Do you want some dried fruit?" Julia asked, dangling a plastic bag filled with the snack toward her.

Becca took an apricot.

"Shouldn't we have seen them by now?" Julia asked with a crinkle of plastic. She hadn't wanted to leave base camp and hike out to meet the Silver Bend crew. Julia was a sweet thing until she left her comfort zone.

Ironically, the great out-of-doors seemed beyond Julia's comfort zone. It was an aspect of Julia's character that frustrated Becca, yet she felt her assistant would overcome it. After all, there was no way Julia could have assumed a Fire Behavior Analyst would work in a nice air-conditioned office, was there?

"Why don't we rest here and take a reading?" Becca suggested, ignoring Julia's question. She slung her lightweight backpack to the ground and dug around until she found her handheld weather meter, grateful to be distracted from thoughts of Aiden.

Ninety-two degrees. Sixty-five percent humidity. Wind speed five. That and the extra pregnancy pounds she carried explained the sheen of sweat covering Becca's body. She recorded the results in her small notebook, balancing the sheets of paper on her belly, then tucked everything back in her pack.

She bent awkwardly to pick up a handful of spruce needles. "Look at how easily these snap." She held the needles out to Julia, wanting her to experience the forest fuels first-hand, but Julia looked at the crushed needles as if Becca held a rattlesnake.

Trying not to frown, Becca continued to teach. "Too little rain this past year has left the forest dry and the floor covered in combustible fuels, making it a prime target for a lightning strike. What do you suppose it's like farther up the mountain?"

"I'm not going to have to find out, am I?" Julia wiped at her eyes.

"Walking the woods brings the topography to life. The more you know of the terrain, the better your predictions." Disappointed in Julia's lack of interest, Becca shouldered her pack and continued up the trail. She was determined to find a way to wean Julia's dependence on computers for fire prediction.

"What makes you think this fire is a sleeper?"

Atta girl. Curiosity led to growth in a job like theirs.

With a small smile, Becca glanced up at what little smoky skyline was visible through the trees. "First, the slopes on these ridges aren't gradual or smooth. As wind speed picks up, it can really blow in some places and not at all in others." She paused to catch her breath.

"And second?"

"For the most part, the westerly winds are working for us." Filling her lungs with air, Becca continued up the slope. "But, I was talking to some of the local kitchen crew yesterday and they say that when the heat breaks at the end of summer it's because the wind shifts to come from the north. There are a couple of valleys back here that open up onto the highway to the south. With the right northerly wind, there'd be no natural barriers in a fire's way."

"Locals?" Julia couldn't disguise her disbelief. "You asked a local fry cook? You can't be serious."

Becca kept the impatience out of her voice because she remembered when she'd been young, immortal and perfect, too. "Locals are a great source of information. And these locals are Native Americans who've passed weather knowledge down through the generations."

Julia tilted her head as she pondered that bit of knowledge, before falling back on what she knew. "Carl will let us know if the wind is about to shift, won't he?"

"I hope so." Carl had yet to prove himself worthy of Becca's trust. Despite the heat, she shivered. Becca didn't want to think about firefighters in the fire's path if they didn't have advance warning.

Julia was silent for a bit, lagging behind, and then she fell into step with Becca, rubbing at her nose. "What if Silver Bend took a shortcut? What if they've hitched a ride back to camp?"

Becca heaved a sigh of defeat. Maybe this aversion Julia had to the outdoors wasn't going to be as easy to beat as she'd thought.

She was sure she'd run into the Silver Bend team on the trail, but just in case, she should have a backup plan. "Why don't you go back? You can wait for them in Medical in case I'm wrong."

Julia perked right up, and then had the grace to look embarrassed. "If you're sure," she added hesitantly, running a finger underneath one eye and glancing downhill. "I mean, you'll be alone up here."

"I'm used to it. You go on."

"I'll check the satellite feed and print out a fire update so you can review it when you get back," Julia said with a wave.

Alone, Becca looked up at the trees towering against a sky blanketed with a thick layer of brownish-gray wood smoke; stroked her belly and took in the grandeur of the forest. Julia didn't understand what she was missing.

A quarter of a mile later, Becca was puffing, limping and wishing she'd gone back with Julia. She stopped to take a reading.

Eighty-nine degrees. Seventy percent humidity. Wind speed ten. The fire wasn't affecting the temperature and humidity as much this far from the front. The higher she went, the cooler and more humid the air.

Becca shaded her eyes and scanned as much of the ridge above her as she could see. Her stomach grumbled. Her leg still felt weird. Doubt taunted her tired body. Maybe she had missed the Hot Shots. Maybe she should give up. She glanced back, knowing her stubborn pride wouldn't let her return just yet. Her mother used to say that pride would one day be Becca's downfall. That might be true, but willpower and pride had certainly taken Becca far in a field dominated by men.

She started climbing again. It was slow going. The trail steepened and wove through a patch of boulders. She could walk between some and gingerly climb over others where they overlapped or nearly kissed.

Aiden had been a great kisser.

Becca walked faster, despite having to angle her belly this way and that to get through nature's rock garden. She thought about the baby inside her. Aiden had done his job and they'd both moved on. She'd hardly spared him a thought all these months until she'd seen him on this fire.

Except she often dreamed about him at night.

She shook her head, trying to dispel those unsettling thoughts and concentrate on the task at hand.

A sound on the slope above drew her attention. With images of Aiden still lingering, Becca was startled by a vision of him running over the boulders ahead of her wearing boots and boxers, and carrying his backpack.

And then her foot slipped and her stomach churned with sickening certainty.

She was going to fall.

The baby...

She cocooned her belly with her arms. Her left elbow scraped across a tall boulder as she stumbled cockeyed, and her temple connected with a sickening thud on that same rock.

Becca landed with an air-stealing thump on the ground.

CHAPTER TWO

"WHOA! WHOA! EVERYBODY SLOW UP. Big Mama down." Spider leaped across a couple of boulders just as a pregnant woman with a long blond braid stood on shaky legs.

"Take it easy, Big Mama." Spider hopped to the ground next to her.

She took a step back, her blue eyes widening at the sight of him. Or maybe it was at the sound of thundering booted feet on rock as the rest of the Hot Shots approached.

"You're bleeding." Without sparing a glance at the crew, he yelled, "Doc, get down here!"

Blood spurted over the side of her face, but that didn't seem to shake her. "Did you just call me big?"

"I don't know," Spider hedged. His grandmother would tan his hide if she'd heard him disrespect a woman like that. But the woman was big. And carrying…a baby.

She raised her eyebrows at Spider with the disbelieving expression of a school principal, challenging him to tell the truth.

Spider lasted another ten seconds before he crumbled. "Okay, I might have."

She huffed. "Were you raised by wolves? Never call a pregnant woman big."

"I didn't mean anything by it."

But she was on the offensive now. "Are you so blind that you can't see a pregnant woman in front of you?"

Spider took a step back. "Hey, these boulders are ten feet tall. I couldn't see a bear hiding down here."

"I wasn't hiding." She crossed her arms over her large—really large—stomach, which only plumped up her prime-size breasts. "A gentleman wouldn't knock someone over, call them names and then accuse them of hiding."

"I never said you were hiding." Spider kept backpedaling. Pregnant women, as a rule, made him nervous. Sex was supposed to be fun, not result in…in…*that.* "I'm just trying to make sure you're okay. Doc!" he yelled again. Sheesh, where were your friends when you needed them?

"I'm fine."

Dang, she was stubborn. He stared into her ice-blue eyes and almost believed her despite the blood trail on half her face. She wasn't kidding. She thought she was fine.

He took a finger and ran it over her plump cheek, turning his bloodstained finger in her direction. "That would seem to indicate otherwise."

Cool as you please, she lifted a hand toward her forehead. He caught her wrist before she could touch the wound.

"Aw-aw-aw. You might have germs on those fingers. Let's have a medic look at it." He craned his neck around, reluctantly taking his eyes off her. Most of the guys were standing up on the boulder in their Skivvies, looking down on them with concern. Some were yanking off their boots and pulling on their pants. Arms crossed, Victoria stood apart from the rest in full field gear. She didn't understand that making a game of racing down to the base-camp showers would ease the tension from the crappy day they'd had.

Doc landed on the ground next to Spider with his pants on. Spider suddenly felt a bit underdressed. Air-conditioned, but definitely underdressed.

Lifting her blond bangs out of the way, Doc examined the cut on the pregnant woman's temple. "It's already slowing down on the leakage department, but you're going to need a stitch or two."

Blond Mama frowned. At Spider. As if it were his fault.

"I don't know why you were out here hiking in your condition." He was compelled to say it, although normally, he'd be a little kinder to a damsel in distress, especially one with a bun in the oven. Yet, there was something about this woman that wouldn't let him be her hero. "There's a wildfire raging up there." Spider pointed behind him. "And it's not safe for anyone, especially a woman as pregnant as you, to be out here."

She glared at him in a way that made him wonder how she'd ever gotten pregnant in the first place. He could almost imagine her saying "Oh, you are so dead when I get you alone."

Really. It was as if he could hear that smooth voice filled with playful disdain, as if he'd heard her say those words before or something like them, although he heard a more loaded, sexy undertone in his head.

Sexy? The Ice Mama?

Ignoring her back-off stare, Spider leaned closer and peered at her in the hopes that he'd figure out who she was. She was almost as tall as Spider, and full of chutzpah, not backing down from his scrutiny. They would have gone on staring at each other all day if Doc hadn't elbowed him aside.

"Give me some space to work, man," Doc mumbled as he swabbed her wound with an antiseptic wipe and then applied a butterfly bandage.

She drummed her fingers on the huge rise of her belly. She had long, dexterous fingers. Something in Spider's memory hiccuped. He knew this woman. "Don't I—"

"No," she cut him off emphatically, as if reading his mind.

"Isn't that the Fire Behavior Analyst?" someone asked from the boulder above them.

Spider looked at her again. In her khaki shorts, white T-shirt and sturdy boots, she looked like your average hiker, except for the baby in her belly. He hadn't noticed she was pregnant, but he'd only been to one base-camp briefing and he'd been at the back of the throng of teams.

Had he seen her somewhere else? He would have remembered talking to a pregnant woman, right?

Well, not usually.

But there was something naggingly familiar about this one.

IT WAS HIM.

Black hair and intense black eyes. All five foot ten inches of sculpted, sexy man.

Not only was it him, but Aiden Rodas had looked her in the eye as if she were some irresponsible, idiotic woman who had caused her own accident. He had filled her nights with pleasurable memories that came pressing back on her now, heating her from the inside out. And he…

Didn't even recognize her.

While the man they called Doc applied a bandage to her temple, Becca's foolish pride steamed. Aiden didn't recognize her. Had he really been that drunk when they'd met? She hadn't thought so. She should be grateful he didn't recognize her. It made everything that much easier.

Still, Becca didn't want to be just another notch on his bedpost.

The baby kicked her belly in Aiden's direction, a proverbial wave to garner his attention. Becca ran a hand over her tummy, trying to satisfy the urge to shush her little one. There were plenty of reasons why Aiden didn't need to know of his role in creating this child. But she wouldn't waste any more time on Aidan. She'd found the Silver Bend Hot Shots and now had the ideal opportunity to figure out what had happened up there on the mountain.

Becca managed to collect herself enough to get down to business. "I hear you saw some excitement today."

"Man, did we ever," Doc chuckled. "I've never seen anything like it."

"And I'd prefer not to see anything like it again," someone on the boulders above clarified, and received many jibes for their honesty.

Ignoring her wound, her twinging leg and heavy belly, Becca couldn't contain her curiosity about the runaway fire. "I'd love to hear about it."

"Is this our debrief?" Aiden asked, a suspicious expression clouding his face. He'd put on the forest-green pants and yellow shirt that was the Hot Shot uniform.

"No," Becca protested, holding out her scraped elbow to be swabbed with an antiseptic wipe by Doc, unable to keep from making a face when his ministrations stung. "We just happened to bump into each other—"

"Stumbled upon is more like it," Aiden mumbled, still eyeing her as if she were the enemy.

"—and I'm just naturally curious."

Aiden wasn't buying it. He frowned at her before turning away, climbing to the top of the boulder and disappearing on the other side.

"All done here and ready to move." Doc snapped his first-aid kit shut.

With a sigh of relief, Becca thanked Doc and followed him

with ginger steps down the trail, asking about the fire just as carefully. She didn't see Aiden, but felt his disapproving presence somewhere behind her.

"DO YOU BELIEVE HER?" Spider asked Chainsaw from the back of the single-file line of Hot Shots wending their way the last mile into camp. Ahead of them, he occasionally caught a glimpse of golden hair and a swinging braid through the trees. The two men were lagging behind mostly because Spider was dragging his feet.

"No, as pregnant as she is, I can't believe she hiked up here. She's like Super Pregnant Woman or something," Chainsaw observed.

"That's not what I meant," Spider snapped. "She came up here just to interview us personally, before anyone else could."

"You are so paranoid," Chainsaw chuckled. "The Fire Behavior team hikes all over the place. They also go on the helicopter and airplane flybys with Incident Command."

"And it just so happens that we meet her on the trail coming down from nearly getting burned over?" Spider wasn't buying it.

"Crazier things have happened," Chainsaw said.

"The trouble with you is, you're too trusting," Spider complained. "I bet she missed something in her analysis and she's trying to cover for it. I think I've seen her somewhere before, too."

"The trouble with you is, you've seen too many bad conspiracy movies and now you can't trust anyone. Come on, she was probably just doing her job. Get over it."

"You're a pushover."

"And you're jaded beyond belief."

Despite himself, Spider grinned. He was jaded and suspicious by nature, a product of a father who'd made too many empty promises. His grin faded. He'd met the Fire Behavior Analyst before. Sooner or later, he'd figure out where and when. Until then, he wasn't trusting her as far as he could throw her…so to speak.

"SO YOU HAD NO WARNING? No wind kicked up?" Carl was trying to probe the crew into saying weather had nothing to do with the dangerous situation they'd found themselves in.

Half of the Silver Bend Hot Shots were crowded into the Medical tent. The other half had already been questioned, examined, observed by a stress counselor and released to the chow line. Becca had been smart to meet the team up on the mountain. The mood in the tent was more like that of an interrogation than a debrief, thanks mostly to Carl.

"We noticed the wind about the time we noticed the flames were riled up," the broad man they called Chainsaw answered. The rest of the firefighters had grown silent the more Carl questioned them.

"So the wind did blow." Carl nodded, scribbling something onto his notepad. "And then what happened?"

"We ran like hell was on our heels." Aiden stood with his arms crossed, only giving Carl half his attention. The other half kept lasering over to Becca.

"And what do you mean by that?" Carl was persistent. Getting on everyone's nerves, but persistent.

Aiden pushed up his shirt sleeves with sharp movements. "I mean we had no time to stop and take a reading of the wind speed. It was as if someone flipped the toaster switch to on, and we were the toast."

"You'll need to head into town for a sonogram and an

X ray," Maxine, the paramedic on duty said softly, staring at Becca over the rim of her bifocals.

Becca avoided acknowledging the ache in her head, avoided looking at Aiden. The way he kept staring at her had her jumpy enough to want to disappear. Her gaze fell upon a woman in Aiden's Hot Shot crew who had bright red hair and burns on her wrists.

"I fell on my butt, Maxine, not my belly. The only thing bruised is my behind. I'll pass on the hospital," Becca whispered back, because other than her head, she did feel fine. That's all she needed was a trip to the hospital during a fire. She'd be branded as weak and ineffective quicker than she could refresh her parched lips with Chapstick.

Near enough to hear their discussion, the female Hot Shot smiled as if in approval of Becca's decision. Becca smiled back. The two women shared something unique—both operated in a man's world where any reminder that they were the weaker sex was unwelcome.

"What about your head?" Maxine snapped off her gloves and put her hands on her hips, no longer quiet now.

It hurt, but Becca would never admit it, or the way her stomach was starting to rumble with hunger.

"It'll take more than a bonk on a boulder to send me to the hospital in the middle of a fire." Becca slid off the examining table—almost gracefully—and with a nod in the female Hot Shot's direction, made to leave. "If you'll excuse me, I need to get back to work. The evening briefing is in about ninety minutes."

"I'll need to run this by Sirus," Maxine warned, clearly not approving.

"Of course." Becca understood about liability and, if ordered by the Incident Commander, she'd go to the doctor.

But until then, it was business as usual.

"I'm off as well," the Hot Shot with the burns on her wrists announced.

"Not much I can do for you anyway. Doc did a good job on your bandages." Maxine patted Doc on the back as she went to greet a man limping into the tent. "Make sure you wear those gloves properly in the future."

With a brief thank you to Doc for cleaning her up on the mountainside, Becca was out of there, somehow managing to exit the tent without having to look at Aiden again. Her head pounded, her back ached and her ankles were swollen. She'd gotten much more out of the Hot Shots as they'd escorted her back to camp than Carl was getting from them now. The airflow had come from above them, although some had felt light breezes from the direction of the creek. Almost without warning, the winds had come from over the mountain, driving the fire down on top of them like one big blanket of flame.

Becca shivered, despite the oppressive mountain heat. They'd been lucky to have Jackson Garrett as their leader. The Hot Shots nicknamed him Golden because of his knack for reading fire situations before they became deadly. According to Golden, he'd felt the pressure change and the winds stir around him, and watched the flames leap up then retreat in an area above them. He'd given the order to pull back just as the fire had roared to life at their backs.

Becca saw some of the Incident Command team grouping down by the chow line. She'd still have time to check the weather satellite one more time and start a draft of her report on what had happened to Silver Bend before the briefing.

"Excuse me."

Becca's shoulders tensed. There was still plenty to do and

by now the rest of Incident Command would have heard of her accident, so she had to prove that the pregnant Fire Behavior Analyst was as tough as any man. A bump on her noggin? Wouldn't slow Becca down. But the interruption came from someone she couldn't easily ignore.

Becca turned around to see what the female Hot Shot wanted.

"What you did back there in Medical was…great. You made taking control look so simple." The Hot Shot shifted her feet and jiggled her fire helmet with one hand as if she were nervous. "My name is Victoria…The Queen." Self-consciously, she touched her red hair. "Would you like to have some dinner? I could use the company."

There was an informal sisterhood in the fire community. Women helped each other with moral support, advice and a safe place to vent. But the Hot Shot's timing was off. Becca's job was calling, her credibility at stake. If she wanted that promotion in Boise, she had to perform above excellent, above what a man could do.

Becca opened her mouth to refuse, to suggest they catch a cup of coffee in the morning, but then she caught Aiden's disapproving stare as he came out of the Medical tent. His attention seemed to be aimed at both Becca and the Hot Shot with her, which pushed Becca's nurturing instincts into overdrive. He clearly disapproved of Victoria, who might have approached Becca to talk about how to deal with Aiden.

Becca sighed. Her conscience wouldn't let her leave this until later. Besides, her stomach growled again; the baby needed to be fed.

"Can we make it quick? I still have plenty to do before the IC team meets to set up their plan of attack."

"I appreciate it. I need to stand in line for the shower anyway." The Hot Shot ran a hand over her hair. At some point, it had been in an intricate French braid. Now red hair hung in limp strands around her dirt-streaked face.

The last glimpse Becca had of Aiden was of his frowning countenance as they made their way to the chow line.

The sight made her smile.

"YOU COMING TO EAT, Roadhouse?" Bart asked as he wiped his face with a worn blue bandana and made to follow the rest of the Montana #5 ground crew into the chow line.

"In a minute." Roadhouse wanted to make sure his son, Aiden, was okay. He'd heard about the Silver Bend crew's close call on the mountain. He'd even heard there were no severe injuries. But that didn't stop him from worrying, or ignoring his empty belly and walking on stiff knees through camp looking for his son.

Roadhouse was on a private fire crew—second-class citizens to the likes of Aiden on their Department of Forestry firefighting teams, even though the pay was better in private crews and the work often farther from the front line. DoF Hot Shot crews got the prime jobs on wildland fires, except in situations like this one, where bodies were scarce.

Non-fire civilians might say Roadhouse was lucky to be away from the action most of the time, but when fire ran in your veins, you wanted to be at the front line, with adrenaline and the dragon roaring in your ears. Why suit up otherwise?

Before he'd rounded camp once, he saw Aiden step out of the Medical tent. His heart nearly stopped. Other Silver Bend members were filing out as well. What had happened to his boy?

"Roadhouse," a deep, familiar voice called out behind him. Roadhouse glanced around, knowing he had to give Socrates, one of NIFC's most respected Incident Commanders, his full attention, but unwilling to take his eyes off his kid.

"How was it out there?" Socrates didn't call him "Old Timer" like some of the kids on the crews, because he'd been fighting fires longer than Roadhouse. He had the gray hair and scars to prove it.

"It's a sleeper, sir," Roadhouse stated bluntly. Wouldn't do to hold back with Socrates. "The fire seems tame, but it'll surprise us all at the end. You can sense it up on the line." He could have griped about the gasoline, but Roadhouse wouldn't complain about having to hike five additional miles to base camp. Back in the early days, firefighting in the mountains was more of a survivalist challenge. A bit of hiking was nothing in comparison.

Socrates stared long and hard at Roadhouse before admitting, "Someone finally agrees with the Fire Behavior Analyst." Socrates scanned the camp. From the rise where they stood, they could see most of the mess area, tables filled with grubby, hungry firefighters, the Medical tent, the staging area where trucks unloaded men and equipment, and the command tents.

Aiden started up the hill toward them with the Silver Bend superintendent, Golden. Roadhouse turned around, pretending to look up the mountain, hoping his son wouldn't recognize him with all the grime and his long hair tucked beneath his helmet. Desperate for Aiden's company, Roadhouse had resorted to dropping into Aiden's path when he least expected it—only because Aiden would vanish if he saw Roadhouse first. When that happened, it nearly broke Roadhouse's heart all over again.

"Golden," Socrates nodded to his stepson when he stopped a few feet away.

Still in his prime and liked by many, Golden was fast becoming a legend. People would tell stories about Golden around fire camps long after he was gone.

No one would remember Roadhouse when he was six feet under, fondly or otherwise, least of all his son.

Hearing a second set of footsteps, Roadhouse turned around with a sinking heart, meeting Aiden's curious gaze, watching it harden with recognition.

When would his son learn to forgive?

WHAT A LOVELY little family reunion. Spider pulled his helmet off and wiped the sweat from his forehead. Wasn't he just a luck magnet today?

"You know Roadhouse, don't you, Spider?" Socrates asked with an arched brow. To an outsider, it might appear that Socrates was being polite, making sure they all knew each other. But every one of the men standing on the knoll knew that Roadhouse was Spider's dad. Just like every one of them knew that Spider and Roadhouse had a shaky past, if you could call neglect and abandonment shaky.

"Yeah, we've met," Spider answered coolly, wishing he'd recognized his father as he'd walked up. He would have walked on, and let Golden talk to their commander alone. "We've come to check in." This last part came out a little belligerently. It wasn't every day that a man watched a woman get burned, ran down a mountain in his boxers and startled a pregnant woman, then had to face his father. Spider was dirty, tired and not in the mood for pleasantries.

"Come to gripe a bit?" Socrates raised a white eyebrow. He'd been the Silver Bend superintendent before Golden and had trained many of the Hot Shots in the Idaho region, including Spider. He cut right through the bullshit and didn't let anyone give him undeserved grief.

"No, sir." Golden shook his head, ever the politician, spinning his wedding band, a movement that reminded Spider how much his friend loved his wife.

"Hey, I'll gripe if you'll let me. But I'd rather hear about the latest on the fire," Spider said, giving Socrates a halfhearted grin, waiting to see if they were sparring or playing nice.

"I'm sure you could have been briefed by Becca Thomas when you ran her over on the hill today." Socrates shook his head. "Spider, when are you going to grow up and learn to think about the consequences of your actions?"

So, they were sparring.

"I was just telling him—" Golden began.

Socrates cut his stepson off with a wave of his hand and a disapproving glance. "There are women in NIFC and the fire crews now. Did you happen to think that running down the mountain half-naked might be considered harassment by one of them? Perhaps by the woman in your own crew? Either one of you?"

Spider avoided the Incident Commander's hard stare, but somehow managed to catch his dad's disapproving shake of the head. Spider drew his shoulders up so that he was at least even in height to his dad, even if he was still shorter than Socrates and Golden. He'd just been trying to lighten Silver Bird's spirits.

"Morale is a little low in the field, which is understandable given that this is the end of the season and crews, including ours, are burnt out," Golden spoke defensively. "What are we doing on this fire? Setting up a perimeter and picking our noses while it gains momentum? Or are we trying to put it out?"

Socrates looked pretty damn grim as he stared at them, which gave Spider a funny feeling in his stomach, but he chose to focus on Golden. "I wanted to pull you onto the IC team, Golden. That'll be awfully hard to justify after a stunt like this."

"I don't want to be part of Incident Command, so maybe it's for the best." Golden looked frustrated. "I've told you that before and I thought we agreed that my skills were best used in the field."

"We're not likely to get much more in the way of resources and you're good at creative ways to fight fire. I could use some help in planning the attack."

"Try someone else on our crew, like Spider." Golden was being uncommonly stubborn considering what they'd just been through, and that he had a wife and two kids back in Silver Bend to consider.

"Ding-ding-ding! Round over. Gentlemen to your corners." Forcing a grin on his face, Spider stepped between the two men. "We're here for some relaxation, a shower and some real food. It'd help morale a heck of a lot more than me running around half-naked, treading on the politically correct line you seem to have drawn in the sand, Socrates, if you'd just let us know what help we can expect on this beast."

The Incident Commander considered them silently for several seconds before admitting, "You won't be getting much help. Based on the Fire Behavior Analyst's recommendation, I've requested more air support and crews." He didn't sound as if he'd put much stock in his request. "But resources are stretched thin this time of year and we're not exactly defending anything from the fire. There are no government logging contracts or public structures in this fire's path."

"We're risking our lives for nothing? That bites." Spider scanned the picnic tables below them. A blonde and a redhead caught his eye amid the sea of yellow shirts and fire helmets. What were those two women up to?

"You'll be happy to hear we've solved the gas supply dilemma." Socrates' voice dripped with sarcasm.

"A little hiking never did anyone any harm," Roadhouse added, as if defending Socrates, who sure as shooting didn't need any defending. The man was tough.

"Considering the way Spider hikes these woods, we'd all feel better if he went from here to the DP in a vehicle." The severity of the Incident Commander's tone left little room for argument.

CHAPTER THREE

"THAT WAS FUN," Spider mumbled to Golden as they made their way back slowly to the mess area.

"Oh, yeah. Pulling teeth should be this fun," Golden answered. "If Lexie's been talking to Socrates about getting me into a *safer* job—"

"Your wife wouldn't do that," Spider quickly cut Golden off. "She's *so* not like that."

Golden sighed. "I know."

"But I feel for you, man. It would really suck to be on the IC team right now."

"Not that your opinion means much, Spider." Socrates spoke dryly as he passed the pair. "I'd even pull you on to the IC team if I thought your antics would do us any good. In fact, just so you get a taste of it, I'd like you to discuss your experience today with Becca Thomas before you head out tomorrow. The more she knows about this fire, the better off we'll be."

Spider swore under his breath and stopped in his tracks, letting Socrates proceed alone. Had the Fire Behavior Analyst requested he talk to her since he'd avoided her all afternoon? Was this her way of punishing him for her injury?

"Damn, Spider. You really know how to put your foot in your mouth." Golden laughed. "He's gonna put you on the IC team just for spite."

"That's not funny." Like most Hot Shots, just the thought of being corralled in camp gave Spider the hives. He'd become a Hot Shot because he loved the physical challenge, the adrenaline rush and being outdoors six to eight months a year.

Golden looked relaxed now that it seemed Spider might be the Incident Commander's minion of choice. "Socrates is right about one thing. You need to stop and think every once in awhile. I'm glad the race downhill wasn't my idea."

Spider tossed up his hands in mock innocence. "First you egg me on, then you abandon my tactics. Thanks for the support, fearless leader."

"You know what I mean. You and The Queen weren't getting along before this. Socrates is right. With no love lost between you, she could file a harassment claim against you."

Spider had first noticed Victoria slacking just before they'd been certified in the spring. He'd mentioned it to Golden back then, but he'd told Spider he thought it was preseason jitters. That hadn't been the case. Now at the end of the season, Victoria was endangering her life and those of the crew with every mistake she made.

"I saved her bacon on the mountain today. Maybe she needs more training. Maybe sooner rather than next year."

"Maybe." Golden almost sounded convinced. "She was fine earlier this season, but she's struggled through the past couple of fires."

Relief teased at Spider's tired brain. Sure, there were a couple of rookies he worried about, but no one on his unit of eight men—half of the Silver Bend crew—made him more anxious than Victoria. If he could get her out of danger, the team would be that much stronger. Maybe this fire assignment wasn't so bad after all. "Okay, let's send her back home or something."

"I don't think we need to go that far."

Spider stopped and grabbed Golden's shoulder. He'd been so close to improving their crew's safety. "Whoa. She's a liability, man. One mistake after another. She's not cutting it with Logan's unit."

"I know. That's why I'm going to shift her into yours." Golden grinned.

"What?" It was bad enough to have a royal screwup on your crew, add that to the fact that she was the girliest girl in the history of the Hot Shots and that she was reporting to him. Uh-uh.

"Here's your chance to put your money where your mouth is, Spider," Golden goaded. "You always said it's your fault if someone on your unit isn't performing."

"But this is different. We're in the field and she'd dead weight." Spider looked around searching for any reason Victoria shouldn't report to him. He'd only worry more, which would affect his performance. Pretty soon, Golden would be sending Spider to be retrained. Being sent to extra training courses at NIFC when you weren't switching jobs was like stamping a big "L" on your forehead. So, he reached for the first thing that came to mind—to stop Victoria from being assigned to him. "For crying out loud, Golden, she's got nail polish on."

"Yeah, and she uses a napkin and a fork." Golden shook his head. "Come on, let's go tell her."

"Now?" Victoria was sitting with the pregnant Fire Behavior Analyst, the one person he bet could influence Socrates when it came to base camp special assignments.

This day kept getting better and better.

"HOW DID YOU MANAGE IT?" Victoria asked Becca. They sat with full plates in front of them at one of the picnic tables NIFC had set up in a small clearing, surrounded by towering pine trees.

Becca had to chew the rubbery spaghetti a bit before she could reply. "Manage what?"

"To last so long in a man's world."

"It's not a man's world anymore." Becca struggled to make her words sound convincing. The farther she climbed up the management ladder, the less she could say about the way it really was in the system. She didn't know Victoria at all, and, much as she wanted to, she wasn't going to agree with her about the barriers women still faced in wildland firefighting ten minutes after meeting her.

Becca picked up an apple and wiped it with a napkin to keep herself from admitting anything. She'd accepted her dinner invitation to help Victoria, not ruin her chances at that promotion. A quick glance showed her that all the men in IC, including Carl, were congregated at a table on the other side of the mess area.

Victoria looked at her closely, then sighed. "So if I say I'm going to file a harassment suit against the Department of Forestry because my crew ran down the mountain, flags waving out of their boxers, you're going to tell me I should, right?" Despite the bandages around her wrists, Victoria had delicate hands with short nails painted a beautiful shade of red. She pointed at Becca, her disappointment evident in every word. "You don't understand. It's different out there."

Becca did understand. It wasn't that different in base camp. To succeed, a woman had to have a nearly squeaky-clean reputation, look the other way seventy-five percent of the time, as well as be quicker, smarter and tougher than a man. Becca stroked a hand around her belly. Try outdoing a man while being pregnant.

"Forget it," Victoria said, turning her attention to her meal. The Hot Shot's disappointment stung because Becca and this woman had a lot in common. Both were struggling to appear as strong and capable as any man. Keeping up the facade was a tough job. For the first time since joining NIFC, Becca was tired of doing it. Granted, the pregnancy was sapping her staying power, and her pounding head wound wasn't helping her energy level today, but mentally, Becca needed time away to regroup, even if it was only an afternoon. Time was something she didn't have in base camp, not when she didn't have an accomplished assistant.

While Becca stared at Victoria's nail polish, the baby kicked her ribs as if in reprimand. Still she hesitated.

"So much for the myth of the sisterhood," Victoria mumbled with a shake of her head.

Becca had watched out for her female colleagues most of her life. And, in their own way, they'd watched out for Becca. There were some things that only another woman would understand. The Hot Shot was right—in a man's world, women needed to support each other.

"Off the record—" Becca put her fork down, glancing around to make sure they wouldn't be overheard "—you and I both know you can't file a claim." She'd be labeled *trouble*, and no one would hire her after that.

"I know." Victoria pushed her spaghetti around her plate. "This is my second year as a Hot Shot. I thought the first year was tough but this year is different. Everything seems to be going wrong. Everything," she repeated, a dejected gloss in her eyes.

"You just need to find your rhythm, that's all." Becca had been right to spend time with Victoria. She seemed to need a friend.

"Do you really think so?"

Becca put her hand on Victoria's, careful of the bandages around her wrist. "Hey, if it's worth it to you, it's worth the sacrifice—the dirty jokes, the way they act like fifteen-year-old boys, even the skinny-dipping in that mountain stream—all the things they can do together that you can't because you're a woman. If you want to fight fires that much, it's just like having a bad commute or a crummy office—you put up with it, because you're good at it and you want this more than anything."

"I can't see myself doing something else. It's stupid, but I feel as if I was destined to do it, even though it's harder than anything I've ever tried before." Victoria's smile elicited one from Becca, who knew exactly what the Hot Shot meant. "Some of the assistant supers, well, just one of the assistant supers, gives me a pretty hard time. He's not in charge of my unit, thank heavens, but he…" She glanced up. "Here he comes."

To Becca's dismay, Aiden was bearing down upon them with Jackson. She swung one leg over the bench to leave. She'd been lucky—if offended—so far in that Aiden didn't remember her. Just how far would luck take her?

"Don't go," Victoria whispered, a plea in her eyes that Becca wanted to ignore. The woman needed more backbone if she wanted to succeed out here.

Becca hesitated long enough for the men to stop at their table. If she left now, she'd have to acknowledge Aiden. Sensing her agitation, the baby hiccuped. Maybe if she sat really still, they'd ignore her.

"How are you feeling?" Jackson asked Becca as he stopped near her with a friendly smile.

Trying not to grit her teeth, she reassured Jackson that she was fine and bit into her apple, carefully wiping the juice from the corners of her mouth. Out of the corner of her eye, Becca caught Aiden looking at her with his now familiar scowl.

The baby hiccuped again.

Becca stared at her plate. How dare he not remember her? How dare he not remember the way she'd taken him to the limits of his willpower and beyond. She just had to look at him and she was flooded with memories.

And an unwanted sense of longing.

She arched her back as the baby hiccuped a third time. Aiden probably dismissed her as just another old, pregnant woman, of no more interest to him than a heavily veiled nun.

Without preamble, Jackson got down to business. "Victoria, I think you might benefit from a change. I'm assigning you to Spider's unit."

Victoria appeared stricken. "Why?"

"Maybe he thinks I'll whip you into shape," Spider said, arms crossed over his chest. He didn't smile or reassure Victoria in any way. He clearly did not want Victoria reporting to him and Becca felt sorry for her all over again.

She willed Victoria to fling a snappy retort at him, but Victoria didn't move or speak. Without thinking, Becca stepped up for her new friend. "Maybe Jackson thinks Victoria will whip you into shape, Aiden." Then, because she was a little surprised at herself and wanted to soften her words, Becca gave him a cordial smile.

Jackson and Aiden were momentarily speechless.

"I think the team would benefit from the change." Jackson finally filled the awkward silence. Then he touched Victoria's shoulder. "You'll be fine."

Victoria's curt nod and downcast eyes broadcast how hurt she was by the move. Aiden had gone back to scowling.

"Get some rest. We'll see you in the morning." Jackson bid them good-night.

"Socrates…er, Sirus, asked me to talk to you about our experience today," Aiden said with a stubborn set to his chin.

Becca managed to choke out, "Perhaps I can find some time for you after the briefing." Drat. It was the last thing she wanted to do.

With a brief nod in Becca's direction, Aiden followed Jackson up to the dinner line.

"Thanks." Victoria groaned. "Spider hates me."

"Don't give him an inch. Guys like him look for weakness, especially in women out here." Becca wasn't going to let Aiden find her weakness, her secret. The baby shimmied around, making her dizzy for a few seconds.

"Oh, great. Just what I need to top my day." Victoria ducked her head. "There's that creepy old guy."

"Who?" Becca glanced around, one hand splayed protectively across her belly.

Victoria made a face. "That guy with shaggy hair standing at the end of this row of tables."

Becca tried to look casually in that direction. She spotted a beaten-looking firefighting veteran. He was gazing at them with a dull expression on his lined face, then he turned his attention to Jackson and Aiden.

"I've seen him around fire camps this year," Victoria whispered, barely moving now, as if keeping still might make her invisible. "He seems to stare at our crew a lot. It creeps me out."

Out of the corner of her eye, Becca saw Aiden turn and lock his gaze on her. She was suddenly able to relate to Victoria as a target of unwanted attention. She rubbed the baby in her tummy with one hand, trying to reassure herself that he didn't recognize her, although it was disappointing that he didn't. She'd thought they'd been spectacular together.

It was hard to believe that her impression had been wrong. Maybe…she sucked in bed.

Becca shied away from the embarrassing notion. It didn't matter that she was nothing to Aiden or any other man, for that matter. She'd gotten what she wanted.

Becca patted her belly again.

"I KNOW HER," SPIDER SAID as he trudged back up the hill with Golden to the supper line. The afternoon breeze had died down and the oppressive heat was making one last run before the sun sank low on the horizon. "She knew my name." Few people in the fire community knew his given name.

"The Fire Behavior Analyst?" Golden asked. "You might. She's been around for years and years. I hear her brother was a Hot Shot a long time ago."

"She's not that old," Spider grumbled, not knowing why he felt the need to stick up for her. "Have we been on other fires with her?"

"Probably not. She's California Overhead." Meaning the California division of Incident Command. "Socrates picked her up as an end-of-the season replacement. I've heard she's one of the best FBANS around, though."

Spider wasn't impressed. He'd heard too many times before about "the best" and found them sorely lacking in the field. He looked at Becca again. Where had he seen her? And why was the memory bugging him?

"This fire's going to be a tough one. I'll need your help keeping the team's spirits up, including tonight," Golden clarified, with a glance back at the Fire Behavior Analyst. "Don't get distracted."

"She's hardly my type," Spider said too quickly, unable to resist looking back, too. Pregnant and bossy. Not his style at all.

With long fingers, Becca twisted and tucked stray golden

strands of hair behind her ears, and blinked heavily at Victoria as if she were fighting off fatigue.

"Oh, man," Spider said under his breath as the images flooded his brain. He'd met her in Vegas—a tall, blond goddess who'd seduced him while he was at a firefighting convention the day after New Year's. He'd been nursing one in a string of too many beers, trying unsuccessfully to forget what his father had just told him—about a half brother and a half sister he hadn't known existed, two children Randy Rodas had fathered while married to Spider's mom.

Becca Thomas had worn this amazing, flimsy white dress that had clung to her curves and exposed most of her creamy skin and long legs. She'd walked over to him, sizing him up, taking his measure and finding him wanting...her.

Spider wasn't normally picky about a woman's intellect, as long as her features caught his attention. But his nameless goddess was no slouch in the brains department and had a face that was proud with high cheekbones and bright blue eyes. The sex had been great. The conversation had been great.

And come morning, she'd disappeared without so much as a "thanks, it's been fun." Not that he was complaining. Earth-shattering sex and no complications was primo. He just wasn't used to being the one who woke up alone.

No wonder he hadn't recognized Becca at first. Her body was plumped up from the pregnancy, from her ankles to her cheeks. But the hair was the same, her gestures were the same and her sharp wit was the same. Only she looked about ready to give birth, too far along to be carrying something he'd left behind. She had to have been pregnant before they'd met. An older woman like her didn't just get pregnant unless they were married.

Spider squinted at Becca, angry now. She hadn't mentioned

she was married in Vegas. Spider didn't screw around with married women. That was just wrong. Unlike his father, he considered marriage as something sacred, to be honored. If Spider even spotted a glimmer of a ring on a woman's finger, it was a no-go.

Becca Thomas had used him for her own purposes, whatever those might be, and had made him into a filthy, stinkin' cheater.

"SIRUS REVIEWED HOW THIS FIRE made a large, hot run this afternoon," Becca spoke into the portable microphone outside the Incident Command tent as she began her part in the evening-shift briefing.

Blanketed in thick smoke, the sun was receding behind the towering Flathead mountain ridges. It would still bathe them in soft light for another hour, but already the air was cooling. Once the teams were briefed, the crews on the evening shift were heading up to the drop point. Often the winds lessened or died down at night, so some of the best suppression efforts on the ground were possible when the sun went down. Those crews on R & R tended to come over to listen to the brief, to hear the latest on the fire, which was why the group was larger than the number of men and women going out to fight the fire this evening.

Aiden stood at the back of the crowd, probably waiting to talk with her. She tried not to let his stare intimidate her. He was probably still irritated at her snappy comeback in Victoria's defense.

Becca's head pounded beneath her stitches. It didn't matter that Fire Camp Aiden was cold and cocky, vastly different from the Aiden that had charmed her in Las Vegas. As long as Aiden didn't remember her, he could glower as much as he liked.

"I'm here to tell you that we can expect to see the fire make even more runs." Becca hated delivering bad news, especially when this fire seemed so low in priority to NIFC that the resources they needed to contain the fire weren't readily available.

"The winds are predicted to continue to come from the north, hot and dry, which means we'll have to be vigilant on the south slopes where the fuels are drier still. As you've probably heard, these winds kick up without much warning as the temperature rises in the afternoon. I know I don't need to tell you to set a lookout, but—" she paused to pat her belly "—you'll forgive me if I sound a little maternal toward you all. Please be careful."

As she'd hoped, that elicited chuckles from the group.

"Now, as for the conditions you're likely to encounter out there tonight…" Becca proceeded to go over the possible scenarios the crews were going to be working in that night, as well as trigger points—the geographical limit where a fire became unsafe for the manpower assigned and a retreat was ordered.

She could remember when she'd first started as a Fire Behavior Analyst. She'd been too earnest, all monotone urgency. The fire crews hadn't paid much attention to her at all. It had scared her to death. If she couldn't get through to them, their risk of injury increased. Now, after fifteen years of fire prediction, Becca knew how to keep their attention.

When the briefing ended, Becca asked Sirus to walk with her back through the sea of tents to the Fire Behavior tent, hoping to talk to him more about an idea she had to contain the fire—an idea the IC team hadn't been receptive to—as well as a more personal issue.

Energetic crews were loading into trucks and heading up

the mountain. Becca had to give it to the firefighters. They couldn't wait to get out there and risk their lives. They thrived on the kind of danger she tried to help them avoid.

And, even though she knew so few of them personally, she knew them in spirit. Firefighters with mothers and fathers, brothers and sisters, spouses and lovers at home in their air-conditioned houses, hoping for their safe return. Becca hoped she was doing her part to see they made it home unscathed.

"Have you worked a lot in Montana?" she asked Sirus.

"Some," he admitted. "But not in the fall. NIFC usually has me shifting to special projects by then. Desk work." This last was said with the distaste of a man who loved the outdoors. "Why do you ask?"

"I was just wondering what you knew about the weather here this time of year. Some of the locals have been saying the wind shifts when the temperature cools off. With the steepness of these ridges, we could be putting a lot of people at risk if we aren't careful. Perhaps we should pull back. You know, build a line in a place where we know we can stop it." This was her first experience working for Sirus. She'd served on special committees with him in the past and had learned the value of Sirus's opinion. He knew how to work the politics and the crews without losing the respect and liking of either side of the fire line, and he cut right to the chase—no hidden agendas.

He slanted a dark glance her way. "Do you have solid information about the weather that Carl or I don't have?"

Ignoring the implied warning, Becca pressed on. She desperately wanted Sirus to see the logic of her thinking. "Historical weather patterns can be tremendously helpful—"

"I know you want to change tactics on this fire, Becca, but you're one voice of several that I have to listen to as I decide what we'll do. Don't push me," he snapped. After a moment,

Sirus sighed and when he spoke again, his words were calmer. "Sorry. Lack of sleep tends to give me a short fuse. Look, if they send us more support for the fire, or if you can get Carl on your side, I'm more likely to reconsider that idea of yours. It's just too soon to change tactics."

Their current strategy was to fight the fire close to the flame. Becca believed pulling back and preparing for it was a safer strategy, and gave them a better chance to contain the fire with the resources they had to fight it.

It was going to take a good bit of convincing to get Carl to believe in her theory. Perhaps her hopes were better placed on NIFC. "Do you think NIFC will change their minds about this fire?"

"And give us more support?" Sirus shook his head. "Most additional resources are going to that huge fire in Washington. Fires are burning all across the western states, most are closer to the urban interface, threatening homes and small towns. There's nothing here but a national forest in one of the least populous states in the union. What do you think our chances are of getting more support?"

"Pretty slim." Becca's belly seemed weighted down by the news. "It's depressing. Even though it's only been a few days, it's at the end of the season on a tough fire. You can feel the hopelessness in everyone, from the firefighters to the support staff here in camp."

Sirus frowned. Glancing around, Becca was relieved to find they were alone, despite the fact that crews strode with purpose past them in both directions. It was probably the best opportunity she'd get to speak to Sirus about more personal matters. He was on the hiring committee for the Boise job, which was one of the reasons she'd accepted the Flathead fire assignment.

"Speaking of chances," Becca began, "what do you think my chances are for that Fire Behavior management position in Boise?" She barely made it out of the way of a rowdy crew carrying shovels and Pulaskis, striding toward the parking lot and their transport to the DP.

At the door to the Fire Behavior tent, Becca looked up at Sirus, who still hadn't answered her question. His expression wasn't encouraging. Her hopes suddenly sank to her toes.

"They're not going to give it to me, are they?" Becca managed to say.

"I'm sorry," Sirus said, looking steadily into her eyes. She admired his directness, even as she dreaded his take on the situation. "You have everything they're looking for—education, experience, and years with NIFC. And you've earned a lot of respect for your creative, if sometimes conservative, fire strategies."

Ignoring the label that she was too conservative—who could be too conservative when lives were at stake?—Becca waited for the *but*.

She glanced down at her belly. It had to be because she was pregnant. Some good old boy who had a friend on the interviewing committee and who let the simulation program do his work for him was going to get the job. It really was a man's world.

Still, she had to ask, "Why?"

He didn't hesitate. "It's your management skills."

"My…my what?" Becca couldn't believe her ears. "How could they say that? Every one of my direct reports has gone on to do well."

The expression on Sirus's face was solemn. "Many of your direct reports have gone on to do well in other fields."

Becca's equilibrium shifted, although her instability had nothing to do with the baby. What did you say in a situation like this? Defend yourself? Or crawl in some hole and lick your wounds?

"They weren't suited to the work." Becca lifted her chin, hugging her clipboard so tightly that the baby tried to elbow it aside. She loosened her grip while she tried to make Sirus see things from her perspective. "Most of these people—let's face it, they send kids out here most of the time—don't know what they want to be when they grow up." Julia came to mind, bright, but with a mindset closed to less high-tech methods of information gathering.

Becca glanced around, but her assistant was nowhere in sight. "Too many see it as a step up in pay grade rather than a calling. They seem surprised when they realize the day doesn't begin at eight and end at five, or that they can't just bring a printout to a meeting and read from it."

Sirus regarded her silently for a moment before looking away. "You know how things are around here. We have to deal with body count and open slots. If NIFC gets someone in the position, they'd rather not have them looking to move or quit after their first season."

"You're saying that I scare these people out of the job?" She refused to believe that. She tried so hard to help her direct reports improve on their weaknesses, to weed out the ones she felt weren't suited to the work, and this was the thanks she got?

He touched her shoulder ever so briefly—a condolence gesture. "What you've told me makes a lot of sense and gives me a new perspective, but—"

"That's the way they see it back in Boise." She bit her lip looking anywhere but at him. What was she going to do? "I'm pregnant," she let slip lamely, her nose stinging with the desire to cry. That's all she needed, a breakdown in front of her boss.

"There are other positions in Boise that need good people," Sirus suggested gently. "I'm sure they'd love to have you somewhere."

"Somewhere not in my field." Someplace she wouldn't as directly watch over the safety of firefighters.

NIFC didn't like the way she managed. They considered that her weakness.

Because they sent her people like Julia and had never seen her manage top-notch employees.

The baby shifted and Becca took a step back to regain her balance. How was she going to support herself and the baby? And the little house on the outskirts of Boise was definitely out of reach. All of her plans…

"Have they…" She could barely bring herself to ask. "Have they made a final decision?"

"No, but when I was in Boise last week, that was where they were leaning."

"So, there's still a chance," Becca whispered.

Sirus made a face. "It's pretty slim. You'd have to prove that you can effectively manage." He gestured to her tent, presumably where Julia was. "And that's all you've got to work with."

Sirus was right. Becca wasn't getting that job.

CHAPTER FOUR

"I'D LIKE A WORD WITH YOU." Stepping into her path, Aiden gripped Becca's arm when she came out of the Fire Behavior tent nearly an hour later. Without waiting for her assent, he pulled her away from the main camp and into the shadows of the night.

Panic shivered through Becca's system, making her knees like jelly.

He knew. What was she going to do?

Her throat closed up. She placed one hand over her belly, over the baby who she'd hoped wouldn't have to suffer an emotional tug-of-war. This close to him, she could smell the soap he'd used. It reminded her of his body pressed against hers, all hard planes and wiry muscle.

When he didn't say anything, Becca fought back her panic. They were beyond the parking area now, beyond where anyone else was. The portable lamps mounted on twenty-foot poles cast light beyond the camp's borders into the woods. Maybe he didn't know.

Then why was he dragging her away?

"If you want to talk about the fire today, I'll need my notepad." The pounding from the cut in her temple that had finally receded to a dull ache resurfaced with a vengeance.

"You're not going to want to take notes on anything I have

to say." Aiden kept on marching as they entered the edge of the forest. He wore a fresh pair of fire-resistant, forest-green Nomex pants and a Nomex yellow button-down shirt, while she was still in her sweaty, smelly shorts and bloodstained T-shirt, covered only with a worn, red fleece vest.

They moved past pungent, fresh bear scat. Becca shivered, her gaze alternately darting from the ground, looking for bear tracks, and into the shadows, looking for bear. Grizzlies were common in this part of the country and had discovered base camp early, testing the patience and locks of the caterers. There was no food allowed in tents or base-camp packs on this fire, but that regulation hadn't kept the bears away.

"If you've got to talk to me, just say it here." She struggled to keep her voice even. Between the bear and Aiden, she was trembling.

With a sound of disgust, Aiden released Becca and stepped away. "I've been trying for the past two hours to figure out why you did it."

Still panting for breath, Becca struggled to formulate an answer. Going to bed with Aiden, a stranger, to get pregnant had seemed logical at the time, but now? Staring into his dark, angry eyes, it seemed incredibly foolish.

He circled her. "You must have thought I was stupid. Did I look like an easy mark? That older woman, younger man thing?"

Mutely, Becca shook her head. He'd been perfect until the point she'd discovered he was a Hot Shot. His team logo—a tree centered on an orange flame—had been permanently etched in Becca's mind when she'd seen it on a T-shirt on his bathroom floor.

Becca continued to watch him, flooded with feelings of

shame, but she would not share this baby with a stranger. She would not stand by and let some man treat her child like a piece of property to be divided, as was happening with her nephew. Nor would she sink to fighting over her child, making them an emotional wreck.

"Why'd you do it? Why'd you make me into a *cheater?*" He leaned in closer. "Did you have a little spat with your husband? Was he cheating on *you?* You didn't even tell me to give me a choice."

"Hu-husband?"

"Did you know you were pregnant when we slept together?" He was pacing around her. "You must have known because you said you had the birth control covered. I don't sleep around with married women, lady, especially a pregnant one. You've made me something I *so* did not want to be. Man, this sucks."

Never much good at lying, Becca's mouth was still hanging open when Aiden halted his tirade.

"Well?" he prompted.

"You thought I was married?"

He scowled. "Not then. But when I saw you here—pregnant as a house—what was I supposed to think?"

"Uh…" It finally registered in Becca's tired, stressed-out brain. He thought she'd been cheating on her husband. He didn't know she didn't have a husband. He didn't suspect the baby was his.

A nervous, relieved laugh escaped before she could stop herself.

"Wait a minute." He peered at her in the gathering darkness. Then he snatched up her left hand. "You're not wearing a ring."

Becca pulled her fingers back. "I'm not married." It was

too late for that. While she'd been focusing on her career, her friends and siblings had been getting married, and having babies. She'd just played a little catch-up and skipped a step or two—dating, engagement, marriage. At thirty-eight, she couldn't wait for Mr. Right.

"But if you're not married, whose baby is that?" He pointed at the baby nestled in her belly as if it were repugnant to him.

"It's mine." Not Aiden's. She wrapped her arms around her belly as if she could prevent him taking the baby from her.

Under the orange, fire-lit sky, Becca watched the wheels turn in Aiden's mind.

"Tell me that baby isn't mine," he demanded slowly in a voice shaking with anger.

"This baby is *mine,*" Becca repeated, staunchly walking the line between lying to him and admitting the truth.

"That's not an answer." Despite his youth, he was annoyingly smart.

Becca stepped sideways, toward the makeshift parking area. "It shouldn't matter to you who the biological father *was.* I'm raising this baby alone."

He shifted his stance, but kept his dark gaze on her. "Every baby needs a father."

"Not this baby." Becca lifted her chin. From what she knew of Aiden—his sleeping around, his wild behavior—she suspected he didn't really want to know if his sperm had helped create the little one inside her. If she told him, it would only weigh on his conscience, if not now, then later, when he got older. And she didn't want to open her door one day ten years from now to find Aiden demanding things like visitation and partial custody.

Instead of being relieved as she'd thought he'd be, Aiden grabbed her by the shoulders, tugging her forward until her face was near his. "Who fathered *your* baby?"

"None of your business. And even if it was, I wouldn't want anything from you." Becca's knees crumpled and she would have fallen if Aiden hadn't turned his grip from cruel to supportive.

"Too late." His voice crackled with anger. "You took something from me in Vegas—a choice. And now I have a different choice to make, don't I?"

SPIDER SANK AGAINST a sturdy spruce as he watched Becca walk back to camp. She moved slowly across the uneven ground as if she were afraid to fall.

Damn her.

Oh, she hadn't come out and admitted the baby was his. In fact, she'd gone out of her way to give him an out, to let him think what he wanted, as if he were the kind of guy who wouldn't step up when something like this happened.

He'd decided long ago that he'd never have kids. His father, a career Hot Shot, had been the worst excuse for a dad ever known to man.

His mother, perhaps recognizing too late that Randy Rodas was poor parenting material and that she was no better, had left Spider with his grandmother one fire season and never been seen or heard from since. At first, Randy sometimes made it home for a brief visit around Christmas, leaving as quickly and unexpectedly as he'd come. And then there'd been nothing but a card with a twenty-dollar bill to validate that Spider had a dad. It was the revelation that his father had been spending his holidays and winters with his other families—other kids that he obviously loved more—that had sent Spider into a tailspin in Vegas.

He'd have to do the right thing, whatever that was. Only the right thing looked pretty damn unpleasant at the moment.

He could just see coming to Becca's house to pick up the kid on a Sunday. She'd be cold, looking down that finely chiseled nose of hers as if he weren't good enough for her or their kid. And the kid would look at him as if he were a stranger.

Double damn.

The one time he'd trusted a woman with birth control—an older woman who should have known better—he'd fathered a child. If his dad was any indication, he'd make a horrible father.

History had a sick way of repeating itself.

"THAT WENT WELL," Becca mumbled to herself as she sank onto her cot. At least Aiden hadn't demanded parental rights. He was too busy recovering from the double whammy discovery that he wasn't an adulterer and that he *might* be responsible for Becca's pregnancy.

"What went well?" Julia lifted her head out of her sleeping bag and opened puffy eyes.

"The day. Don't you think?" Becca covered quickly, inwardly ruing the fact that she had to share a small tent on this assignment. At this stage of her pregnancy, she was uncomfortable all night long, tossing and turning. With Julia in the cot next to her, Becca's burps, stomach gurgles and worse had to be controlled or embarrassingly revealed.

After her confrontation with Aiden, Becca's stomach had twisted into knots. Add the baby bouncing on top of that and she wasn't going to be the quietest roommate in camp tonight.

"Do you really think the fire's going to jump the highway?" Julia asked in a voice less sleepy than her eyes indicated.

It was comments like this that gave away Julia's love of their work, that gave Becca hope for Julia's goals and her own.

"If the winds shift the way they usually do this time of year and we don't get more help, yes." There'd be no stopping the fire's rampage down the mountainside and through a narrow valley a few miles east of their camp.

"I think you're wrong," Julia said, then added, "But you're never wrong." There was a trace of bitterness in Julia's voice that nearly smothered Becca's hope for the Boise job completely.

So, her assistant disagreed with Becca's assessment. Julia had rarely hiked these woods, rarely got her hands dirty in the field, touching the dry earth, snapping the spruce and pine needles, filling her nose with the parched air, seeing in her mind's eye how ready it was to burn or fight for life.

If Becca's assistant spent half as much time studying the maps of the area, local history and weather updates as she did on her makeup, she'd do fine. She had the credentials for the work. She had the interest. She just lacked the drive. And for that, Becca would push Julia until she reached her potential.

The fire business was tough. You either knuckled down or stepped down. People's lives were at stake. The firefighters and people who lived in the area were all at risk. There was little room for error.

At the memory of her parents standing at her brother's grave, familiar frustration churned in Becca's belly. Her mother had never been the same after Jason had died while fighting a wildland fire. Becca hadn't even decided on an area of study in college until he'd been killed. His death had inspired her to try and save others.

"I'd rather be wrong and prevent someone's death, than ignore the signs. A man can't outrun a ninety-mile-an-hour, eighty-foot wall of flame on a flat course, much less a seventy-five-percent grade." The frustration of the Boise job being just out of reach combined with the shattering revelation of Aiden recognizing her pushed Becca over the edge. "Or maybe you like to gamble your ego against the life of someone you know," she snapped, immediately regretting her harsh words, but reluctant to take them back.

Without a word, Julia rolled over, leaving Becca with the sour feeling of her assistant's resentment.

Well, Becca couldn't please everyone. Least of all Aiden. But she wouldn't give up—not on this fire, not on Julia, and not on her plans for a safe, independent future.

Aiden had been angry over the idea that she'd made him into something he wasn't. Becca hated to admit it was a bit of a relief to know he was a choosy womanizer.

She'd left him at the edge of the forest without giving him a chance to say that he wanted nothing to do with her baby. From what she knew of him, he wouldn't relish his role as a father. He was young, far younger than she was. Not just in years, because he had to be about thirty, but in the way he behaved.

Running down the mountain in his boxers. Becca scoffed. High-school hijinx, that's what it was.

Aiden Rodas a father?

No, Becca comforted herself as she struggled to unlace her boots, leaning around her belly. Aiden wasn't ready to be a father. He was a typical, carefree bachelor, predictable in his desire to remain responsibility free. He'd accept her wish to raise the baby on her own, and she'd continue with her plans.

At least, she hoped that's how it all happened.

"HEY, SON." ROADHOUSE FELL into step with Aiden at the edge of camp, dodging a man carrying two chainsaws. Darkness didn't bring much calm to base camp. There were still people everywhere.

"Don't call me that." Aiden scowled, almost making Roadhouse regret that he'd even attempted to talk to his son.

"Won't," Roadhouse mumbled, but he kept his legs moving in step with Aiden's, ignoring the ache in his knees.

"If it's money you want, I don't have anything larger than a ten on me." Aiden walked faster.

Roadhouse wished he could turn back the clock, wished that he'd never asked Aiden for money years ago.

"I don't need any money. I was just wondering…" What happened to you today? But Roadhouse couldn't ask that. Aiden would bite his head off if he tried to get too personal. Instead, he said, "Heard you saw a bit of action today."

"Too much," Aiden replied almost under his breath, making Roadhouse wonder what was wrong. Hot Shots lived to fight fires. They never complained about seeing too much action. No. Something wasn't right.

The crew Roadhouse served on had been lucky enough to battle the fire up close these past few shifts. If more Hot Shot crews were assigned to the Flathead fire, the non-DoF crews were going to be assigned mop-up work—cold trailing burned-over areas to make sure it didn't flare to life again.

A fire could dance through the treetops and leave the forest floor relatively unscathed, or race along the ground, singeing the lower tree branches. In either case, a tree root or trunk could smolder for days before deciding to give the fire a second chance at life. Mop up was tedious, boring, necessary work, but seemed to be in Roadhouse's future.

It took Roadhouse about twenty paces to work up enough saliva to ask, "Something bothering you?"

"Wouldn't tell you if there was. You gave up that right a long time ago, starting with my first birthday." Aiden didn't look at Roadhouse. In fact, he looked away, to the orange glow of the fire on the horizon. "Haven't seen you at a birthday since."

"Suppose I did give somethin' up," Roadhouse admitted,

half under his breath. When Maria had left, her mother had taken over the daily duty of raising Aiden and had been adamant that Roadhouse not undermine her authority or spoil his son on his sporadic visits. He'd never gotten along with his mother-in-law to begin with. After Maria had left, things had become unbearable, until Roadhouse had stopped visiting Aiden altogether. Yet, he never stopped thinking about his firstborn.

If asked, he'd admit he didn't know how to be a good dad. But he'd always thought fondly of his kids—even wrote them letters.

He just never sent them.

He wanted his parental rights back. Forget that Aiden was thirty, Roadhouse wanted to be a part of his life. Ever since his mother-in-law had died, he'd made an effort to be on teams that operated in or near Idaho. He'd told Aiden about his other two children in Vegas, hoping the truth would bring them closer, only to have Aiden seem to resent him even more. Still, he wouldn't give up.

But he could tell by the set of Aiden's expression that now wasn't the time for bonding, so he let Aiden walk away, back into camp, alone with his thoughts.

Roadhouse headed to the rise where he'd talked to Sirus earlier. He squatted on the ground beneath the generators, heedless of the noise created by the machinery. From this point, he could see the various areas where fire crews were bedded down for the night and the tents off to the right of the IC and base-camp staff tents. Behind him was a harsh medley of sound—the washers and dryers chugging away in the laundry trailer, metal grinding on metal as Pulaskis, chainsaws and shovels were sharpened for another day of work—battling to be heard over the hum of generators.

Rummaging in his pack, Roadhouse pulled out a plastic

bag stuffed with dog-eared letters. Carefully, he sorted through the envelopes until he found one in particular, pulling it out as gently as if it were a precious piece of antique glass. He withdrew the folded paper from the envelope and started reading the scrawled handwriting slowly, as if every word weren't already etched in his memory.

Aiden,
We saved a family from the fire today. Their little boy had dark eyes, like yours. It made me wonder how you're doing. Are you behaving for Abuelita? Are you riding the red bike I got you for Christmas? If you were here, I'd ask you to play catch. I'd show you off to my friends and then tuck you into a sleeping bag under the stars. The stars are so close up here at night that you can almost touch them. If you were here, things would be different.

He'd scribbled "Love, Dad" as illegibly as he could beneath the brief missive. It was the way he signed all of his letters, as if he weren't sure he deserved the title or the right to express the sentiment after all the mistakes he'd made.

Ignoring the ache in his knees that had become as painful as the emptiness in his heart, Roadhouse continued to stare at the paper and dwell on the lost opportunities of his youth. He'd never thought he'd end up like this—alone, having nearly outlived his usefulness and with no place to go. He doubted he'd be able to pass the stringent physical exams next year. The time had come to retire.

Too soon.

Someone laughed across the compound. Roadhouse looked up in time to see Aiden take off his boots and slide into his sleeping bag on the ground. Weather permitting, Hot

Shots slept out under the stars. Tents took time to pack and space to transport, not to mention they were stifling in the heat. Roadhouse tilted his gaze up to the sky, where only a few stars peeked through the blanket of smoke.

He'd seen Aiden walking with the pregnant Fire Behavior Analyst. It was unlikely that Aiden saw any action from the woman. But he had been with her. And now he was upset.

Looking down on base camp, Roadhouse wondered what that might mean.

A flicker of hope ignited in his chest.

"COME ON, QUEEN, LET'S SEE what you've got," Spider challenged his new charge as they clawed a hand line out of the mountainside the next afternoon, trying not to think about his meeting with Becca the night before.

The Silver Bend Hot Shots had been ordered to build a firebreak on the safer western boundary of the fire, this time with the aid of two other Hot Shot crews. Once it was done, they'd burn the area from their line to the advancing fire, halting its progress in this direction. "Or are you a little princess with nothing left to give?"

Victoria hacked at the ground with her Pulaski with a fervor that would leave her running on empty in another twenty minutes. The heat and unyielding ground would take the steam out of her arms quickly.

"Don't worry about me. I've got enough juice to clear a path to that ridge," Victoria assured him, although her voice lacked the conviction to inspire confidence.

"We'll see." Spider glanced over to the ridge. Smoke rose in deceptive puffs, as if the fire were gasping its last breath. Spider wasn't fooled. Becca was just as deceptive, and every time he thought of her carrying his child, he had the same sense of doom he felt when working on this fire.

The blaze was stalled a half mile to the north. Spider knew it was just teasing them, waiting for the right moment to roar back to life. In which case, Spider and his team, including Victoria, had to be ready to make for safe ground.

Where was the safe ground with Becca?

Victoria was at the front of a group of five Silver Bend Hot Shots hacking away on the bushes and tree roots in their path. The ridge was still a good hundred yards ahead of them, beyond a thick stand of pine trees. Leading the team, Chainsaw cut trees out of their way while Golden kept lookout. Behind them, five of the crew dug away what was left of the roots and brush with shovels, and five raked the debris with Mc-Cloeds, a compact, sturdy rake. Logan brought up the rear, raking any missed debris out of the way.

They operated efficiently when everyone pulled their weight. Spider was going to make sure Victoria understood this, otherwise she'd have to quit.

"Don't let him beat you, Queenie," someone encouraged from the back of the line.

Eyeing the group, Spider walked uphill until he stood next to Golden.

"If this is your new way of keeping their spirits up…man." Golden shook his head, and then continued quietly. "Don't break her. We need her. I don't want to get classified 'ineffective' because we can't field a full crew, and be sent home early. This is my last shot at overtime this season, and I don't want to come home without a full wallet. Lighten up."

Under the burden of his discovery about Becca, Spider found it impossible to be upbeat. He didn't want to be a father. He wasn't the fatherly type. Being a father meant the end of…of…the life he loved. More than anything, he wanted to hear Becca say that the baby she was carrying wasn't his. And if she said otherwise…well, he'd do what had to be done, whatever that was. He just wasn't ready to think about that yet.

He looked over to where Victoria worked. Keeping her and the others on the crew safe was what was important. Distractions, like the possibility of fatherhood and deceitful, beautiful women, had no place out here. "I don't want Victoria to snap either. She'll either bend or break. If she can't cut it, so be it. I'm not going to go easy on her."

"I never took you for such an ass." Golden had a way of staring at you that made you want to confess all your secrets and sins.

"Yeah." Spider forced a grin on his face and kept his sins to himself. "You just thought I was an everyday, ordinary ass. But I'm not going to let her slide just because the season's nearly over and I'm not going to let her assume her performance is acceptable. You know out here that one screw up multiplies until the entire team is at risk."

"That's cold, man." Golden shook his head.

"Is it? Do you remember the first fire of the season? The one right after we found Logan's Aunt Glen in the mountains?" Spider looked at Victoria, then at the rookie next to her, O'Reilly. Should he be worrying about the rookie, too? He had a kid, didn't he? And he'd frozen when the order had first been given to run the other day.

Damn. Now he was seeing weakness everywhere.

"Technically, Thea and Logan found her," Golden corrected, pulling Aiden's attention back from his mini-panic attack.

Spider waved that small detail aside. "They got lucky.

Anyway, we went to New Mexico afterwards for that fire and Victoria choked."

"She did not choke," Golden protested, a note of warning in his voice. There were limits to his patience. "I'd know if she choked."

With a quick shake of his head, Spider defended his assessment. "That was the first time I realized she wasn't cut out for the Hot Shots. She kept falling behind as we hiked out of there, until she just wasn't behind me anymore." It was Spider's job to bring up the rear and account for stragglers, regardless of whose unit they were in. "So I backtracked until I found her and I waited while she puked her guts out trailside." Spider dropped his voice as if someone could have heard them over the chainsaw. "You don't do that unless you're losing your nerve."

"Come on, you've been on her case from day one." Golden wasn't buying it. "Face it, she's the first female Hot Shot we've had and you don't accept her because she's a woman."

Spider had no problem with her being a woman. Yet, he knew that Golden wouldn't want to hear about Spider's worries concerning their safety on this fire. The men didn't talk about their fears. So without a word, Spider moved back to the line, stopping behind Victoria to hack at a root with his Pulaski. Sure, she'd had a solid first year, but being a Hot Shot was about endurance.

"You need to ease up," he said quietly. "You can't push yourself to the limit, without keeping something in reserve." The way she was pushing herself, she'd never make it if they had to run for a safety zone.

"You can't break me," she said just as softly.

Spider wasn't so sure.

"Hey, Spider, I saw you last night with the Fire Behavior Analyst," O'Reilly called out after a few minutes. With little to occupy their minds during such physical tasks, wildland firefighters were notorious talkers and latched onto any event as a source of entertainment. "Has your taste in women changed?"

So much for having a private conversation with Becca at base camp. At least no one suspected Becca might be carrying his kid.

Hell, who was he kidding? She hadn't come out and said it, but that kid was his. Spider still couldn't believe she'd offered him a way out. It was tough raising kids. For all her holier-than-thou attitude, she ought to know that she shouldn't be doing it alone.

The question was: How badly did Spider want to be a father? That is, a better father than his dad had been, because Spider wouldn't repeat his father's parenting mistakes and have his kid resent him.

A father. The idea was horrifyingly intimidating.

"His taste has changed, alright. To *older,* pregnant women," Doc said, as if Spider needed clarification. "This winter, he'll be cruising the retirement village for dates."

The countercomments and rounds of laughter indicated the mood on the crew had shifted, lightened. At Spider's expense.

"Might want to save your breath, Doc," Spider warned, a bit of venom in his tone. "As soon as Victoria burns out, you're switching spots."

"I'm not burning out." Victoria stood, wiping sweat from her brow.

"She won't burn out. She's tough," Doc defended her.

"Why don't you switch with her now, Romeo? Yeah, I'm not kidding. Make the switch." Victoria was visibly slowing and the last thing Spider needed was Doc, with his suave ways, making a play for his teammate. A within-team romance was the last distraction they needed right now.

Victoria would be royally pissed at anyone Spider sent to replace her. Anger kept you going.

Yeah, Doc was the perfect choice.

CHAPTER FIVE

"THIS IS THE KIND OF FIRE you tell stories about to your grand-kids, eh, Roadhouse? Wicked slopes, out in the middle of no-where, inaccessible by fire-engine crews, forced to engage in fire-at-your-boots combat. It's my kind of heaven." From his place in line next to Roadhouse, Bart sighed happily, wiping his forehead with his blue bandana. Why wouldn't he be happy? At forty, he had a wife and two kids ready to spend the winter listening to his stories.

Roadhouse grunted. Had he been ten or twenty years younger with a family at home, he would have reveled in this fire and the challenge it presented, too.

As it was, Roadhouse couldn't wait for it to be over! His knees traitorously ached with every move he made. He want-ed to sit in a chair somewhere for a day with his feet propped up, talking to Aiden, making up for the mistakes of his youth.

Only, Roadhouse didn't want the fire to be over because this was almost certainly his last one. This close to the flames, the smoke hung heavy around them. He filled his lungs with gray-brown air, savoring it as a smoker about to quit smok-ing might his last cigarette.

Days after Aiden and his team had nearly been consumed by a tunnel of fire, Roadhouse found his team assigned near Aiden's. The fire burned low meadow brush thirty feet away as gentle as a ringed campfire. His team had eked out fifty feet of brush across a rise on this southern edge of the blaze, working their way down toward the Silver Bend Hot Shots. Hopefully, the fire wouldn't be able to cross the line they were building. With little more than a puff of wind in the air, barely more than five miles an hour, the fire was currently a tame beast heeling upon command.

The superintendent of Montana #5, Jack Strand, thought that meant the fire would soon be contained. Roadhouse knew better. There was a perverse character to this fire, as if it had split personalities.

Working with deliberate movements, Roadhouse kept one eye on the ground fire. According to the Fire Behavior Analyst, the winds could pick up late in the day, creating wind tunnels that would fan the meek morning embers into more than one hundred and fifty terrifying feet of flame, gobbling whatever lay before them in mere seconds.

Jack laughed somewhere farther down the line, pointing to a grizzly lumbering through the stand of pine trees below them. Roadhouse shook his head in disgust. The superintendent wasn't even radioing the other teams in the area to warn them that a bear was making its way out of the fire's path. Jack was so irritating that no one had come up with a nickname for him. Privately, Roadhouse thought of him as Jack-ass. Roadhouse had never wanted the responsibility of leadership, but that didn't mean he didn't know what it took to be a good leader.

A super should position himself higher than the rest of the crew where he'd be more likely to notice any abnormal activity on the fire or feel the stirrings of the wind. Instead, this moron stood at the bottom of the line, joking with his buddies and letting Incident Command—miles below them, valleys between them—determine when conditions turned dangerous.

About sixty feet down the mountainside, Roadhouse noticed a flash of yellow in the trees. It was Golden, wearing a yellow fire helmet, doing an advance scout ahead of his crew, as a good leader should. After staring a few moments at the fire, he turned his face skyward as if reading the weather. On a quick turn of his heel, Golden returned the way he'd come.

Something about the way he moved, quickly and with purpose, worried Roadhouse.

Aiden was down there, working along the edge of that large stand of pine trees. It was dangerous to be working blind like that without a good superintendent to watch over you. Roadhouse tried not to worry about Aiden, but it was hard not to when you knew the potential danger of an unpredictable wildfire. He'd lost too many friends over the years to take the job of wildland firefighter lightly, and he had too many regrets about his kids already.

"Do you need an engraved invitation to move, Monsieur Roadhouse?" Bart asked from behind him, with a poor imitation of a French accent. "Or do I need to kick your butt outta my way?"

Roadhouse ignored him, lifting his face to the heavens as Golden had done. No wind caressed his face. The crackle of the ground fire was gentle, almost lazy.

What had spooked Golden? Or was it his own overactive imagination reading more into Golden's action than there was? Perhaps some misplaced desire to watch over Aiden as he should have done years ago?

Just one hundred feet and they'd have completed the first successful firebreak on the southern boundary. Bending to his task, Roadhouse tried not to worry. Even now, he could hear the grind of chainsaw against wood as Silver Bend cleared a ten-foot wide path through the trees.

The Fire Behavior Analyst hadn't been happy that they planned to hem in the fire on this slope. He'd seen her frown when the IC announced the day's duties. There was risk here.

Roadhouse worked faster, ignoring the pain in his knees. According to the meteorologist, the afternoon wind would kick up in the late afternoon. It was barely two-thirty now.

Something orange danced into his line of vision. Roadhouse looked up from his work.

Feather-light embers floated and twirled across their line. A breeze brushed tauntingly against his cheek, then returned with a much stronger caress.

The afternoon wind was early.

Had Golden sensed the change? Would Aiden be pulled back to safety or be trapped in the trees below?

A quick glance revealed the obvious—Jack-ass had no clue yet. Roadhouse waved him over, gestured to the fire with a nod of his head. "The wind's starting to pick up."

Jack gazed around, sniffed the air, seemingly unconcerned. "So?"

"So? Don't you think we ought to consider pulling out?" It pained Roadhouse to even suggest it, but Aiden—

"Hell, no. You don't see Silver Bend retreating to a safe zone, do you?"

"Not yet." But he hoped it wouldn't be long before they did.

"Let me tell you something, old-timer. We don't pull out until the DoF crews do. Wouldn't want a reputation as a chicken, now would we?" Jack-ass slapped Roadhouse on the shoulder.

There was a difference on the fire line between being brave

and being stupid. Jack-ass hadn't learned that difference, had probably never scrambled up a steep slope praying that he could outrun the fiery dragon at his heels. To him, being cautious was a sign of weakness.

Roadhouse was helpless to do anything but his own task, because the only way to ensure Aiden was safe—other than to retreat—was to complete the line. Roadhouse bent and scraped at brush, ignoring the feeling that the wind was increasing, that the fire had suddenly awakened and was doing more than creeping toward them.

"SPIDER, A WORD." Socrates waved Spider over as the team came into base camp after another wasted day fighting the fire. Silver Bend and Montana #5 had hiked in before dawn to defend a ridge. Ten hours and one bear sighting later, they hadn't been able to finish their line and start back-burning since the fire had raced down the mountain in the early afternoon, cutting them off above and below, nearly trapping them in a triangle of fire on that tricky slope.

Squinting in the late afternoon sunlight, Spider had been casually looking around to see if his father's team was in base camp, which would mean the old man was okay. They'd been cut off from the Montana #5 team and Spider hadn't seen them anywhere yet. A quick glance at the expression on the Incident Commander's face, however, and a feeling of dread rippled through Spider's gut. Socrates was about to deliver bad news, information Spider was going to reject. His dad couldn't have been trapped in the fire. He was too seasoned for that, even if his team was under-trained.

He gave Socrates his complete attention.

"I'm pulling you onto IC for a couple of days."

Expecting bad news of a more personal nature, Spider's

jaw clenched as his entire body went rigid with relief and dread. He bit back a smart-ass reply, managing one word instead. "Why?"

"Morale is low and you've proven…*insightful* when it comes to creative ways to keep a team's spirits up."

Translation: You're good at making an ass of yourself.

Spider frowned. Was that the reputation he'd created for himself after ten years of firefighting? Or was Socrates just trying to make him toe the line? The old man wasn't beyond giving out duties that were meant to put you in your place.

He caught a glimpse of his dad limping over by the laundry tent, looking relatively unscathed.

Spider was going to be a father soon, whether he liked it or not. Good fathers were upstanding citizens, serious, responsible, early risers. Did Socrates see any of that in Spider?

Probably not. Socrates was constantly telling Spider to grow up.

It was this attitude toward Spider that convinced him this "assignment" was his punishment for the boxer incident, perhaps Becca even had a hand in it. Of course, she had. He clamped his lips together to keep from swearing and making things worse.

Socrates clarified, "I'm making use of your talents. There haven't been any fights yet, but the tension level in camp is ratcheting so high I expect one at any time."

That was too much for Spider's short fuse. "You know I'm much better at starting fights then stopping them." As a thin, wiry guy in school and then a thin, wiry man on the Hot Shot roster, Spider was often seen as an easy target. He'd learned early that he couldn't let people push him around or he'd forever be looking over his shoulder.

Socrates narrowed his eyes and Spider found himself

caught in the older man's gaze. When Socrates finally spoke, his words dripped with warning. "You'll be serving as my assistant for a few days. I need you to work with the support units here in base camp, find out what they need help with, and tell them what it's like up there without being the voice of doom." He glanced around. "The last thing we want is people making decisions without hope. Got it?"

"Yes, sir." Spider did get it. He had to take his punishment like a man, jump when Socrates snapped his fingers, and hide his frustration behind a pleasant smile. He just didn't believe he could play the obedient assistant for longer than a day or so. There was, after all, one heck of a fire on this mountain, and even though it made him nervous, he'd rather be nervous out there than shackled here in base camp.

"Start with the Fire Behavior team." Socrates pinned him with a cool stare. "I believe you still owe Becca Thomas a debrief on that blowup a few days ago."

Spider couldn't suppress a groan. Cheer up Becca? That would be awfully hard to do when he hadn't decided whether to forget that her baby was his, as she seemed to want him to do, or tackle the enormous role of fatherhood—a role as doomed to fail as this bogus assistant assignment.

"THINK ABOUT IT, JULIA," Becca prompted for what felt like the umpteenth time in five minutes, trying to keep her eyes open against the pregnancy fatigue that usually swept over her in the afternoon. "What's the fire going to do tonight?"

"I thought you already ran the simulations," Julia said instead of answering the question. "Can't we just go with those predictions?"

"Systems crash, bugs appear and inputs can be wrong." The baby played her ribs like a bass drum, eliciting a weary smile from Becca. The underside of her bra and the back of her shirt were damp with sweat. Becca wanted out of the stuffy tent, longed to step out into the late afternoon breeze. It would still be hot, but at least the air would be moving. She shifted in her chair as best she could with her swollen ankles propped on an empty milk crate, wondering, despite herself, where Aiden and Victoria were and if they were safe. "So, what's this fire going to do tonight?"

"It's going to burn something. All it's been doing is eating up acres." Twenty thousand so far.

"The satellite picture shows where the fire burns hottest," Becca prompted patiently, giving Julia a huge clue. If Becca couldn't get the management job without Julia excelling, Julia would excel. Becca wouldn't accept failure. She'd mold Julia into a success story if both she and Julia had to go without sleep every night. "Where are the winds?"

Julia let out a ponderous sigh and rubbed her eyes. Becca must have been keeping her up at night with her frequent trips to the bathroom and tossing on the narrow cot, because Julia's eyes were puffy again.

"Hello, ladies."

Aiden's voice.

Becca went cold. The baby quivered deep inside her, as if anticipating its daddy.

Be calm.

But her heart raced. And her eyes were wide open now.

Julia spun around, releasing a breathy *Oh,* the word so loaded with welcome that Becca believed Aiden was here to see her assistant.

With as much grace as Becca could muster past her suddenly bruised, stupid ego—because she had no right to feel slighted that Aiden found Julia attractive—Becca lifted her puffy ankles off the milk crate and turned to face the man who had the power to make her life as a mother miserable.

He looked like hell in his grimy uniform, with a face smudged with dirt and sweat, and eyes drooping from exhaustion. Becca knew Silver Bend and another crew had been sent out last night for a double shift in the hopes of creating a fire line before the afternoon winds picked up. She tried not to sympathize with Aiden because he looked like every other firefighter just off a long shift. Yet, there was a mantle of defeat that seemed to weigh him down and tugged at her heartstrings.

Needing something to do other than sit and stare at Aiden, Becca gathered up the pencils and maps on her desk. "We're busy. Maybe you could come back to see Julia later."

He opened his mouth to speak, then closed it and stared at her. Finally, he shook his head. "I've been sent over by Socrates. He wants you to pick my brain about the fire since you've only seen it on a computer screen."

Becca's skin grew hot. "If you're implying we sit down here in base camp with our eyes glued to the computer screen—"

"And your feet propped up? Which is just the way I found you."

"—then you need to learn what a Fire Behavior Analyst really does."

"And if you think I've got nothing to bring to this tea party, then you need to learn what a Hot Shot really does." And then he smiled, as if he were a used-car salesman and she were an easy mark.

To think that he'd fathered her child.

Irrationally, Becca wished she had something more lethal than a pencil to throw at Aiden. She gave him what she hoped was an intimidating glare, wishing him gone.

Her glare was so powerful, he didn't even blink. They stared at each other for what seemed like an hour of tense silence until Becca realized that Julia was a rapt spectator of the pair of them making fools of themselves.

Sirus stuck his head in the tent. "Everything all right in here?"

"Sirus." Ignoring Aiden, Becca walked out the door with ungainly steps, forcing Sirus to move back. "Can you explain to me why I need a Hot Shot?"

He gazed down at Becca for a long time, his expression closed, before saying, "He's here to help."

"Help with what?"

"Download his experiences and give his perspective. Look, you've relied on firefighters for information before, haven't you?"

"Yes, but—"

"You're always talking about information you've collected from places other than the computer, right?"

"Yes, but—"

Someone called to Sirus, and he almost looked relieved as he stepped back. "He's here to help. Use him." And then he left her standing alone in front of the tent.

"So, Sirus sent you." Becca tapped her chin with her forefinger after she returned to the tent. If Sirus thought Becca needed a Hot Shot, she'd go along with it until she could get rid of Aiden. And if she couldn't get rid of her Hot Shot, maybe Becca could convince Sirus that Aiden wasn't the right Hot Shot to help her. Becca drew a deep breath, attempting to swallow her pride.

Think of the job in Boise.

"Yes, Socrates sent me." With a disdainful grimace, Aiden looked just as unhappy to be here as she was to have him. Hot

Shots were such pompous pains in the ass. Most believed they were a class above the overhead and support crews in base camp simply because they fought fires up close and personal.

"Well, since you're here and we've got a *few* minutes, why don't you tell us all you know." Becca mirrored his earlier smile with one of her own. She could be professional and courteous, and still be a bit intimidating. They weren't going to be best buddies after this assignment, or ever.

Aiden's lips stretched as he struggled to hold his smile. "Wow. It might take me more than a few minutes to share it all, especially if you don't get it on the first try."

"I'd love to hear what you have to say." Julia gazed up at Aiden as if he were a Greek god, clearly not helping Becca's case. Not that this was a surprise.

Aiden cocked an eyebrow in Becca's direction, waiting for her assent.

A large map was tacked onto the back of the door. The body of the fire was indicated by red lines and in a very few places on its northern flank where they'd contained it, there were lines formed by thick black *X*s.

Part of her wanted nothing more than to kick him out—not wise when she was looking to impress Sirus or when she was trying to curtail Aiden's involvement with her baby. Part of her wondered about what he had to say, what he'd been through. She was curious about his curt, smart-ass answers to Carl at the debrief the other day. Had he noticed something more than he'd admitted to?

With a reluctant nod of her head, Becca indicated Aiden should begin. "Why don't you start with today's map."

"You were making a fire line out on the southern flank today, right?" The assistant Fire Behavior Analyst asked with eyes as large as big blue quarters, just begging for Spider's attention.

"Right." Out of courtesy, he thrust his hand in her direction and introduced himself, promptly forgetting her name because his attention was on Becca Thomas.

This close, it struck him again that she was very pregnant. Her green T-shirt was a bit snug, revealing curves where Becca hadn't had any before, curves that beckoned to be explored by a man's hand. Yet, her legs looked almost as fit and trim beneath her black shorts as they had several months ago. Except for a fringe of bangs over her stitches, her blond hair was pulled back into that thick braid she seemed to prefer, taming those long, wild locks into something more civilized.

Pregnant and sexy. There was a new one for Spider. When he noticed pregnant women, if he noticed them at all, he wasn't aroused.

Becca took a step closer to the map with her belly thrust forward and a crease in her brow as if she didn't quite trust him.

Not trust him? Now that was a laugh. He was sure she was the reason he'd been given this assignment. She probably wanted to exert control over him. Fat chance.

"The way I figure it, the line we were working on today is in the middle of the black right now," he said, meaning the burned-over ground that was the fire's wake. "We were working in the trees when they started going up like Roman candles. We had to make a hasty retreat."

The winds had picked up in the early afternoon and breathed energy into the fire. A couple of the newer Silver Bend Hot Shots were complaining that the IC was building fire lines too close to the front. They hadn't yet realized how frequently they'd be working in the fire's shadow. With more seasons under his belt, Spider knew the tricky, angled terrain made fire prediction, and weather prediction for that matter, a crapshoot. You made do with the information you had.

"Was anyone hurt?" Becca asked, looking him over—not in the come-to-me way her assistant had—but with concern, as if checking for injuries, as if she cared.

The notion that Becca might not want to see him drop off the face of the earth gave him pause. Women he'd slept with didn't usually look at him with tender emotion, perhaps because he didn't usually pursue a relationship after the itch had been scratched.

"We're all safe and accounted for," he told her. Once more, he'd practically dragged Victoria to the safety zone.

Instead of snapping back at him, Becca moved with swaying steps over to one of the desks and began flipping through stacks of paper, mumbling, "Wind shifts? Ridge incline? Fuels?"

He looked at her assistant, who shrugged and said, "She talks to herself a lot."

"I heard that." Becca turned to Spider. "Where did we go wrong?"

"The winds whipped up." Trying to be casual, he shrugged. "By the time it reached the trigger point, it had quite a bit of speed and height." That was certainly an understatement.

Although the meteorologist had predicted the winds would pick up this afternoon, he couldn't predict the exact hour or give the task a time tag, indicating when they should retreat.

The women looked at him expectantly. He'd said his piece and they didn't appear any more upbeat than when he'd come in. That seemed to be about all Spider had to contribute. Sirus would consider this a failure.

Spider almost smiled. Failing at a bogus assignment wasn't really failure, was it?

Becca passed a hand over her belly, bringing his thoughts away from the fire.

She's carrying my baby.

He had to decide what his role would be. If he chose fatherhood, there'd be custody to explore, financial support to arrange, not to mention a lot of learning on his part about how to be a dad. No more late-night parties or taking off for days with no plan and nothing more than his car keys, because dads didn't do things like that. A myriad of next steps and potential lifestyle changes awaited his decision of whether or not to be involved in his child's life.

Spider's shoulders tensed and knotted as reality struck. What could Spider offer his kid that Becca couldn't? She was educated, classy and capable. He didn't even know how a diaper worked. He stared stupidly at Becca as feelings of inadequacy washed over him. Hell, he couldn't even handle a simple base camp assignment.

In the midst of his circuit-frying thoughts, he caught Becca mumble, "Hopeless."

Her defeated tone of voice shocked him out of his stupor. According to his grandmother, nothing was hopeless. Maybe Socrates had been right. Morale really was low. Spider was needed here. He'd been given a legit assignment. He straightened and looked at Becca in a new light, energized now that he believed there was something to be done here. There was a difference between being needed and being put in his place by a vengeful woman.

This should be easy enough. After all, he was used to building morale for his own team. A little positive reinforcement, a joke or two, bonding over a beer with some of the other support staff and snap—job done, back to the fire line.

Besides, it was to his advantage to make nice with Becca.

He eyed Becca speculatively. She looked like a nice girl, like someone who'd respect a guy who dealt with her fairly. Nice girls played fair, didn't they? If only Spider could forget a few details, like Vegas, or that Becca hadn't told him about the baby.

Spider put on his best trustworthy smile. "I think you ladies have been doing a great job. It's not your fault that this fire changes its mind as often as a woman changes her hair color. So, let's get to work. I'm here to help in whatever way you need me to."

Becca's expression turned stony, the woman knew how to give a visual put-down, and even her assistant looked at Spider as if he'd stripped down to a dirty pair of Skivvies. Again, he felt useless.

"And just what do you expect to do to help us? Choose a new hair color?" Becca's stare might have daunted a lesser man, but Spider was used to rebounding from adversity.

Fighting the feeling that he was failing, he kept his smile in place. A good joke always diffused the tension. "I'm more qualified to choose nail color, but we can talk about that later. Don't you want to ask me about my opinion and experiences on this fire?"

"No." Becca moved over to a desk and began sorting a stack of paper, probably one that didn't need sorting.

"No?" Socrates was going to have Spider's hide if she refused his help. His smile faltered. Who was she to say he couldn't help her—either with that kid or strategizing about the fire?

"No," Becca reaffirmed. "We've heard all you've got to say. Now, if you'll excuse us, we need to finalize our fire predictions before we meet the meteorologist."

She was dismissing him? No way.

Becca glanced up, one eyebrow raised beneath that bandage, her unspoken question was clearly *Why are you still here?*

He'd heard it said that there was just so much a man could take before he threw in the towel.

A glutton for punishment, Spider wasn't even close to that point. He had a purpose here in camp, and the sooner he accomplished it, the sooner he'd be back where he belonged.

"Maybe if I hang around awhile, I'll have a few questions." With a smile that now felt like a grimace, he sat down on Becca's chair, propped his aching dogs up on the milk crate as she'd done and let Becca know that he wasn't about to be pushed aside like an errand boy.

"I SUPPOSE THE WINDS will blow it somewhere around here," Julia observed, pointing to an area at the southern tip of the fire on the map.

"Yes, it's nearly at the head of this west-facing ridge. It could head anywhere and everywhere." Becca tried hard to ignore Aiden—hard to do under normal circumstances, but harder still when he was reclining in her space. If he said anything to give away her secret, she'd...she'd...Well, she'd make him sorry. If it got back to Boise that he'd fathered her child, her chances at the management job would be ruined. Men could sleep around with younger women, but Becca was certain that the conservative NIFC wouldn't accept the reverse. Oh, if NIFC found out, they'd come up with some legitimate excuse for not offering Becca the job, but she'd know the real reason.

"What do you think the fire will do, Julia?" Becca asked

Julia shrugged and Becca wanted to strangle her. The baby bopped her belly, as if advising her to be patient. To keep herself from answering for Julia or cracking under the pressure of anticipation that Aiden would expose her, Becca took a swig of water. Then another.

"I suppose…with these winds…it would head south faster." There was the slightest hint of interest in her voice, almost as if Julia were afraid to show it.

"Good," Becca encouraged. "Why?"

"The southern exposure from the sun will have dried the forest out more than on the northern side. Winds blowing in from the west would push a fire quicker, possibly creating a crown fire on the drier face of the ridge." The words spilled out of Julia quicker toward the end of her speech, and then Julia looked as surprised as Becca was.

Of course, there was no one important around to notice how much progress Becca was making with Julia. Just Aiden.

"Good answer, don't you think, Bec?" Aiden said, sounding like a bad imitation of a motivational speaker.

"Let's compare that to the model." Becca was pleased with Julia's answer. She was certainly on the right track. For a moment, there was hope…if she could just forget that Aiden could ruin things for her with NIFC…or the possibility that he might want this baby.

"The model doesn't predict the winds as accurately as they have on other fires I've been on," Julia noted a few minutes later.

Becca almost fainted with relief at Julia's revelation. "It's the slopes. All bets are off on ground-wind prediction when the topography is so severe." Okay, that was a bit of an overstatement, but wind predictions certainly hadn't been accurate here.

Aiden raised his eyebrows with a quirky smile and a nod,

indicating this was not news. Becca ignored him. She couldn't admit that Carl was pulling predictions out of his worn baseball cap.

"Why don't we hike up the ridge a bit and take some readings? Carl's going to be up there, and you might change your predictions after being out in the field," Becca suggested when they'd reviewed the model some more. She wanted to show both Julia and Carl the dangers of keeping to their current strategy, and hoped Carl would agree to support her recommended strategy in front of Sirus.

With Aiden in camp, she didn't fear getting run over by a Hot Shot crew this evening. The gas supply had been restored and crews were being carried to and from the drop point by truck. Besides, Aiden looked exhausted, so a hike was probably the last thing on his agenda. Becca could relax once he wasn't sitting within five feet of her watching every move she made.

Julia almost pouted, her lip drawing down, but in the end she didn't argue. "I suppose there's time before dinner. Would you like to come?" Julia asked Aiden.

"Sure," Aiden stood with envious energy, as if he hadn't been working on a fire since the wee hours of the morning.

Pressing her lips tightly together so that she wouldn't release a primal yowl of frustration, Becca gathered up her instruments and walked away, not waiting to see if Julia and Aiden would follow her. Only when she was trudging up the path did she look back. Julia was trailing along as if she were the older, pregnant woman, not Becca. Aiden walked just a few steps behind, calling out greetings to friends as he passed, then pausing to share a joke with one of the equipment managers.

Why hadn't she noticed in Las Vegas that he was a louder, more comedic version of Colin Farrell? Too much energy. Too much volume. Too young. Too much a danger for her peace of mind. What would Sirus say if he knew Aiden had fathered this baby? He'd forget about ever thinking she deserved a chance at that Boise job, that's what.

That's when Becca saw that Sirus was watching them.

And he wasn't smiling.

CHAPTER SIX

"I SENT JULIA BACK." Aiden strode past Becca on the trail, barely breathing hard.

"You what?" She leaned one hand against a tree, unable to take as deep a breath as she needed since the baby stretched and elbowed her lungs. Becca didn't know who to be angrier at—Julia and her aversion to the woods, or Aiden for casually dismissing her.

The Boise job was slipping through her fingers.

Aiden paused mid-stride to look back down on Becca. "Julia was congested and having trouble keeping up. And, you know, if she can't keep up with *you,* something's gotta be wrong."

"You insufferable idiot!" She was ten times angrier at Aiden than she ever could have been at Julia.

"Hey, I was being nice." Aiden had the nerve to look offended.

Becca found it hard to draw enough breath to chew his irritating butt out, which was good because she couldn't afford to start a fight with him. He might bring up the topic she most wanted to avoid—her baby. Becca straightened, trying to make room between the baby and her lungs, releasing a groan of frustration. How she longed to tell Aiden what she really thought of him.

"Hey." He peered at her. "You don't look so good. Let's take a breather." Aiden stepped closer, towering above her only because of the steep incline. He held out his canteen.

"I've got water, thanks." Somehow, she managed to regain her composure, although she had to clench her teeth to do so. Without accepting his canteen or reaching for her own water, she looked at her watch, still unable to believe he'd sent Julia back. Why would he do that without asking her? "I'm running late." This was her chance to talk some sense into Carl. It was clear they weren't getting any air support from NIFC.

Canteen still in hand, Aiden glanced at his own watch. "What's your hurry? Everybody needs a breather now and then, especially a pregnant woman. Let's just sit down and talk until you're ready to go again."

And then Becca realized why he'd sent Julia back. He wanted to talk to her about the baby. He couldn't do that with Julia tagging along.

She slapped his canteen away and tried to step past him. "You'll have to do better than that."

"Calm down," he advised with his arms spread to block her way, as if he actually cared what happened to her, sounding and looking so sincere that Becca almost believed him, until the baby kicked her.

He was sneaky all right. If she didn't watch out, he'd tell everyone in the fire industry what they'd done in Las Vegas, destroying her credibility, making her unemployable. Then he'd take this baby from her.

A pregnant woman's paranoid delusions? Hardly. What did she really know about Aiden? And if he trapped her into some kind of visitation or custody agreement, she had no way of knowing what kind of father he'd be.

Becca's breath came in quick, shallow gasps now. Too much air. She was going to have a panic attack. All because of him.

"Hey, slow down. This is how accidents happen." Aiden spread his arms out again and wouldn't let her pass.

"If you don't move out of my way," she managed to pant, "what happens next will be no accident." She'd taken self-defense. Perhaps it was time to put it to good use, although she couldn't imagine doing much damage in her current pregnant state.

Her distress must have penetrated that thick skull of his because Aiden moved aside. "Okay, how much farther until we reach Carl?"

"Another ten to fifteen minutes." She puffed past Aiden, barely able to resist slapping at him, which was so unlike her that she nearly stumbled. Her cheeks felt hot and her eyes filled with tears. The dratted hormones, the plans she had for the future at risk, and Aiden's knowing the truth had made her into a paranoid, monster-woman. It wasn't the best of moods to confront Carl.

Aiden didn't say a word, but she could hear his booted feet following her up the ever-steepening trail. She was giving him a great view of her wide ass-ets, when her best feature was now her bountiful boobs—not that she wanted him looking at those either. At any moment, she expected him to ask about Las Vegas or the baby, until she became so taut and filled with tension that she wanted to scream. At any moment—

"I was wondering—"

"Don't." Becca spun, fully intending to cut off any attempt for the talk to become personal, but she lost her footing and slid down into him.

"All right, let's sit down." Aiden put a hand on her arm and firmly guided Becca down to the ground, squatting in front of her. "Trust me. Don't push it in the mountains. The meteorologist will wait. It's time for a drink."

"I don't want a drink." And Becca hadn't a minute ago, but as she looked into his dark eyes, her mouth seemed to dry out. She sat awkwardly on the ground, her knees tight together. With her belly so large, the baby practically rested in her lap, quiet now as if hunkered down against Becca's stormy, unpredictable temper. "And I don't want to talk about my baby."

His expression turned deadly, black brows pulling low. He opened his mouth as if about to swear at her. Then he looked at her stomach, pressed his lips firmly together and shook his head. "I admit. I have questions. But I don't want to go into it right now when you're obviously upset and we're miles from camp. I can't exactly carry you down the mountain by myself. Now, take a drink."

On top of sending Julia back, he was accusing her of being fat? "Of all the nerve. I don't want—"

"Yes, you do." He cut her off and sighed, closing his eyes as he worked his expression into something less threatening. When he reopened them, Aiden's smile was gentle, nothing resembling the cocky smile he'd given her down in camp. "I have a feeling that pride of yours doesn't get thirsty, but the rest of you does."

He was right. She'd been pushing herself hard, ignoring her body's and her baby's needs in her desire not to let anyone down on the fire. Becca found his canteen in her hands and without much thought, she lifted it to her lips, never taking her eyes off Aiden. She couldn't figure him out. Everyone had an agenda.

She shifted her bottom on the hard ground and narrowed her eyes. "What are you up to?"

"I don't know what you mean."

"You're being nice." If she ignored the fact that he'd sent Julia back, if she believed him about her needing to go slow, and shoved the paranoid monster to the back of her mind, she might possibly have considered him a good guy.

As Aiden squatted at her feet, Becca could almost feel the compassion in his eyes racing through her blood, heating her neck, her skin and elsewhere. On some level, he seemed to care about her, even if it was only as a pregnant woman who seemed to need watching over. She didn't want Aiden to be nice to her. She couldn't afford him to be nice to her.

"I'm just doing my job. Sometimes you just do what they tell you." He tried to smile but couldn't quite. "Socrates wanted me to tell you about what happened on the mountain the other day. He thought it would help you fight this fire. Admittedly, I've let this—" he gestured in the direction of the baby "—get in the way. I'm not usually so…difficult. I do have friends, you know."

Aiden was being civil, and she liked him when he wasn't scowling at her, which just wouldn't do. It made her vulnerable. She reminded herself to be tough. "I don't understand why Sirus picked you. When they've sent me firefighters in the past, they've been crew bosses, like Jackson…I mean, Golden." She tilted her head. "Your job is up there, fighting fires." Far, far away from her.

Aiden shrugged. "Not today. Today my job is to help the Incident Command team…to help you." There was something about the way he said it, perhaps because he looked away, that led her to believe he didn't want to be here—with her—any more than she wanted to be with him.

The rejection hurt, poking her irritation back to the surface. "That's ridiculous. How are you supposed to help me? You know nothing about weather patterns, fuels and fire behavior."

Quick as a shot, he stood, looming over her. "Don't I? I've been a Hot Shot for close to ten years. I've fought fires that were as predictable as my grandmother's casserole, as ornery as a bull and as determined to put something deadly over on us as this fire is." His eyes blazed with anger and his words with passion. "It's always rough being among the first ground-pounder crews out on a fire. You don't know what to expect. I'm in charge of the safety of my unit. I have to listen to what fire experts, like you, said twelve hours ago and put it in the context of what the fire's doing now. So, don't presume that I can't help you or don't know anything just because I'm not a legend, like Golden. I know a hell of a lot more than you think. If Socrates thinks I can help you, then you better believe that I can help you."

Rarely had a man spoken to Becca with such intense emotion. She could sense his frustration with her and his pride in being a firefighter.

Unaccountably, she wanted to kiss him.

Instead, she nodded slowly, trying not to think of him as more than a colleague, trying not to remember the frenzied way his hands felt on her body. Becca could control a physical attraction. She focused on breathing steadily and on what Sirus expected of her—to be a good manager and team player. "All right. Tell me. Tell me about that fire a few days ago."

Aiden stared at his boots for a minute as if composing himself and then cleared his throat. "We hiked up to the ridge and took stock of the fire. It looked peaceful enough, so we chose an anchor point—the little creek—and we started to clear a line. The brush was only four-foot high, dry as a bone and easy to dig out by the roots. We made good distance until after lunch." He paused, looking up at the sky. "I'd like to say it was me that noticed something was wrong, but it wasn't. It was Golden. Several times in the past, he's noticed when a fire's about to wake up and get dangerous."

She could sense by the way he stared at the smoke-strewn sky that he wasn't telling her everything. She wanted him to share everything. "Golden may have called you to action, but you noticed something as well, didn't you?"

Aiden met Becca's gaze. After some hesitation, he nodded, backing away a bit as if uncomfortable. "I'm not psychic or anything. The fire kept changing. I'd look over and it would be crackling, as tame as you please. And then the next minute it would…I don't know…dance or something, flaring several feet into the air." His brow wrinkled.

That wrinkle was the tip-off. "And…"

"And what?" He tried to look as if there were nothing else to tell, but she knew better.

"You may as well tell me the rest of it," she prompted, willing to wait.

It took a moment for Aiden to cave in, during which time he stared off to the side. "It's nothing really. Just a feeling, like when you dive too deep in the water and you feel pressure in your ears."

That wasn't good. Not his ability, but the abrupt pressure buildup. Sleeper fires had that characteristic.

"I didn't feel anything like that today," he added quickly, trying to make light of a skill few firefighters had. "You know, if this fire keeps this up, it might be as tricky as some of the deadlier fires I've worked on."

"Deadly fires?" Becca echoed, a knot forming in her stomach. She'd been on a few of those herself and still carried the sorrow and doubt. Could she have done anything differently to prevent their deaths?

"I was down in southern California a couple of years ago

when things got out of control," Aiden said, his eyes drawn back to hers. "I was on the Ruby fire when we lost a smoke jumper. And the Coyote fire that trapped two engine crews several years back."

"We lost two," Becca murmured.

"Yeah." Aiden knelt back down, examining her expression. "Were you there?"

She had been, but she could barely bring herself to admit it with a nod. It was the one fire—the only fire—where she'd relied on a new computer-simulation program without a back-up system in place. The fire had taken advantage of the mis-calculation. Two people had died. Even now, four years later, Becca's stomach churned.

She'd do anything to keep firefighters safe, even if it meant depriving herself of food and sleep, and driving those that worked for her to pursue other, easier roles in NIFC. Even if it meant putting up with egotistical meteorologists.

"Bad calls made on that fire," Aiden said quietly.

Again, Becca could only nod. She couldn't even look at him. He'd been out there, too. He had every right to point the finger of blame her way.

"It's like I said. We deal with a lot out in the field. Besides, those firefighters took a chance. They made a choice and it didn't work for them." Briefly, he touched her hand, the first indication she'd had from any firefighter on the Coyote fire that she wasn't to blame.

Selfishly, she wouldn't have minded a hug about now, a physical touch to absolve her soul of guilt. It was hard to think about the people she hadn't saved, their families, their futures cut short.

"Hey, it's not as if bad calls never happen. Look at this fire."

"Are you saying that you think Incident Command gives orders that endanger you? How dare you?" She scrambled to her feet, grabbing onto a tree trunk for support. She wanted to run, but she was almost eight months pregnant, on a steep slope and had already nearly taken a tumble today.

"No, no. It's just… Becca, give your pride some breathing room." He got to his feet, studying her as he did so. "It's not as if anyone blames you. Don't go looking for heartache where there is none. You'll kill yourself." His words unexpectedly soothed her indignation, but the burning feeling turned into something worse.

No one had blamed her. Becca just blamed herself. She regularly donated to a memorial fund for both firefighters who'd perished. "But decisions are based off recommendations, and they listened to my recommendation on the Coyote fire to deadly consequences. It could have been you who died. Your friends—Jackson and the rest."

"But it wasn't. You helped make sure most of the men and woman on that fire made it home. You helped keep me safe." He ran his palm down her arm, giving her hand a gentle squeeze, easing her burden with a compassion she hadn't received before. "According to Chainsaw, each fire we survive means we've got a task left to fulfill."

"Quite a prophet, this Chainsaw." After the Coyote fire, she'd met Aiden in Las Vegas and he'd helped her create a baby. What other tasks did he have left to fulfill?

"He is that. Now, if there's one thing I've learned about fire, it's that it's unpredictable, like me." He grinned, transforming himself into the charmer she'd fallen for in Las Vegas.

His assessment of himself was so far off that she laughed, an abrupt release of her heavy mood. "You are very predictable."

"Prove it." He raised his dark eyebrows, his smile turning lopsided, an invitation for mischief that was predictable.

Becca ticked off the first few things that came to mind. "You don't own a house or a condo. I'm sure you drive a truck, probably black. You like to have sex with women you barely know, but aren't interested in a relationship or responsibility. You didn't even recognize me at first. Face it. You're a predictable, firefighting bachelor under the age of thirty." A man totally inappropriate for Becca, who was interested in climbing the management ladder at NIFC, where aspects of your life other than your job performance mattered.

"I'm not under the age of thirty, and I am not predictable." His chin jutted out.

"You can't be more than thirty." At least eight years separated them. She hadn't thought about his age in Las Vegas. She'd been thinking that he was a delicious stranger who seemed to want her as much as she wanted him, and that she'd never see him again. He'd been perfect. "But that's not the point. The point is that you're more predictable than this fire."

"If I'm so predictable, what am I thinking?" His grin was devilish.

Too easy. "You're wondering if the baby is yours. And you won't listen when I say you don't need to worry about it."

He rubbed the back of his neck. Clearly, she'd burst his bubble. "Okay, you're half right, but since you've opened up the topic, let's talk." He cradled one elbow in his palm, propped his chin on his fist and regarded her with a serious expression. He just didn't give up. "I know we created that baby together. There's no use denying it. And I know you don't expect me to want to be a part of his life, but I'll make you a deal. You admit that baby is mine and I'll agree to whatever parental terms you want. Sundays only. Once a month. I don't care what limitations you set. I want to be a father to this baby."

She didn't immediately reject him, as she should have, because his desire to be involved with the baby was unexpected. "Why?"

"Because I don't want this child to wonder if I care about him or not. If I'm more than a faceless, nameless sperm donor to him, he'll at least know where he stands with me, that he can call me anytime and I'll be there." She realized his eyes were the most telling feature on his face, and now they were filled with an earnest sadness.

Becca was speechless. The baby kicked and she placed both hands on her belly, drawing his eyes to their child…her child. The decision she was about to make would change her life and the baby's forever. If he'd been at all like his reputation, she would have immediately refused; but he was a caring, compassionate man, and she couldn't get past the guilt of denying such a man minimal contact with his child.

"It's that important to you?" she finally managed to ask in a half whisper.

"Yes."

"And you'll agree to any terms."

"Anything."

For some cockeyed reason, she believed him, still… "Why is this so important to you?"

"If you knew my dad, you'd understand. The short of it is, he was never there for me." He washed a hand over his face, and when he spoke, his words were very low. "I never knew if he cared."

Becca's heart went out to him. What he said made so much sense. She hadn't considered the implications of keeping her baby's parentage secret on her child. But she needed that Boise job and he could ruin it for her. "And you wouldn't tell anyone?"

"Is that one of your conditions?" Aiden frowned. "Isn't that a bit unrealistic?"

"You can't tell anyone yet. I'm up for a desk job in Boise. I can't possibly continue working in the field with a baby." She drew a deep breath before rushing through the tricky part. "I'm sure you understand. I mean, it doesn't look so good, me having a baby with someone like—"

"Me?" He drew back in apparent shock. "Because I'm a ground-pounding grunt who uses any excuse to pick a fight?"

"No." Although, the Silver Bend Hot Shots were known to be a physical team, as were many of the younger crews. Fighting fires created a lot of stress and it wasn't surprising, although more rare nowadays, to have fights break out between or within crews.

"Because I don't have a college education?"

"No."

"It's because I'm younger than you are." It wasn't a question. He slanted her a disapproving glance. "Because I'm a predictable, young stud who likes to sleep with women…or shall we say nameless bimbos?"

He'd certainly—bluntly—struck the nail on the head, although the bimbo label stung. Becca's cheeks heated with a combination of embarrassment and shame. Age shouldn't matter. Yet she knew when it came to this situation and her career, it did. Looking at him now, standing before her in his forest-green pants and yellow button-down fire garb, looking as if he'd been dragged through the dirt, yet with a strong set to his shoulders and proud lift to his chin, Becca found herself wanting him all over again. And it wasn't just because he was forbidden fruit.

She liked him as a person, as a firefighter, possibly something more, something dangerously more if she didn't remember her goals and what she'd be losing by pursuing such a relationship.

When she didn't immediately answer, he swore. "And they say Hot Shots are stuck-up snobs. The pregnancy was an accident, Becca. You should be admired for standing up and doing the right thing no matter what age you are and what age I am. Who cares what people think?"

Aiden was wrong. Her getting pregnant had been no accident. Becca's cheeks burned with guilt. She'd gone to Las Vegas at the height of her fertility cycle without birth control, and with the goal of finding a man to father a child. Yet, he was right about one thing. She couldn't keep his identity a secret if she was allowing him some kind of role in her baby's life. And she wouldn't riddle her child with doubt by keeping Aiden's identity and his desire to have some kind of relationship a secret.

"Tell me the truth, and then we'll meet with the meteorologist and I'll get you back in time for dinner and a rest."

Becca's mind told her to stop, but her conscience wouldn't let her. She chose her words very carefully. "Aiden Rodas, if you agree to tell no one until I get this job…"

He nodded and leaned forward.

"…I'll admit that your sperm helped create my baby. When we get back to the real world, we'll talk about what that means."

The blood drained from his face and he swayed just a bit before going rigid. He made a lame attempt at a recovery. "That wasn't so bad, was it?"

Becca had a feeling that it wasn't so bad. Something in her gut told her it was worse, much worse.

"I'M GOING TO BE A DAD," Spider whispered to himself.

He wanted to collapse on shaky knees, but he kept putting

one foot in front of the other, following Becca uphill. Spider was bringing a kid into a world that suddenly seemed large and threatening. Jeez, he was worried about his dad and about Victoria on this fire. How was he going to keep from worrying about his own kid every day? Choosing the right preschool, getting him safely across the street, driving responsibly when he turned sixteen. And Aiden didn't even want to think about what he'd do if the baby was a girl. He was assailed with a ton of worries he hadn't been ready to deal with, until his heart was hammering against his chest.

Becca grabbed hold of a tree and used it for support as she stepped over a fallen log. His hand reached out impulsively to steady her. She was carrying his baby. She had to be more careful. She hiked around here by herself. She breathed the smoky air. She always looked tired. Becca wasn't taking care of herself or his baby.

Leaping over the log, he moved right up behind Becca on the trail in case she slipped again. She stopped and he almost bowled her over.

"What are you doing?" She half turned, a frown on her face.

"I'm just…making sure you don't fall."

Becca scanned the trail ahead and the ground at her feet for a few moments before asking, "Why?"

"In case you slip," he explained, feeling a bit foolish. "You know, being a gentleman." She'd accused him of lacking those qualities when she'd hit her head the other day.

"Don't do that. Pregnant women need space." She climbed on. "Even from gentlemen."

Spider was the first to admit he lacked experience with pregnant women. "What else do they need?"

"Peace and quiet."

"Is that a hint?"

"Not if I need to explain it." There was no humor in her reply.

"You're not smiling. Are you regretting your decision?" He could tell she was by the resigned set of her shoulders.

"There's a time and place for everything." They entered a clearing at the crest of the mountain. The meteorologist sat on a boulder on the far side of the clearing. Becca tossed Aiden a serious look over her shoulder. "Let's see what you've got, Mr. Predictable."

SPIDER HAD NOTHING.

No skills. No tricks up his sleeve. And his knowledge of fire seemed to have deserted him the moment Becca admitted he'd fathered that baby she was carrying. She thought he was young and foolish. He could live with that. She'd called him predictable. He resented the label. He was predictable in that he enjoyed life to the fullest. But he'd be old and gimpy before anyone called him predictable again.

A father. Oh, boy. Heavy stuff.

Wouldn't she be surprised to know that Spider needed an outlet for all the pent up emotion churning his gut?

Spider tried to focus and think of something to say. They stood on a ridge overlooking an as-yet-untouched green valley. The fire was two valleys east of their location, a distance of perhaps thirty miles as the crow flies, with base camp behind them to the west. Carl, the gratingly obtuse meteorologist, and Becca were deep in discussion about humidity and wind speed, a conversation in which Becca totally ignored Spider.

And why shouldn't she? He knew nothing about the technical side of things. He'd been pissed off when Becca had insinuated he was worthless to her. What was he supposed to say? That he'd been sent to boost her spirits and make her laugh? How demeaning. Becca believed he was there to offer technical expertise. If she knew the truth—that he'd been assigned to help people lighten up, he'd feel that much more unworthy of being a dad.

Carl, on the other hand, seemed to think he knew a lot about fire. Spider had seen him around camps for the first time this summer on other IC teams. The guy had *know-it-all rookie* written all over him. A few months ago, he'd looked Spider up and down, and immediately dismissed him. Somebody needed to take him down a peg or two, and Spider wouldn't mind being the one to do it. In his early forties, with a soft build and a friar's dome that he tried to hide by shaving his head and wearing a baseball hat, Carl was just the kind of man Becca probably looked at as prime dating material—a guy she could boss around, a guy she could shove into a corner or leave behind until she needed him for sperm donations.

She better not think of Spider that way.

Spider burned with anger while he listened to her intelligent discussion, looked at the soft curves of Becca's body and the proud way she carried herself. She had thought of Spider that way.

"You think the wind's gonna whip the fire across two valleys to this one in a matter of days?" Carl didn't give Becca much respect, but he did eye her as if she were something tasty he'd like to sample. "So what if it does?"

What an ass. Carl had a lot to learn about fires. Thirty miles in three days was not out of the question with the right winds and the wrong defenses. And, if Carl wanted Becca, he wasn't going about it in the right way. Spider would have laughed if he hadn't been so friggin' frustrated with himself and his brain-freeze. The only bright spot on the horizon was Becca's sure-to-come put-down.

But instead of putting Carl in his place as she'd often done to Spider, Becca made a small noise to indicate that she'd heard the meteorologist. Silently she just kept looking out over the valley, making Spider wonder what she found so interesting that would silence that sharp tongue of hers. Ignoring the fact that he was bone tired and keyed up tighter than a spring, he moved just behind her so that he might see the view and understand what fascinated her so.

Trees towered thickly above the valley floor. Although the terrain was deep, narrow and stretched for miles north to south, Spider had fought fires on worse terrain. He'd been in places like this when the wind channeled to the bottom of the valley, picked up speed and blew a fire all along its width—

"To the road," Spider said in awe. He stepped past Becca, closer to the edge of the ridge.

"Aiden, what did you say?" Becca asked, her hand briefly touching his shoulder.

Absorbed in his thoughts, Spider suddenly realized it was the second time she'd asked him. "It's the only one of the three valleys in the fire's immediate path that isn't hemmed in on the south by a ridge. If the fire tops that crest and comes down the slope, the right winds will send it to the south, to the highway with no natural barriers to stop it." Nothing except the firefighters who would most likely stand in its path.

A hungry fire...

Aiden looked at Becca, jaw tense, ready to argue with her if she thought he was wrong.

Instead, Becca lifted one corner of her lips in an almost smile. "That's what I thought, too."

Spider hadn't anticipated how a near-positive reaction from Becca would lighten his mood. He felt as if they'd connected, like that night in Vegas. He felt as if he knew this woman like no other.

Which was no help whatsoever.

CHAPTER SEVEN

"So, WHAT IF THE FIRE MAKES IT through those two valleys and gets here?" Carl shrugged. "Then we make a stand here."

Aiden paced. Becca held onto her temper by digging her fingernails into her palms. If she could just make Carl see the logic of the fire's progression, they could convince Sirus to defend this ridge. They could pull back the firefighters and set up a break at a safe distance. "Carl, the difference is that our current efforts aren't containing the fire. It'll just tire out the crews as it makes its way here, where it will gain strength and run away."

She ground her fists into her aching back. She needed to sit down. Her ankles were swelling. The baby squirmed, then settled into a different position. Becca hoped her little one would forgive her for pushing herself so hard, but lives were at stake.

"Now, Becca, this scenario of yours only happens if the wind changes." Carl shielded his eyes from the sun as he gave Becca a look as indulgent as one gave a child who'd just said something pie-in-the-sky ridiculous. He was such a condescending, self-important jerk. "Sorry, Becca, you've come up with a worst-case scenario and I think it's unnecessary. We'll stop it long before it reaches that ridge with either reinforcements or rain."

"Bullshit!" Aiden couldn't contain himself any longer. "You said last night that there's no rain on the horizon."

Becca held up a hand in Aiden's direction, unable to contain a slight frown. Nothing would be solved with a loss of temper. Carl would just close his mind even further, if that was possible.

"You and I both know that our current strategy isn't working and endangers lives every day." Becca tugged down her T-shirt with a warning glance at Aiden, who couldn't seem to stand still. "If we had more manpower, it would be different. I'm asking you to do the right thing for those out on the line. You mentioned that you thought the heat was going to break in five to seven days."

Carl adjusted the brim of his baseball cap. "Even if the heat breaks, I don't see the winds shifting."

But Becca did. "The locals say—"

"Locals?" Carl cut her off, shaking his head resolutely.

"I hope you're right. Really I do." Becca managed to speak calmly. "But—"

Carl cut her off again. "You're proposing we let thousands of acres burn? Are you willing to take the blame for such a loss, Becca? Because I'm not. And that's what it comes down to."

"Carl—" Becca wouldn't give up.

"No, I'm through talking." He rubbed his stomach as it growled, then smiled as if they'd just come to an amicable agreement. "Hey, what do you say we head down for dinner? All this fresh air has made me really hungry. It's not candlelight or anything, but we could get to know each other better."

A feral sound came from Aiden's direction, which should have warned her, except Becca was so repulsed by Carl's interest that she froze. He wasn't extending an invitation that included Aiden. He was asking Becca out.

"Dinner? We're not done here, Romeo." Spider stepped between Carl and Becca, his body taut and ready to spring. "We've tried blocking the front. In six days, that fire has overrun us two times."

"That's what I'm saying." Carl smiled easily as if he weren't aware of Aiden's tension. "Why set us up for failure again? If we back off from the fire, it could move in any direction, gain momentum and blow right through this valley or miss it altogether," Carl argued, stubbornly rocking back and forth on his squeaky new boots. "Forget this foolishness. We need to be conservative."

Hoping she appeared calm, Becca stepped in front of Aiden for one last try. "This is conservative, Carl. Hopefully, the fire won't reach this valley for days. If we build our defenses this far back, we'll have time to stop it." Becca tried her best to ignore how Carl was patronizing her and trying to hit on her at the same time, while hoping her calm demeanor would help to diffuse Aiden's bloodlust.

"I'm willing to take responsibility for those two valleys burning. Are you willing to take responsibility for the fire jumping the highway?" Becca fought to keep the frustration from her voice.

"Holy crap. Can't you see she's right?" Aiden cracked his knuckles. "With a shortage of teams and the vindictiveness of this fire, we're screwed with our current attack strategy. Even an idiot can see that."

"Slow down, fella." Carl smiled at Becca as if sharing a secret that excluded Aiden. "All the weather reports indicate that we won't get a new front in for days and even then, it's not a sure thing. It could stall out over Canada. But it's not going to cause a dramatic shift in the wind. Hell, why the worry? It's a long shot, but you and your boys may even contain it before it hits that ridge."

Becca couldn't miss that the whole boy/fella bit didn't sit well with Aiden.

"Shit, Carl. What do we need you for? You're not a fire expert. How many years have you been working fire?" Aiden faced Becca. "I say we ditch Carl and just watch the local weatherman for his report."

"Becca, don't listen to him."

"Becca's trying to save lives here, not pretending to be something more important than she is. Maybe if you listened to her, you'd learn something."

The air crackled with animosity and testosterone.

"I don't have to take this from you." Carl's face was beet-red.

"What's wrong? Run out of illogical reasons to disagree with Becca?"

Carl made a grunting noise and threw down his clipboard like a twelve-year-old. "I know how you settle things out here. Come on. You don't scare me."

"Aiden! Carl!" Becca tried to stand between the two men.

Aiden gently but firmly pushed her behind him, even though she resisted. It was hard to win a shoving match with a watermelon-sized belly.

"I am so tired of you Hot Shots thinking you're untouchable and all-knowing. You aren't God. Heck, most of you haven't even graduated from college." Carl advanced. "You can't predict the weather or the fire. You're only qualified to shovel dirt."

"Don't you hit him," Becca warned Aiden. Every time she tried to step around him, he moved in her way.

Carl turned his baseball cap backward. "I'm not gonna hit him—"

"I think she was talking to me, weatherman." Becca could tell Aiden was smiling by the bravado in his voice.

"—I'm gonna throw him off the mountain." Carl crouched and spread his arms. He glanced at Becca. "Stand back, Becca. I know what I'm doing. I was all-state wrestling champ."

"You two are not going to fight," Becca commanded. If Aiden pounded Carl, the meteorologist would never align with her.

"Oh, yes. We are." Then Carl laughed, as if he had no clue he didn't stand a chance.

Becca grabbed Aiden's arm, because Carl would never listen to her. "Touch him, and I take it back. All of it," Becca warned, knowing he'd understand she was talking about the baby. "I mean it."

Aiden half turned and stared at her. His jaw was tense and his eyes were blazing with the need to smash his fist into somebody.

"Please," Becca pleaded softly, not moving from his side.

"Come on," Carl encouraged Aiden forward with one hand. "You're not going to listen to a *girl,* are you, *Spider?*"

Aiden glanced back at Becca one more time, his fists clenching and unclenching.

"You are *so* not worth it, Carl." Aiden turned on his heel and left.

As she watched Aiden disappear into the trees, Becca's heart swelled with pride. It took a man with a ton of courage to walk away from a fight he was sure to win.

"No guts." Carl stood, righted his baseball cap and grinned. "I thought so."

All the frustration and anger from their argument made

Becca tremble. She wanted to tell Carl what a jerk he was, but she knew it would only fall on deaf ears. Carl was a legend in his own mind.

"He's right, you know," was all Becca said before she followed Aiden back to camp.

Fighting Carl wasn't worth the energy. She'd convince Sirus on her own.

The startling revelation was that it took Aiden to point that out to her.

"FINALLY, A DISPLAY of common sense," Becca called as she stood precariously on the slope above Spider. If she lost her footing, she'd come tumbling down—not such a good idea for a pregnant woman, especially one carrying his child.

It scared the hell out of Spider. He should have known when he'd taken off that she'd follow, despite his breakneck pace. Only when he'd walked away, he couldn't help but realize that Carl wasn't worth fighting, but Becca just might be worth fighting for. She'd been calm and determined in her struggle to open Carl's shortsighted eyes, and do what was best to contain the fire and keep firefighters safe. He had to admire that.

"Becca, stay right where you are," Spider commanded and then he ran uphill to her, even when all he wanted was to gain some much needed space from her and Carl. He took Becca by the arm. "Are you crazy?"

"Me?" she squeaked. "I'm not the one starting fights for no reason."

Unbelievable. Even when he did the right thing, she gave him grief. "I didn't start a fight. I'm the one who walked away, remember?" And if Carl told anyone about it…Spider ground his teeth.

"Men," Becca huffed. "You wanted to fight him. Heck, you

wanted to hit a tree five minutes after we got there and you weren't paying attention to Carl then." She tried to shrug out of Spider's grip.

"Oh, no you don't." He wasn't letting her hike out of here alone. "Wait a minute. How did you know what I wanted to do?"

She arched a brow at him.

The superior triumph in her expression grated on his ego. "I can't be that predictable."

Her expression softened. "You're upset."

"Hell, yes, I'm upset. Nothing about this day has been par for the course. Not the fire, not my assignment, not Carl, and most certainly, not you." Why had he walked away from Carl? All he'd wanted to do was smash Carl's face with his fist. And then she'd asked him not to. It had taken every ounce of self-control he possessed to walk away.

She stared at him as if not sure what to think, standing next to him with her lips parted, breathing heavily, her breasts rising and falling in a seductive rhythm. Instinctively, he leaned forward to kiss her, then stopped himself. Barely.

Could she tell that he wanted to kiss her? Did he care if she knew?

At the moment, no.

"You're evil," Becca said under her breath, eyes locked onto his. She knew what he was thinking all right, but she didn't call him on it.

On the contrary, she wasn't backing down at all. He could kiss her if he wanted to. He could wrap one hand around her soft braid, tilt her head back to deepen the kiss, and direct one hand lower, over her tantalizing curves.

Reality set in and it was Spider who pulled back. Only slightly though. Wouldn't do to let on that she rattled him.

"It's a guy thing. Deal with it." Spider shifted awkwardly, still holding her arm.

Blinking, as if she just realized what had almost happened, Becca somehow managed to get out of his grip and stubbornly lead the way back.

He was left watching her hike in front of him as the silence stretched between them. The way she walked was oddly graceful—a big woman moving at a slow and certain pace, her hips swaying as gently as the long blond braid down her back. The only way he could tell she was hurt was by the stiff set of her shoulders.

A gentleman would apologize.

That had to be his Abuelita talking, not Becca.

Spider frowned, not sure. Becca had accused him of not being a gentleman the day she'd fallen.

Damn. What had happened here? He wasn't making choices to please her, was he? Sure, he'd seen the hurt in the way Becca had stood, so strong, yet so fragile as she'd tried to talk sense into Carl. In hindsight, she hadn't been as calm as she'd appeared. So what if he'd discovered she was a fire-prediction savant, or that Becca could turn him on with a word? She'd still handled this baby business all wrong and would probably continue to do so. Spider couldn't afford to give her an inch of leeway in this parenting relationship. He'd blow everything if he gave in to this kinky desire he had for her.

All he had to do was keep quiet for forty minutes while they hiked down the hill and he'd be okay.

AIDEN CURSED ON THE trail behind Becca. "I was always a talker in school. Couldn't stand the silence."

"With that kind of language, you probably spent a lot of time in detention."

"Language didn't get me into detention."

Becca stopped herself from asking him what had, although she was dying to know. It was Las Vegas all over again—him intriguing her, creating a desire to know him better.

Lucky for her, before she could ask, Aiden changed the subject. "My grandmother always taught me to acknowledge hard work and give credit where credit was due. So…that was pretty impressive back there."

Becca's heart pounded in her chest. She had to steady herself with one hand on a tree trunk midstep. Was he talking about their almost kiss?

"The way you figured out what the fire would do was awesome," Aiden clarified. "I'm usually a step ahead of guessing where the fire might go. And you're like three or four steps beyond me with all the facts to back it up."

Not the kiss. Becca didn't know whether to laugh with relief or groan with frustration. The way Aiden had looked at her a few minutes ago was nothing close to the lecherous way Carl had stared at her. When Aiden had looked at her, he'd let her see who he was, holding nothing back—pain, anger and desire were all there, raw and powerful. It was more intimate than watching him shed his clothes. And yet, she couldn't touch him.

"This is where you fill in the silence with a response." When she still said nothing, he added, "Or can't you accept that your prediction was poetry?"

Reminding herself that colleagues didn't lust after one another, she sighed. "Carl wasn't buying it."

"Carl was blinded by your beauty in about the same way I was blown away by your intelligence. That accounts for his drop in intellect when he's around you."

"Ha! You are so full of it. It's closer to the truth to say that

Carl would never believe in something he didn't come up with first." She wasn't amused with Aiden's attempts to lighten her mood. Or was he flirting? She'd know if she turned around and looked in his eyes.

Becca hesitated mid-step. It didn't matter if Aiden was flirting or not, either way he was off limits, a hazard, a line she should not cross.

Aiden caught up to her. "He'd have realized your insight sooner or later."

"I'll bet on never." Becca's shoulders tensed. The more he talked about Carl, the more uptight she became.

"That's all right. Unlike you, Carl will never be the sharpest tool in the shed."

Compliments didn't mean much when Becca didn't have anything to show for the afternoon, except for her renewed determination to convince Sirus to change attack strategies on her own.

"That was a compliment. One usually responds to a compliment with a thank you."

Becca stopped and squared off with Aiden, tossing her braid over her shoulder. "I'd thank you except for the fact that I wanted Julia to see the ridge. I was hoping she'd come to the same conclusion as you and I did. I was hoping she'd help me convince Carl." She tossed her hands in frustration. "Oh, and, I'd thank you for helping me enlighten Carl, only you ruined it by wanting to pound the living daylights out of him!"

"Wow, you don't keep it all inside, do you?" The teasing glint in his eye was too much.

"This isn't a game, Aiden. There are lives at stake." Not just on the mountain, but inside her belly. What the two of them said and did had profound implications on the future. Would Aiden honor his word and keep her secret?

"Oh, come on. You think Socrates is going to take Carl's word over yours? Give the man more credit."

Recalling her conversation a few days ago where Sirus had refused to talk about new strategies, Becca crossed her arms, dropped her chin and stared at Aiden.

His grin faded. "No way. You told Socrates and he ignored you?"

"Contrary to what you might think, no one takes my recommendations all the time. Everyone advises the Incident Commander. I'm a voice of one." Turning away, she blinked back the tears, unaccountably feeling beaten.

It must have sunk in to Aiden that she was upset, because he was taking her awkwardly in his arms before she knew what was happening. Her belly and their baby bumped into him. A woman with sense would have put distance between them.

But Becca craved a little tender loving care. She was tired of pushing herself, tired of putting on the indestructible front for everyone in camp, and ruing the day she'd taken this assignment. As Aiden's hands roamed across her back, leaving a welcome heat in their wake, she didn't pull away.

Strong, independent woman that she was, Becca sighed and melted further into him.

"I'm sorry, Bec. I had no idea how important this meeting with Carl was. I'll admit I was wrong in sending Julia back, but don't blame me for what happened with Carl. He wanted to fight as much as I did, probably more."

"If you think an apology is going to smooth things over, you're sadly mistaken." Weakling that she'd become, she sniffed against his shoulder.

"How about a kiss to make it better?"

"I don't think that's such a good idea." Still, she found herself raising her head. Just so she could gaze into his eyes and tell if he was serious or not.

His eyes were black, brimming with desire. Places that shouldn't get warm sparked to life.

"It's just a kiss, Bec." And to prove it, he placed a gentle kiss on her nose.

No fair! Becca wanted to cry out that she'd been cheated. Her body nearly trembled with wanting more of Aiden's touch. It was just a kiss, after all. Nothing bad ever came of kissing, except the crankiness from not getting one, right?

She had to admit that he was right to limit their kiss. They shouldn't have any contact at all until she landed the Boise job. After that, they shouldn't exchange more than friendly handshakes if they were to create a healthier environment for the good of their child. Aiden was just being a gentleman and offering emotional support during her breakdown. Becca was the one reading more into it. She was the one wanting more of his forbidden fruit.

Becca was about to pull away and try to console herself that she'd escaped with her dignity intact when his lips moved onto hers. She gave a breathy moan as her eyes drifted closed and she surrendered to the remembered taste of him, his warmth and the feel of his firm body.

Pulling her closer, Aiden kissed her fatigue away, gave her strength and made her want to continue fighting the system for safer, saner ways to fight fire.

Safer. Saner.

Was she insane?

Becca stumbled back, shrugging off Aiden's steadying hand, immediately missing his touch.

"A-A-AY!" She yelled, regretting that she had no sense of self-preservation.

Even now, staring at Aiden, she throbbed with the call of her body to his. Enticing him into bed when she'd needed his sperm was one thing. Inviting him in for no other reason than their mutual pleasure was another.

"Your communication skills could be improved," Spider tried to make light of the situation. So they'd kissed. They'd kissed before.

And fallen into bed for a glorious evening.

He stood rigidly at attention just remembering Vegas, further charged by the residual effect of the sizzling kiss they'd just shared.

"I…I…I…" Becca stammered.

Spider couldn't stop the proud smile on his face. He had quite an effect on this woman, as she did on him. Pregnant or not, she made him feel hot-hot-hot.

"Don't you wish that we'd met under different circumstances?" Spider could imagine how great it would have been to have dated Becca. She was smart, beautiful, challenging, and a babe. He let his gaze run over her soft, tempting curves. Yep. Even pregnant, she was a babe. "Maybe we could go out sometime." To her place. To a motel.

Suddenly, coming to visit his kid took on a new dimension. Being a dad wasn't going to crimp his lifestyle. Becca would greet him at the door with that sultry smile. And nap time. Whoa. Nap time was going to be—

"No!" she practically shouted. "We can't date. Have you lost your mind?"

"No. I'm just…" *Fantasizing?* God, no. She'd kill him if he said that. Backpedal! *Almost having a wet daydream?*

Even worse. Think faster! "Uh… Trying to make the best of the situation."

Becca narrowed her eyes. "Just because we're having a baby doesn't mean I'm stupid enough to sleep with you again."

Ouch. Anger kicked in and overrode mind-numbing desire. "Maybe I thought we should get to know each other better. Jeez, I wasn't looking for a good time." Liar, liar, pants on fire.

"Thanks for the compliment." She did the crossed-arms, chin-cocked stare. She really had that move nailed.

"I didn't mean it wasn't good…I mean, it was great, like old times." Smooth, he wasn't.

"You are so out of control. They let you manage and take responsibility? You don't do so well under pressure."

She couldn't just insult him like that. Not when he was still straining against his zipper, damn it. "Oh, I do very well under certain kinds of pressure. What about you? Having trouble managing?" Clearly, Julia was a challenge for Becca.

The color in her face faded, but she kept her game face on. "Like your management skills are stellar."

"Hey, I tell my team what to do and don't put up with any shit. Being straight up has worked wonders. You ought to try it with Julia."

"Really? Are you straight up with Victoria?"

He held up a hand. "That's a different thing entirely. She's not performing. I've saved her butt twice this week and by being tough, I'm hoping she'll save her own life next time." Why was everyone defending Victoria? First Golden, then Doc and now Becca.

"You'd help her out if she were a man," Becca said over her shoulder as she headed down the trail.

"No. I'd be just as quick to get a man off the team. Incompetence is deadly." Especially on a fire as deceptive as this one, where there was little warning before the dragon attacked.

"And if you argued with Victoria, you wouldn't try to beat your opinion into her, like you did with Carl?"

"I did *not* fight Carl. You know I'm never going to hear the end of what happened up there from Mr. Weatherman. You emasculated me!" He caught her surprised backward glance. "Yes, I know what that big word means. And don't go accusing me of being a chauvinist, because I'm not."

Spider shook his finger at Becca, which did no good because she was now three steps ahead of him and he was pointing at her back. The adrenaline was pumping through his veins so quickly now, his thoughts bounced from one topic to another. "Besides, don't think I didn't notice how you tried to sway Carl up there. Women are always trying to manipulate men in one way or another. You were waiting for the right moment to move in for the kill, only you miscalculated how thick-headed he was."

Spider drew a quick breath before she could get a word in. "If I hadn't forced the issue, you'd probably still be up there, batting your eyes and trying patiently to get Carl to see it your way. You let him talk down to you, just like you let Julia give you grief. Jeez, Bec, she's your direct report, and he's just a washed-up weatherman. You know what you're doing. Force the issue with them, for once, instead of being so passive."

She turned to face him. "I think I've had enough for one day."

"Still don't believe me?" He shook his head. Man, she was stubborn. "Well, let me give you one more thing to think about. I forced the discussion about the baby with you. If I didn't press it, you wouldn't have confessed. And I'll keep being proactive because I go after what I want." He stared at her for a few seconds before he realized that he'd stopped talking because his gaze had started to drift over those curves. He swallowed, trying to regain his composure. "So, one more question. What's it going to take to get you to explain the terms of fatherhood to me?"

She didn't even hesitate. "Quiet time and space."

Those were two things he wasn't going to give her.

"QUIET TIME AND SPACE," Becca repeated just to make sure he understood. Then she started toward camp again. Passive? She was far from passive. She went after what she wanted. Didn't she?

Well, maybe not with the in-your-face bravado that Aiden did, but she didn't think she was as passive as he made her sound. She was trying to protect her plans. How could that be passive?

"You do get the strangest ideas." Aiden's reply was laden with sarcasm. "When is the baby due? You can at least tell me that."

If she could have walked off and left him, she would have. Because she couldn't, she had to answer. "October. Can't you hold off talking about this until then? The more you talk about it, the more likely someone will overhear and find out about you." She'd have to stop soon. Her legs were shaking badly from fatigue. The last thing she needed was to fall down.

Who was she kidding? The last thing she needed was to stop. He'd just get another chance to talk something out of her. Or worse, kiss her senseless again. Despite all he'd said and done today she still craved his touch.

Her foot slipped just a bit.

Aiden steadied her arm from behind before she released her breath.

When had he gotten so close?

"I swear, you're going to kill yourself. Sit down a minute until you calm down." His breath wafted over her ear.

Panicky, sweaty and speechless, but knowing she was a danger to herself and the baby, Becca sat down in the middle of the trail, forcing Aiden to move back or below her. He stepped around a tree and stood below her on the trail, so that the sun was at his back and she sat in his shadow.

"I've gotta admit, I'm learning something about pregnant women." He held up his hand and started ticking off fingers. "Don't surprise them. Don't make them mad. Don't call them big. Give them space, peace and quiet. Anything else I need to know?"

Becca crossed her arms over her belly, refusing to respond to his baiting. The baby had been fairly still all afternoon, possibly because she'd been marching around like a crazy person. "I keep telling you there's nothing you need to concern yourself with. You wanted to know. I told you. We agreed to my terms. Don't rush me." She had to think about this next step very carefully. And she wasn't sure he'd keep the news of his impending fatherhood to himself.

"I admit I never planned on having kids. My parents were less than perfect and I don't want to repeat their mistakes." Aiden sighed, admitting, "And I'm not patient. Once I decide to do something, I take care of it right away. I need to know what my role is going to be or I'll drive myself crazy with wondering, which means I'll drive you crazy with asking."

If he'd been angry or bitterly sarcastic, Becca would have repeated that the baby was her concern, not his. But he wasn't. He was nice again, and the reference to his parents had her imagining a little boy with black hair and eyes, alone and unloved.

Her eyes filled with tears. She was never wishy-washy. It had to be the hormones. It had nothing to do with the way his

dark eyes compelled her to listen and soak him in, as if just
the sound of his voice and the depth of his eyes could reassure
her that things would be all right. Logically, she suspected
things would never be the way she planned now that Aiden
knew her secret, but meeting his gaze was somehow soothing.

"I don't even know you," Becca said steadily, even though
she knew it was a lie. She'd learned more about Aiden in the past
two hours than she'd known when she'd slept with him. But self-
preservation made her press on. "It's hard for me to talk to someone I don't even know about something as personal as my baby.
You agreed that I could set the boundaries. Right or wrong, if
NIFC gets wind of my situation with you, that job I want is in
jeopardy. You're going to have to keep your distance on this fire."

Aiden started to speak, but she cut him off, feeling stronger now that she'd had a few moments off her feet. She needed time to think this through. "That will have to do for now."

"As long as you agree it's only *for now,*" he clarified.

Clinging to silence, Becca would do no such thing.

CHAPTER EIGHT

"I WAS HOPING I'd see you."

Becca glanced up from the worn Realtor flyer she'd been staring at during dinner the next day to find Victoria settling across from her. Since her confrontation with Aiden yesterday, she'd found it hard to concentrate. Sitting at a picnic table in the sunny dining area was making her hot, her pregnant curves and creases damp with sweat.

Although he'd stayed away today, the possibility of Aiden giving her space for the duration of the fire was slim to none. The chance of her landing the Boise job and closing on the house on the flyer even less. She should never have made the offer on the house, at least, not until NIFC had given her the job.

But it was perfect. Two bedrooms, one bath, a fireplace and hardwood floors. A pipe dream if she didn't pull a stellar performance out of Julia or if Aiden divulged her secret. Becca folded the flyer and put it in her pocket with a resigned sigh.

"Are you okay?" Victoria asked. "You look flushed."

"I'm fine," Becca assured her, taking a long drink of water.

Drawing a calming breath, Becca reminded herself to focus on the challenges ahead of her. She needed to develop a strong reason to change attack strategies because no one was going to go to bat with her on this one, certainly not Carl.

And then there was the problem of Julia. Becca refused to believe it was due to her own management style as Sirus seemed to think. Maybe Julia hadn't found her footing. Fire-behavior prediction was a tough field, requiring dedication and effort. If Becca was fair, she had to admit that she hadn't built a strong foundation of confidence in Julia. She had yet to encourage her assistant to speak up in the briefings.

"We had a good day on the fire." Victoria broke into Becca's thoughts.

"So I heard." Becca turned her attention back to the insurmountable pile of broccoli she'd forced herself to put on her plate. What she wouldn't give for some cheese melted on top of it. The thought of eating it plain turned her stomach.

Laughter erupted nearby. Looking up, Becca saw Aiden was still in the food line and joking with members of the IC team and a few female Hot Shots. Becca frowned. Aiden was acting so typical of a Hot Shot—exuberant and strutting around as if women fell into his bed easily—she wouldn't have minded someone putting him in his place, even if it were Carl.

She knew firsthand women did fall into Aiden's bed, and she was grateful he had let her tumble there, but he didn't have to look so…so…young and cocky about his ability. Nor did the women have to hang on his every word. Not that she was jealous.

Aiden hadn't seemed that young as they'd talked out on the mountain. She'd seen the wrinkles at the corners of his dark eyes. Without him standing in front of her, she could convince herself that the wrinkles were probably from too much sun exposure. Certainly not from age or wisdom.

Yet, he'd been solicitous, treating her as carefully as if she were fine china whenever she'd started to slip or do something reckless, like follow Aiden down the trail at top speed because she'd been worried about him. And he'd understood the guilt she carried about the Coyote fire. She'd never spoken to anyone about that before.

Across from her, Victoria rolled her eyes. "Men. There are too many of them out there.".

At least one too many as far as Becca was concerned.

With his back to her, Aiden laughed again. The sound of his laughter did funny things to Becca's insides. She rubbed her belly. More likely it wasn't Aiden giving her these feelings, but the sight of broccoli combined with the baby shifting around making her nauseous. It couldn't be her heart.

"And then," she heard Aiden say, straining to hear the rest of it. "And then I realize the slope isn't too steep, but that I'm too slow, because a snake passes me on the way up." Aiden shook his head ruefully.

He was telling a story about a fire? At his own expense?

She'd liked Aiden in Las Vegas, perhaps too much, because when she'd found out she was pregnant, she'd burned with guilt over not telling him. So, she'd asked around about him. She'd found his reputation to be vastly different from the man she'd met, and that had helped her justify not telling him about the baby, easing her conscience. And now, he was acting just like the man she'd seduced in Las Vegas—caring, charming, yet humble—and nothing like his reputation. Becca found herself liking him all the more, darn him. She was certain that liking Aiden would lead to the downfall of all her plans.

Everyone laughed at Aiden's story. One of the female Hot Shots was short enough that she had to crane her neck to look up at Aiden. The cold claw of jealousy scraped down Becca's spine. He'd kissed her less than twenty-four hours ago.

Someone stepped between Aiden and the Hot Shot to grab a piece of French bread, and then stayed between the two of them. Becca released the air in her lungs. She didn't own Aiden. Far from it. He could talk or flirt or kiss whomever he wanted…as long as it wasn't in front of Becca.

"When's the baby due?" Victoria asked, rearranging her food on her plate into neat piles—salad, steak, raw carrots—drawing Becca's attention back to the table. "You must be excited."

"Yes, my due date is coming up quickly, in October." She had less than two weeks before the deadline the doctor had set when she couldn't work any longer.

"I wish I had a baby," Victoria said wistfully.

"You're too young. And you're still on the fire line. You have plenty of time to wait." Becca couldn't believe she'd said that. Victoria could just as easily end up in a similar situation as Becca. "But don't wait too long," she added.

Pushing her food around her plate, Victoria didn't answer.

Out of the corner of her eye, Becca saw Aiden sit alone at the table behind Victoria, his back toward them.

Victoria sat back, covering her mouth with one delicate hand. "I'm so sorry. I'm not very good company. And I'm tired and worried, and—"

"Don't worry about making conversation. I live alone and I'm used to silence." Becca rubbed the baby in her belly, eliciting a mild kick. She and the baby would be fine alone. Besides, no one could ever live up to the high standards set by Aiden with his dark, soulful eyes.

Becca bit back a groan of frustration, her eyes drifting to Aiden. She had begun to romanticize this baby's conception. She and Aiden had been strangers, and making love to a stranger had gone against everything she'd been taught, everything she was. There was only one explanation for the way she'd been unable to stop thinking about Aiden these past seven months; only one reason she could give for the way she couldn't resist his kiss today. She didn't want their night of lovemaking to have been a one-night stand. She wanted it to have meant something.

First comes love, then comes marriage, then comes baby in a baby carriage. The line from the old school-yard rhyme taunted Becca. She was such a fool. She'd thought she could cheat the system and have a baby without a relationship. What a mess she'd landed herself in. With a word, Aiden could bring her world down.

Victoria contemplated Becca while she chewed her food. "Are you just going to have one baby?"

"That was the plan." She'd spent many a sleepless night the year before second-guessing her life, beating herself up over the choice she'd made—to save lives rather than create lives. She'd ached for a baby of her own. And then she'd realized it didn't have to be an either-or proposition.

The redhead put down her plastic eating utensils, an incredulous look on her face. "Just one?"

She looked so comical that the tension within Becca eased.

"Hmm, let me see. Single woman. *Old.*" She winked at Victoria, trying to lighten what Becca knew Victoria believed was true. "I think one kid is more than enough."

Becca didn't. Not really. She'd loved growing up in a big family. Four kids. Two parents. What was not to like? It was the divorce, custody battles and tug-of-war with a child's affections that she feared. Because Becca had grown used to the fact that a typical family was not in the cards for her, she'd chosen to go it alone, despite the doubts, the fears and the what-ifs.

"Becca, I'm an only child and let me tell you, it's no picnic. There's no one to play with, no one to share secrets with, no one to blame when you break your mother's antique teapot."

Trying not to panic, Becca smiled, knowing the Hot Shot meant well but convinced that Victoria was overdramatizing. "I can assure you—"

"And then there's the social aspect. To this day, it's hard for me to share, or give up on an argument."

Behind Victoria, Aiden turned his head, as if he were listening. If he turned around, Becca wouldn't panic. She'd be civil and act as if he meant nothing to her, so that Victoria wouldn't get the wrong idea.

Becca forced her attention back to her dining companion. "Victoria—"

"You know, when my mom goes, I'll have no one. I never knew my dad. I don't even know his name." Victoria drew a shaky breath, as if trying not to cry. "I do have a picture of my dad in front of the Silver Bend Hot Shot station from before I was born, but my mom won't talk about him. That's why I joined the Hot Shots, to be closer to knowing my dad or at least the type of man he was. Of course, no one's around who knows his name or would recognize my mom. He could be dead for all I know."

Victoria held up a hand. Becca noticed one of her nails was chipped. "Okay, TMI—too much information. But the point is, if I do go first…" Victoria's watery eyes were suddenly locked with Becca's. "If I go first, my mom will have no one. And that's why you need to have more than one baby." She stood abruptly. "Excuse me. I've lost my appetite."

As she watched Victoria walk away, there was a lump in Becca's throat the size of a dry biscuit.

"HEY, DON'T LISTEN TO HER. There are advantages to being an only child." Unable to stand it anymore, Spider picked up his tray and sat across from Becca. The possibility that Becca would take Victoria's advice and perform another standing-ovation, sperm-collecting night of passion with a stranger, giving his kid a half brother or sister, and putting another man in the wings of Becca's life had him on red alert.

"You shouldn't sit here," she told him sternly. "People will talk."

Smiling, he refused to be put off. "So what? I've been assigned to your team. Besides, we need to get to know each other better if we're going to make this work."

Becca lowered her voice and leaned forward, as cool as a cucumber. "I'm under no obligation to make anything work." And he might have believed her, except she couldn't hold his gaze.

Spider switched tactics. "You want to hear that it's okay to be an only child, don't you?"

"You were an only child?" Becca asked, curiosity apparent in her eyes, which was preferable to the Keep Out sign that had been there when he'd first sat down.

"You doubt me?" Spider drew back in mock indignation. Although he'd sat down for his own reasons, once he realized she was upset, he couldn't help but try to lift her spirits.

"Heck, yeah. You're too…" Becca's voice trailed off.

"Good looking? Suave?" Spider picked his best assets.

A fat squirrel scampered across the clearing to forage under the picnic table next to them.

"I think I was going to say *normal*," Becca spoke up at last, a hint of a smile on her full lips.

Something warm invaded his chest at Becca's smile. What

did that mean? She would have given birth to his child without telling him. So why did she spark any reaction other than contempt?

Because he'd seen Becca in action—obstinate, caring and treating him like an equal, sometimes, even when he probably didn't deserve it. And then the future of their baby came between them.... Okay, and maybe that near fight with Carl.

"Or maybe I was going to say *irritatingly* normal," Becca clarified, although she might have been teasing, he couldn't quite tell.

Spider forced his lips to turn upward slowly, although this time it was an uphill battle. "Depends on your definition of normal," he countered, eyes caught, despite his best intentions, on Becca's hands rubbing her belly. Could she feel his child? Would she let him do that?

"All right." Becca took the bait, setting down her fork and focusing only on him. "Describe the *normal* Aiden childhood."

He liked Becca's calm gaze on him. What was happening here? With a shrug, Spider admitted, "My dad had a job that kept him away from home for months at a time."

"Hot Shot, right?" Becca asked, tilting her head.

"Yes," Spider said with a nod. The way Becca looked at him, as if she were interested—which was a damn sight different than the way she'd looked at him when he'd first entered her tent yesterday, as if he were a leper—had Spider adding something more personal. "When I was five, my mom left me with my grandmother and never come back."

"Is that your pickup line?" Becca demanded, suddenly all prickly. "I know you told me about your father, but this is laying it on a bit thick, don't you think?"

"What? You don't believe me? Do you always have to be so suspicious that I'm putting one over on you?" Here he was being honest and she was challenging him like a lawyer, looking for any deception. It sucked. Spider considered leaving, but that would look childish. He'd rather not have Becca think he was someone she could manipulate.

Right, like that hadn't already happened.

Maybe they needed to take a step back and start with the basics. What would earn Becca's respect?

After a moment of hesitation, Spider dug into his wallet for a worn photo. He handed it to Becca.

"That's my Abuelita, my grandmother." The photograph had been taken at his high-school graduation. Spider wore a black button-down shirt and tie, one arm tossed over Abuelita's shoulder. In her waitress uniform with her hair pulled back into a frizzy, silver bun, Abuelita looked like the sweet grandma she'd been.

Becca accepted the photo with a delicate touch. "Come on, you had aunts and cousins at least twice removed, or something. Otherwise, you would have turned out socially awkward, like Victoria."

"Nope. Just me and my grandmother. Besides, Victoria used to be normal with manners and everything. She's just fallen apart this year for some reason." Spider stared at Becca. He thought he'd turned out okay. He had a good set of values, certainly better than Becca's.

But there was something about Becca that contradicted her fast-and-loose behavior in Vegas. Or maybe it was wishful thinking on his part, some weird voodoo because his seed had done the deed.

"Is she still alive?" Becca asked as she handed the photo back. She had the kind of voice that carried authority, making you stop and take notice. If she just learned to use that presence better, she'd be a formidable force. He had to admire her, at least a little, for taking on motherhood alone, even while he resented her for not telling him.

They'd been strangers in Vegas. They'd talked about lots of things, but never exchanged last names, family history or phone numbers. Guys who did that were just liars. She'd left without him knowing how to reach her or vice versa. And he should have been okay with that, but now he realized being dumped had bugged him.

"She's been gone several years now." Spider tucked the photograph back into his wallet. "I miss her a lot. When we had no money in the bank and next to nothing in the cupboard, I'd start whining about things being bad and she'd immediately find some way to give me hope. Pretty soon, we'd be smiling and laughing."

"I'm sorry," Becca said. "She must have been very special."

"She was." But he didn't want to talk about Abuelita. "Are you an only child?"

"I'm the second of four kids," Becca admitted, her expression suddenly becoming guarded.

Sensing her change in mood, the urge to make her smile was strong. "Ahh, a middle child. Always the peacemaker."

"I was hardly the peacemaker." Becca was definitely uncomfortable with the conversation. She was mashing the broccoli with her fork.

"We don't have to talk about it," Spider offered, suddenly remembering that her brother was dead.

"Well, it's really no big deal," Becca shrugged, but her arms encircled her belly, as if seeking comfort. "Both of my parents worked and I had to take care of my younger sisters until they thought they were old enough to take care of themselves. Of course, by that time…" Her smile looked worn out. "They didn't want to listen to anything I had to say. Do you know what it's like to be in charge but have no control over anything?"

"That's the story of a Hot Shot's life, and yours, too, I imagine." Spider tried once more to tease a smile out of her. "Now, about those advantages to being an only child—"

"The number of children I have is really none of your business." Becca glanced around—possibly to see if anyone was listening to them—then gave him an icy, pointed look.

Translation: shut up.

"Hey, you listened to Victoria," Spider protested. This was why he shouldn't have anything to do with Becca. He'd avoided cool, overly educated women like her in the past because they were too much work. "And she was nothing but doom and gloom. The least you can do is hear me out."

"As long as you understand the number of children I have is none of your business." Becca's chin had a stubborn set to it that said she was serious. Spider sat up straighter, grinned wider, trying to look innocent.

This was stupid. He shouldn't care that Becca wasn't interested in his life at all. She seemed to have adjusted to the accident that had created the baby she carried rather well. Of course, she'd had many months to get used to the idea, and he'd had, oh, less than a week.

Becca looked across camp to the Fire Behavior tent, then over to the table with the rest of the IC team. She sighed, fixing her blue-eyed stare on him. "I really need to go. Since you're such a fast talker, you'll be fast, right?"

"Fast." He nodded stupidly, suddenly caught in a memory from Vegas. Her eyes had been locked on him in the heat of making love. They'd explored each other at different speeds—urgently, slower and leisurely. Spider swallowed. Becca was unlike any woman he'd met before, a mix of cool and hot, wit and stubbornness. She was simultaneously intimidating and a turn-on.

"Anytime," Becca prompted, giving him an impatient look.

She was waiting for him to say something about…oh, yeah, the advantages of his nontraditional upbringing.

"Although Victoria would have you believe she had this tragically lonely childhood just because she was the only child in the house, I stand before you, living proof that it's okay to be the only kid around."

"That's it?" Becca frowned, glancing at her watch, reminding Spider that she was an important person who had an evening briefing to conduct soon.

"No, there's more." Spider made the mistake of looking at Becca again. When their eyes met, he could forget that she was higher up the command chain than him, that she was pregnant, that her cheeks and belly had swollen beyond their sleek lines. He could remember that night in Vegas more clearly and how they'd been equals.

He felt himself stir where he shouldn't be stirring—below the belt. He'd spent the past twenty-four hours avoiding Becca and the unsettling way she affected him. That hadn't stopped him from looking for her or listening for the sound of her voice.

And here she was in front of him, turning him on despite her impatient frown. "Ah, anyway. The advantages were that I didn't have to share the television with anyone. I didn't have to eat cornbread—which I don't like—just because someone else in the family did. I could sneak out and no one would tell on me." If she wanted another child, he'd volunteer for duty once again.

Becca arched her brows at him. "So, what you're saying is that I'd better hope for a boy if I'm only going to have one child, so that he can drink, belch, smoke and watch ESPN all day long without any interruptions." Becca's voice definitely held more than a trace of sarcasm.

Spider had never felt so small. What had he expected? To have her throw her pregnant self at him and profess him a wise man? "Yeah, I guess." He gave her a weak smile, hoping to lighten the moment. "Sounds great, huh?"

"I just wanted to be clear," Becca deadpanned. "And according to Victoria, if I have a girl, she'll need more attention and possibly counseling."

Spider felt it wise to keep his mouth shut. Too late, he'd realized he'd crossed a line. She was clearly offended at his advice. Could she tell his opinion was biased by proprietary lust?

"Thank you so much for the insight. Now, if you'll excuse me, I have to finish up the daily forecasts." Becca moved with care, lifting her knees to the side of her belly to get out of the picnic table, taking his baby with her.

"Hey, we both turned out okay," Spider called to Becca's retreating back with a continued feeling of helpless frustration about Becca, his baby and where they went from here.

"HEARD YOU GOT an easy assignment in base camp." Roadhouse settled across from Aiden with his tray of food after the Fire Behavior Analyst left, as the sun began sinking behind the mountains.

Aiden shrugged, staring at his cup of coffee. But he didn't leave.

He didn't leave. Roadhouse couldn't move for a moment. He was making progress.

Roadhouse took a bite of steak, content just to be near his son, content to have him safe.

"Why did you marry my mom?" Aiden asked without looking up from his coffee cup.

The steak got stuck in his throat and Roadhouse had to cough to dislodge it. "Well, I…well…we…we were pregnant. People back then got married if they were pregnant."

Aiden pushed his cup away and pinched the bridge of his nose. "Why did you bother if you didn't plan on honoring your marriage vows?"

"Well, I…" Roadhouse took off his helmet and set it on the bench next to him, then scratched his head. The truth was painful to admit. He blew out a breath. "You don't ask the easiest questions, do you?"

"Do you deserve any easy questions?"

Roadhouse deliberately put a piece of meat in his mouth and chewed slowly. "No, I don't suppose I do," he admitted after swallowing. He was going to be without a job soon, without his few friends in the fire crews. Alone. Losing everything made a man willing to demean himself to get something back, especially when his previous efforts had been met with rejection.

"I wanted my child to have a legitimate last name, which is more than my dad gave me." When he'd grown up, you couldn't escape the label of bastard. He'd spent a better part of his youth running from the stigma. Roadhouse cast his gaze about the tabletop, as if that could help him avoid the harsh memories.

"But you couldn't keep your pants zipped," Aiden noted in a resigned voice.

Roadhouse was surprised that Aiden's comment lacked the bitterness he usually flung his way. It made him continue to try and keep his answers honest.

"I'm not much good at relationships," he explained slowly, because it was difficult for a man to confess his failings to his son. "I'm a bit too selfish about what I want out of life. I never much liked having to tell someone where I'd been or why I was late. And Maria was a jealous woman, who accused me of cheating if I returned a day later than expected from the fire. Back then, there were no cell phones, and pay phones weren't so easy to find out in the forest." Roadhouse drew a deep breath. "I suppose I started looking for something when I realized she never believed what I told her."

"So you became a cheater because she expected you to be one?" Aiden shook his head. "Didn't you have any honor or self-respect?"

"I admit I slept with a married woman while I was still married. Her husband was in the military and gone a lot. We were both feeling lonely and misunderstood by our spouses. She got pregnant and had a little boy," he confessed, then added, "I'm not proud of that." And then when Aiden started to stand, Roadhouse had to say something to keep him near, so he blurted, "I told Maria, and now I've told you."

Aiden's expression was unforgiving. "How do you think that boy feels knowing what you did?"

"I don't know. When Joan's husband came back from overseas she convinced him Mark was his and I left it at that." He tossed up his hands. "He may not even know the truth today. What would be the point in telling him? The truth tends to upset folks." Maria had thrown a frying pan at him, and pretended to forgive him, but then she'd gone out and gotten her revenge by sleeping with someone else and leaving with him. Aiden had walked away from him in Las Vegas after Roadhouse's admission and seemed about to do so again.

Aiden rolled his shoulders and looked away. "And my sister?"

"Ava never wanted to marry me or anybody. She was pretty much her own woman, along with being a free spirit. We had a few good months together one winter and she went to Albuquerque to make pottery." This was the longest conversation he'd had with Aiden ever. That had to mean something. That had to mean they were forming some kind of bond.

Aiden scowled. "So, you just let them go and never looked back? Never worried if your children or their mother needed help? Never wondered if your kids would have been better people if you were around?"

"No. You turned out okay, didn't you? Back then I would have just messed you up, even your Abuelita said so." Especially Abuelita. "I regret taking the easy way out back then. If I had the chance to do things differently, I would."

Aiden didn't say a word as he left, but he didn't have to. Roadhouse was silently berating himself for being a young fool. How was he to know that some mistakes could never be forgiven?

"BEFORE WE CONCLUDE the briefing, let's hear from one of your own—Spider from the Silver Bend Hot Shots," Socrates introduced Spider later that night at the briefing as if he were the evening's entertainment. There was a robust round of applause, followed by a few smart remarks.

"Fellow ground pounders, lend me your ears." Spider hammed it up, spreading his arms out as if he were Caesar addressing his troops. "The time has come to get more serious about this beast. It's the end of the season and I'm ready to go home. How about you?"

There was a rousing round of cheers. When they died down, Spider continued. "We've got to be smart about this fire." He caught Becca's eye, standing with members of the

IC team. She was going to be really happy after his announcement. He could just picture Becca walking toward him afterward with a big smile on her face as she thanked him for helping her convince Sirus to change their attack strategy.

"And apparently, we've got Scrooge…er, Socrates, running things and he says we're due for a short fire. So, without the promise of weeks of overtime, we've got to make our extra money somewhere." Spider avoided looking at Socrates. It was too late to turn back now. If Socrates didn't approve, Spider would pay for it later.

"I'm going to be starting a pool tonight. For a minimum of four bucks, you can bet on when the fire will jump the highway." There was a disapproving murmur from the IC team, but Spider ignored them. "You've heard the predictions of the Fire Behavior Analyst for the next twenty-four hours. What you haven't heard is that she believes the fire's going to jump the highway within the next week if we don't get it contained soon."

There was a collective grumble and many gazes swung Becca's way. A quick glance found her not smiling, but not frowning either. Spider could relate to her numb state of mind. He didn't know whether to take her in his arms and kiss her senseless, or plant both hands on her shoulders and shake her. He'd never felt such a precarious balance between intriguing desire and toss-your-hands-in-the-air frustration toward a woman. Most men might find that grounds for marriage, but Spider was more like his dad than he wanted to admit. What did he know of love from lust?

Still, he wanted to help Becca. After dinner, he'd considered how he could help Becca convince Socrates to listen to her attack strategy. What better way than to get the entire base camp talking about it?

"Half of the proceeds will go to you, and the other half to

the Firefighters National Trust." A good cause that benefited families of fallen firefighters. "Okay, I'm turning it back to IC now, so prepare yourselves for the backlash."

Socrates stepped up next to him and dismissed the group with a frown but he didn't put the kibosh on the betting.

"Becca had a hand in this," Carl accused as he stepped next to Socrates. He jabbed his thumb in the direction of Becca, who looked a bit pale. "They're trying to turn the crews against us."

Well, well. Points to Carl. Spider tried to look aghast that Carl would accuse him of such a thing.

"That's a bit much, even for you to suggest." Socrates's frown deepened to a scowl. "I asked Spider to think of something creative to improve morale. He made a poor choice, that's all. But since it benefits a good cause, we'll go with it for now."

Socrates pulled Spider away from the group. "You've got one day, Spider."

"Fine by me." Spider didn't care if the betting continued or not. His mission was accomplished. Crews would talk. They'd look at the maps. They'd ask questions of their supers, who in turn would question Socrates. He'd just handed Becca a huge trump card.

So, where were his congratulations? Becca seemed to have disappeared.

CHAPTER NINE

"He used me!" Furiously blinking back tears, Becca plopped into her chair in the Fire Behavior tent after Aiden's betting-pool announcement.

He'd mocked everything Becca was trying to accomplish and had turned every firefighter in camp against Becca. Now they all believed she had no faith in their firefighting efforts because she was predicting the fire would overrun them. Who would support her position for a change in tactics now when it was nothing more than a camp joke? The job? The house? Both were lost.

Aiden's betting pool shouldn't have felt like a betrayal, yet it did. She'd been on the verge of liking him. On the verge? Ha! She'd been on the downhill side of the fall into love, her heart finding it harder and harder to ignore the protests of logic and reason. Blame her heart? More than likely, her suddenly overactive libido was to blame.

And yet, there was something more than sexual attraction between them, although she didn't want to admit it. He may be younger than she was, a risk taker when she was risk averse, but he had this uncanny ability to understand what she needed. The way he'd tried to absolve her guilt over the Coyote fire. His advice for handling Julia and Carl better. How he obnoxiously tried to assure her one child was enough. She may not be predictable to him, but that didn't matter, he knew what she needed.

Or at least she'd thought so until this betting business. Aiden's stunt effectively put a halt to that downward slide. Why was it that Aiden was always throwing a wrench into her life? This proved what a romantic fool she'd be to let herself almost fall in love with him.

"Why would Spider use you?" Julia rubbed her nose as Becca began to pace.

"I don't know. Power? Leverage? Stupidity?" They all seemed like good reasons to her. Becca paused, suddenly determined to go find Aiden and give him a hearty slice of her anger. "I know we were supposed to go over the recommendations again for tomorrow morning, but I can't work right now."

"That's all right. I'm fine," Julia assured her. "You go on and get some rest."

Rest was the last thing on Becca's mind.

"AHA!" BECCA FINALLY FOUND Aiden as she came out of the latrines. He had one of his Hot Shot buddies at his side. She tugged her T-shirt impatiently over her belly as she stood in Aiden's path. Thirty minutes after the briefing, Becca was still smarting from the way Aiden had made a fool out of her. "I'd like a word with you." She crossed her arms over her belly.

"Hey, Bec," Aiden shoved his hands into his pockets and gave her a tired smile, not at all like the bundle of energy who'd addressed a crowd at the night's briefing or the cocky man she'd imagined she'd confront. "This is Chainsaw...I mean...Cole."

Cole was as broad as a barn, and fair skinned with short blond hair. She would have known he was a chainsaw swamper even without knowing his nickname because his pants were clean on the front and dirty at the bottom and sides.

Many chainsaw operators wore protective chaps similar to those worn by cowboys. Besides, she'd seen him hefting a chainsaw the day Aiden had run over her on the trail.

With motion made jerky by her anger at Aiden, Becca shook the man's huge hand. His grip was surprisingly gentle, yet firm, not the knuckle-popping grip of some men. "Nice to meet you, Chainsaw."

At the use of his nickname, the big man smiled at her, but his smile couldn't ease the outrage burning through her veins.

"Ma'am." Cole nodded with a twinkle in his eye and a slightly southern twang to his voice. "It's a pleasure to meet such a tough cookie."

Becca's gaze cut to Aiden. Had he told his friend about the baby?

With a shake of his head, Aiden grimaced as if reading her mind. Becca sensed his disappointment that she hadn't believed he'd kept what was between them a secret. She would not let him make her feel guilty. If he hadn't used her fire prediction for some silly bet, she might have trusted him.

"I meant it's admirable that a woman in your condition would still be working fire," Cole clarified, glancing between them as if to try and cover whatever he'd said wrong.

"Sorry. I'm a little tense," Becca admitted. She glared at Aiden, hoping Cole would get the hint that she was furious and leave them alone. "I'm not used to being made fun of."

"Made fun of?" Aiden scowled.

"This silly pool of yours," she clarified.

"You think… You must be kidding." And then Aiden laughed.

"Hey! Hey, FBAN!" Using the Fire Behavior Analyst acronym, a couple of Hot Shots Becca didn't know waved from the bottom of the hill. "We bet on Friday," one of them called out.

"Smile and wave back," Aiden encouraged. "It's good for business."

"Whose business?" Becca crossed her arms over her chest again. "This is out of control."

"But it's got everyone talking," Cole pointed out.

"Bobby!" Aiden greeted the supply officer as he came out of the latrines. "How's the gas supply?"

"Good as gold. No more shortages, I promise." Bobby stopped on his way down the hill and dug into his pocket. "I want four on the fire jumping the highway." He paused, looking expectantly at Becca.

"Don't say a word." Aiden help up a hand in front of her face. "You can't help anybody."

"Ahh, come on," Bobby complained.

Becca batted Aiden's hand away. "And just what am I supposed to tell the IC team?"

"You can tell them anything you want, just don't tell them until the last minute," Cole urged, elbowing Aiden with a wink.

"But you can tell them I told you so when the fire jumps the highway before they get that line built," Aiden advised her.

"I want Saturday." Bobby thrust the bills in Aiden's direction, then smiled at Becca as he returned to the main camp.

Becca was baffled. No one seemed to resent the pool or Becca's prediction. What was going on here? Had everyone fallen under Aiden's spell?

Aiden shook his head as he noted the bet in a small notebook. "I've become a bookie."

Becca's anger may have cooled to a simmer, but she was still angry. "Bookies usually end up in prison." Which was where Aiden belonged if he murdered her career.

"Now, Spider, you've done what Sirus asked you to. The

camp is no longer filled with long, sad faces," Cole clarified. "I'd bet you're the most popular guy in camp."

"Not to everyone," Aiden said, glancing at Becca, making her heart pound even as she willed it not to.

"I can't believe you're encouraging people to bet on me." Becca planted her thumbs into her back, her elbows akimbo.

"Believe it. What's your feeling about Friday? I've got eight dollars on Friday," Cole drawled.

"You're serious?" Becca couldn't believe it. "You want this fire to get the better of us?"

Aiden laughed. "Of course, we're not serious. The last thing this camp needs is more drama."

"The pool is just a distraction." Cole slapped Aiden on the back. "And Spider, here, is our best man when it comes to creating good times and distractions."

"Oh, yeah, that's me," Aiden said, not looking amused in the least. "Mr. Ho-Ho-Ho."

"This is going to backfire." She frowned at Aiden. The baby wiggled over her bladder, making Becca want to return to the latrines, despite the fact that she'd just gone.

"It won't backfire on you," Cole answered for Aiden. "It just makes Spider look bad and he's used to that."

"That's it, rub it in. I'm the risk taker. I admit it." Aiden stepped closer to Becca with a somber look on his face. "Seriously, I'll take the fall if it comes to that."

Unwilling to trust Aiden, Becca took a step back. "You'll take the fall regardless."

"Hey, I thought you'd be happy. At least, they're not betting against you," Aiden said with a slight frown as he watched her. "That would really suck. They know enough to believe you're right. And if they believe, others—more important others—will start to believe as well."

Others...

Could there be a strategy behind Aiden's mad scheme?

A group of firefighters walking by below caught sight of Becca and called out a few good-natured greetings, including requests for insight into the day the fire would jump, and proclamations of the days they'd already chosen.

Relief, when it came, made her feel light-headed. Becca sank down on an old tree stump, barely aware of Cole taking his leave.

They liked her. More important, they believed in her.

"You didn't see that coming, did you?" Aiden followed her over. "Go ahead. Admit it. I'm wicked-smart." Aiden grinned at her, but his eyes held more than a trace of disappointment.

"I don't know what to say." Becca wasn't ready to apologize for thinking the worst. The anger was receding slowly, leaving her drained of all energy, but not yet to a civilized mood.

"A simple thank you will do for now." The cockiness was back in his voice. Moments earlier, he had seemed subdued by the anger she'd made little effort to hide. Or was that just her heart wishing that he cared about her?

"Thank you," she murmured, unable to find any more words as she waded through guilt over her incorrect assumptions, shame over the way she'd behaved, and numbing relief that her career wasn't over. She kept her gaze firmly on the dirt.

"You're most certainly welcome. I hope this makes up for yesterday afternoon, and the day I startled you and you got this scar." He brushed the bangs off her forehead with a touch so gentle that she sighed. "But you've got to admit, it's good to be evil. Unless, of course, you're Carl."

At the mention of Carl's name, Becca became worried again. "What if Carl convinces Sirus that this is some kind of power play?"

Aiden shrugged. "He already tried. You heard him at the briefing."

"He's not the kind to give up that easily."

"You let me worry about Carl. You don't need anything else to worry about." With the light behind Aiden, his expression was barely visible, but his tone was proprietary.

"This isn't your fight," Becca protested, letting anger seep into her tone. She didn't want Aiden's protection. She wanted to erect barriers to keep the chaos that was Aiden Rodas out of her life.

But he didn't do what she expected or wanted. He didn't back off. "My Abuelita used to say that anything worth having wasn't easy getting. You want to fight this fire safely, right?"

"Of course I do."

"My mother was from Mexico. She had no family name." Aiden stepped closer, his voice dropping intimately. "The only thing I remember clearly about her was her temper. When she thought I was too loud, or that I snuck food out of the pantry when she wasn't looking."

Becca listened with interest. "Did you sneak food out of the pantry?"

"No. There wasn't enough food to sneak."

"I don't know know why you're telling me this." But her heart softened and her anger cooled as she imagined a young boy accused of something he hadn't done. She didn't want to feel sorry for Aiden, or get to know him better, at least not here, in the microcosm that was base camp. That would only expose her heart and her baby's future. So, Becca ignored her heart and began walking down the hill to her tent.

Despite the cold shoulder, Aiden kept pace with her, kept talking. "When my dad came home, she was worse with him.

She'd shout about money we didn't have, and how hard I was to watch." He paused before adding, "Part of me was glad when she left."

"Stop," Becca said in a weak voice. She'd heard enough. The more he told her about his childhood, the more she understood him as a man. No wonder he tried to please everyone. He didn't want to relive the rejection of his childhood.

Aiden must have thought she wanted him to stop walking, because he halted, taking hold of her arm and stopping her between the latrines and the command tents.

"I'll want to make sure you don't bow under the pressure like my mom did." Underneath a lamppost, she could see his earnest expression clearly. He wasn't giving up on this. "If I have to step in and make things easier for you and my child, I will."

"You can't…you shouldn't," she said, but her words lacked conviction. She understood Aiden now. He might not have chosen to be a father, but he didn't want his child to suffer the similar fate of being raised by a mother incapable of handling the stress of motherhood alone. It had been a long time since anyone stood up for Becca.

"I'm the father of that baby, so I have every right to butt in and ensure his well-being."

"After they make a decision on the Boise job. *After.*" Becca had spent her late teen years caring for her sisters, and spent the last fifteen years making fire predictions. Both roles required energy and emotional investment. She wouldn't have traded either role, but both lacked control over major decisions. She would not lose control of her attempt for the Boise job, or her child's life. "I'll handle Carl. I need you to respect my wishes and stay away from me for awhile."

"Maybe our meeting again was fate. You're a strong

woman, Becca, and I admire that." His eyes drifted down to her belly. "I'll give you time for this job to come through and for you to make up your mind, but I'm not a patient man and I have strong opinions about how my baby should be raised."

"Fate?" Becca squeaked. If this was fate, the fates were conspiring against her.

SPIDER DUG THROUGH his red pack, the large duffel he kept in base camp, searching for the kit with his extra toothbrush since he'd somehow lost his.

Chainsaw propped himself up on his elbow, his large frame mostly encased in a sleeping bag. The rest of the Silver Bend team snoozed in sleeping bags on the ground around them. "Out taking more bets?"

"No, just thinking." About Becca and how she refused to talk about the baby or her control issues. About how many different ways a parent could screw up a kid. Was he really up to the task? Was Becca?

"Desk jobs'll do that to you, make you think too much." Chainsaw yawned. "Although that Fire Behavior Analyst seems the exception to the rule. She's always tromping up the mountain, scouting things out, looking for trouble spots in the fire."

"You think she looks for trouble?" Spider stopped digging in his pack.

"No, I think she just doesn't back away from it. Like being pregnant and not married. I wonder what her story is?"

Spider wasn't about to enlighten him.

"Make sure you keep an eye on Victoria and the rookies," Spider said. "They'll get too cocky and do something stupid if I'm not around."

"You worry too much." Chainsaw yawned again. He settled back down into his bag. "Want me to wake you for breakfast?"

"No. I'll be in a pre-briefing." Wondering when Becca was going to tell him what she decided about him and the baby, worrying about what she'd decide, nervous about the idea of impending fatherhood. The thought of taking a baby—complete with diapers and bottles and such—out alone scared the heck out of him. Spider knew nothing about babies.

He just had to make sure this baby knew something about him.

"I DON'T WANT TO TALK about changing strategies," Sirus rebuked Aiden as Becca entered the main Incident Command tent for the predawn team briefing.

The air was crisp and cold. The sky was just starting to lighten, bringing the promise of another warm day. Becca had tossed and turned all night, pressured from all aspects of her life. Professionally, she couldn't afford to fail Sirus and the Flathead Fire. Julia had to do well in the pre-briefing this morning. Becca desperately wanted to change attack strategies before they suffered casualties.

On a personal level, she had no idea how was she going to allow Aiden access to their child without giving him the power to manipulate their lives. She'd ached for Aiden and his heartbreaking childhood, unaccountably wanting to bring more love to his life by sharing their child. But letting him into her life was risky to her heart. Once he found out she'd gone looking for a sperm donor, he'd look at her differently.

Becca had no more answers this morning than she'd had last night, and now she had to face the day feeling tired, fat and frumpy.

"Morale is up," Aiden groused. "That's what you wanted, isn't it?"

"Yes, but now everyone and their brother wants to know what I'm going to do about Becca's prediction," Sirus snapped back.

On that cheery note, Becca announced her presence with a soft, "Good morning."

"Morning," Sirus replied with a scowl.

So, Aiden's plan had backfired. She should thank him for trying. The masses may support her theory, but Sirus did not.

"He'll come around," Aiden whispered so close behind Becca that she felt his breath on the back of her neck.

Despite herself, Becca shivered. There was no denying that she still found him attractive, just as there was no denying he'd dug her a deeper hole with Sirus.

More of the team streamed in behind them, ending the confrontation between Aiden and Sirus, but the tension lingered.

"Looks like it's going to be a rough day." Becca said to no one in particular as she pretended to study the morning map with the latest satellite pictures. She pulled at her fleece vest in a futile attempt to close it. Her belly was too large to zip it, not that it would matter soon. In a few hours, it would be so warm that she wouldn't need it.

"No doubt. Another rough one." With a sigh, Aiden sank into a chair next to Becca and began greeting other team members, having something to say for each one.

Becca tried to focus on the map, but all the while she was watching Aiden out of the corner of her eye. Julia came in and Aiden shook her hand in the same businesslike manner he'd greeted her yesterday.

"Let's get down to it." Sirus brought the meeting to order with a nod in Becca's direction. "Start with the latest satellite map."

"The fire was relatively quiet during the night. We built a considerable length of fire line along the north flank." Becca tapped out a line with her pencil on the thick map paper, trying not to think about the recommendation she really wanted to make. "I'd like to propose we keep with this line today, extending it as far as we can for as long as we can before noon. That means building line in the fire's shadow, but we should be all right as long as we stop before the winds gain strength in the afternoon."

Aiden set his coffee aside and leaned over the map. "Three, maybe four Hot Shot crews max, and you could extend the line during the day shift. We'd have to move quickly and finish before noon, mid-afternoon max, like Becca says."

Becca tried to hide her surprise at Aiden's support. She hadn't really believed him when he'd said he'd stand by her.

"Thanks, but I didn't ask for your opinion, Spider." Sirus turned to the meteorologist. "Carl?"

"Winds are going to stall today. It's going to be dry and hot." He shrugged, as if what he was saying didn't have life or death consequences. "I'd give it a go and push it into the evening."

"That's exactly what you said yesterday and the day before, and the wind kicked up on both afternoons," Aiden pointed out before Becca could say the same with more tact.

Carl scowled and tugged on the brim of his baseball cap, but he didn't argue. Everyone knew he'd been wrong.

"Is it worth the risk?" Sirus turned to Becca.

If they built the line quickly and quit before the winds got crazy, yes, but Becca held off answering. Here was her chance to let Julia soar in front of Sirus. They'd talked about various scenarios yesterday. Julia had been reluctant to agree with Becca, but in the end, she had. Becca would have liked to have spoken with Julia again this morning, but her assistant hadn't been ready when Becca had needed to head for the latrines. "Julia, what do you think?"

Julia blinked her carefully lined eyes almost as if she were unable to focus. "Our data indicates this is our chance. With no wind forecast, I say we build as much line as we can all day." She didn't look at Becca.

Sickening anger woke the baby as it charged through her veins. Becca couldn't believe her assistant's betrayal. Julia was basing her decision on computer calculations again. The computer simulation was based in part on Carl's faulty weather predictions. They couldn't rely on Carl anymore. Another meteorologist might have been more creative and adjusted the algorithms for more accurate wind forecasts, but that seemed beyond Carl's capabilities.

"Okay, then, we go all day," Sirus said, frowning at a point to the left of Aiden's shoulder. "If there are no other issues, let's talk staffing and resources."

Becca exchanged a glance with Aiden. Why did Sirus support Carl and Julia?

"It figures," Aiden mumbled.

It didn't. It made no sense. Becca shouldn't say a word. Disagreeing with Julia would only make her look bad. But she couldn't stay quiet. Lives were at risk.

"Wait, we're making a mistake." Becca held up a hand, feeling her cheeks heat. "This fire creates a wind of its own in the mid-afternoon—sometimes gentle, sometimes wild. Carl's outlook may be for no wind, but we've seen wind pick up on more than one occasion out here."

"Why is it creating these winds?" Sirus probed. "Perhaps if the IC team understood these factors better, they'd *agree* with you." He placed a bit too much emphasis on the word *agree,* his irritation palpable.

"The woods are very dry, so they burn hot, sucking oxygen more quickly as the fire grows stronger, creating its own wind. And the terrain is full of abrupt, craggy ridges, which further influences airflow." Becca kept her gaze on Sirus. "All I know is that the computer simulations have been off and we'd be foolish to rely on them again. I'd challenge anyone who believes the winds won't come up today to head out with a fire crew and work next to the belly of the fire." Finally, she looked at Carl and Julia, daring them to dispute her.

Neither one would meet her gaze.

"I can assume you feel strongly about that," Sirus said dryly.

"My vote goes with Becca," Aiden said.

"Your vote doesn't count." Sirus gestured to Carl. "But yours does. We've been here seven days. You've predicted no winds on three of those days and we've been overrun three times because of wind. What do you have to say to that?"

Everyone at the table stilled. Becca held her breath.

"I don't predict the fire, just the weather." Carl fidgeted in his chair and tugged at his yellow Nomex shirt. Becca was the only member who wasn't wearing Nomex, since it didn't come in pregnant sizes.

"Who does predict fire behavior?" Sirus prompted.

"The Fire Behavior Analysts," Carl admitted reluctantly.

Sirus turned his icy stare on Julia. "Did you discuss simulations with your supervisor before this meeting?"

Now it was Julia's turn to look miserable. She sniffed and nodded.

"Did you discuss the simulations then?"

"Yes." Julia looked as if she might cry.

"And did you both agree to a recommended behavior prediction for today?" Sirus was unrelenting.

"Well, I—"

"Did you both agree?" he repeated. It was standard practice for the support crews to align their thoughts prior to meetings.

"Yes."

"And when your supervisor generously asked you to present the Fire Behavior team's recommendation, did you do so?"

"Sirus, this isn't necessary," Becca said. He was only making the situation worse for both herself and Julia. What Julia had done was foolish, but she didn't deserve to be publicly humiliated.

"Yes, it is." Sirus turned to Julia. "Did you?"

"No."

"So, I have to assume that you were grandstanding for your own purposes, even though it would put firefighters at risk, even though it went against your supervisor's better judgment—someone who has years more experience than you do." Sirus stood wearily. "Enough infighting. Deploy four teams to the ridge in sector two and assign a time tag of thirteen hundred hours. No one works past that in sector two. Are we clear?"

"Sirus, wait." Becca hurried after her boss, but he didn't stop until he was outside and several feet from the command tent.

"I'm disappointed in you, Becca." Sirus spun to face her, anger coming off him in waves.

Becca shook her head. "I know, I can't seem to make her understand that fire prediction is about more than reading a computer printout."

"No. You almost let her get away with a lousy prediction you didn't approve of because you wanted her to look good to me, just so you could get my recommendation for that job in Boise. Do you want a repeat of the Coyote fire?"

Becca's spirits sank. He was right. No job was worth risking someone's life.

"But she didn't let Julia get away with it." Aiden stepped next to Becca. "She might not have discredited Julia right away, but Becca didn't let her get away with it. She'd never knowingly put a firefighter at risk."

Sirus seethed silently, regarding them both with a steely stare. Becca wasn't sure whether she should be grateful or resentful for Aiden's intrusion.

Finally, Sirus spoke to Becca. "You really want that job, don't you?"

"Yes, sir, I do." She ran a hand over the baby.

"It shouldn't matter how well Julia does. If anything, Becca's overqualified for the job," Aiden said, staunchly her champion.

Becca held her breath, waiting for Sirus to explode on one or both of them, realizing Aiden had nudged her heart back on that downward descent to deeper feelings for him.

"Thank you, Mr. Incident Commander. The next time I want your opinion, I'll ask for it." With a chilly look at both of them, Sirus turned to go.

But Aiden wasn't done.

"In the spirit of helpfulness and cooperation, I'd rather not delay. There are a couple of suggestions I have to improve things around here that can't wait for hell to freeze over, which is when you'd ask me. You do remember me? Your assistant in base camp?"

After a long, stony stare, Sirus shook his head. "You are full of surprises this morning."

Sirus sighed. "All right, since it seems my pre-brief has been cut short, why don't we talk about your ideas over a cup of coffee."

When Aiden started to follow Sirus, Becca held him back with a light touch on his sleeve. "Thank you."

"It's okay to set aside your pride and get help sometimes." Aiden brushed aside her bangs so he could see her stitches, and then grinned. "Talk to you later."

For once, Becca looked forward to it.

CHAPTER TEN

"I'D THINK YOU'D BE EXHAUSTED by now, running from one team to another telling jokes and collecting bets." Becca kept her smile carefully neutral when Aiden entered the Fire Behavior tent at lunch. She was balancing a small plate with a turkey sandwich and some fresh vegetables on the top of her belly as she sat with her feet propped on the milk crate.

Spider could see the muscles in her legs, even if her ankles were swollen. All that hiking had kept her in shape.

"I'm coming to believe that base camp crews bust hump. I'm just going to hide from Sirus for awhile in here." He thought for sure she'd tell him to go away, but her smile welcomed him. Apparently, the truce they'd reached in the past twenty-four hours still held.

He sat down on the other side of her desk. Her traitorous assistant was nowhere to be seen.

"I've walked more miles this morning than I would have up in the mountains fighting fire." Not true, but it felt like it. "I'd forgotten that Socrates walks faster than anyone I know."

"How are your spirits holding up? It must be hard staying so upbeat when you don't even want to be here."

"I never said I didn't want to be here," Spider hedged.

"No, but you left enough clues. Truthfully, what did Sirus ask you to do here? Whatever it was, he probably didn't mean for you to become my ally." She set aside her plate and steepled her hands over her belly, slouching deeper in the chair, looking as if she'd wait all day for his answer.

"He…uhm…" He wasn't going to tell her.

"The truth." Her blue eyes were piercing, demanding honesty.

"Why are you asking me now?"

She shrugged, and he would have repeated what he'd told her the first day of his assignment—that he was here to help the IC team—but then she raised an eyebrow and smiled at him.

"He thought I'd be able to lift morale. Seeing as how this is the last fire of the season, several crews are ragtag, resources are scarce and he knows that drags spirits down." Spider dropped his helmet to the floor and ran a hand through his hair. "Holy cow, you're better at drawing out the truth than my grandmother."

"I'm not ready for you to change the subject yet." She picked up a carrot. "So why didn't you want the assignment?"

He hesitated too long, trying to decide what to tell her. Besides the fact that he loathed being chained to base camp, he'd also blamed Becca for his assignment.

"And don't give me that line about Hot Shots being underutilized in base camp. There is no *I* in team. If Sirus believes you can help me, then you better believe that you can help me." She tossed his own words back at him.

"It's complicated." Like their relationship. Who knew what that was? And, given his father's inability to honor his marriage vows, what made Spider think he could make monogamy work? Hearing Roadhouse talk…there wasn't much difference between father and son.

"Try me." She crunched on her carrot. Her long braid hung over the back of the chair. He wanted to feel its silky length in his palm.

"I've always been able to liven up a party. I've never really thought about it much." He started out slowly, not really sure how much to tell her.

"And now," she prompted.

"Now…now it's almost as if everyone, from my friends to Incident Command, doesn't see much deeper than that or expect much from me."

"You don't like that, do you?" She creased her forehead, drumming her fingers on her belly. "Does the baby have anything to do with this recent change of heart?"

"No. It started last year. Golden and Logan got hurt, and suddenly I had to be the responsible one." Spider sat up straighter. "I kind of thought it would be a drag, but it wasn't. The biggest change for me was knowing the safety of everyone rested on my shoulders." And then the worry for others shackled itself to his ankle.

"I can relate to that." There was a soft acceptance in her gaze that was new.

"It wasn't as if I stopped cracking jokes. I just downshifted, I guess." He didn't want to come across as a management clone, or even management. He missed the adrenaline rush of the fire, even as he was almost relieved to be removed from the worry that had been riding him on this one.

"So, do you think you've fulfilled Sirus's expectations?"

He shrugged. "Maybe." It had been a good day. Socrates had seemed impressed with Spider's suggestions.

"I heard your pool is a hit. Someone said you've collected a couple hundred bucks. That seems pretty darn successful to me. You should be proud."

He liked that she was interested in what he was doing. Her interest was genuine, not the "I don't care what you say as long as we go to bed later" type of attention he usually encountered from women. "Give the pool a couple of days and Socrates will come around to support you."

Becca didn't seem convinced. "Which day are most people predicting the fire to jump the highway?"

"Friday." Four days from now. Spider hoped to be back out on the line before then.

"I hope they're all wrong." Becca stroked her hand across the swell of her stomach.

"Me, too."

She met his gaze. "Did you hear the latest weather report?"

"Yeah, hot and dry." Perfect conditions for a fire to gobble up acreage. A change of subject was in order. This one was too gloomy. "How's the pregnancy been treating you?"

He would have considered something sappy to describe her, like she glowed, except that she didn't. She looked droopy, as if she could use a few hours sleep.

Her expression became guarded. "I'm fine."

"Is that what you tell Socrates?"

"Every time he asks." She took a drink from a milk carton.

"You need to tell him to let you rest midday. Even firefighters need to take a break." And she wasn't a firefighter. She was a delicate woman. Pregnant women just weren't a good fit on fires. The pace was too demanding and the hours too long.

She stared at him with raised brows until Spider realized he'd spoken this last part out loud.

"You know it's the truth." He wouldn't back down. "Your stubborn streak is showing."

Julia entered the tent, and Becca turned away from him, effectively ending their conversation.

"FEELING BETTER?" Becca asked Julia after Aiden left.

Her assistant had spent most of the day hunkered down in their sleep tent since Sirus had confronted her this morning. Becca knew the younger woman must be upset, but she needed to get over it. Still, Julia's pouting had allowed Becca to enjoy Aiden's company—even the way he looked at her, as if she were some delicious treat—until he'd admitted his prejudice against women working on a fire.

"What did Spider want?" Julia asked instead of answering Becca.

"He and I were going over some fire predictions. He is here to help after all." Okay, so that was a fib. They'd gone over no predictions and if Aiden was here to lift her spirits, he'd fallen far short with his remarks about his limited role as a father and how he didn't want fatherhood standing in the way of his bachelor lifestyle. He may want her, but he didn't want her heart.

"I suppose he agreed with your predictions." Julia slumped into the chair recently vacated by Aiden.

"There are a lot of places he and I disagree." That might be the understatement of the year. Becca tugged at her T-shirt. He was pushing her too fast, too soon. What was his hurry? "But there are a lot of places you and I disagree, too."

Julia wiped at the makeup under her eyes. Becca was convinced her eyes wouldn't be so red if she just quit rubbing them.

"Is he qualified?"

"He has about ten years of fire experience." In some ways, Becca trusted Aiden's judgment more than Julia's.

"What are you going to do if Carl and I are right today?"

Julia had a way of tilting her head down and looking up at Becca that was disconcerting, as if she didn't want Becca to see her face.

"You mean if the simulation is correct in its predictions?"

"Yes."

"Most likely we'll chalk up the day to successful, conservative efforts." It wasn't as if they kept a scorecard with the fire.

"But what will *you* do?"

"Are you asking me if I'll apologize?" To Julia? To Carl?

Julia nodded.

Leaning back in her chair, Becca almost laughed. "For what?"

"For thinking you're always right. No one's right all the time. They can't be."

"Julia, I'm not always right. You know the conditions here in Flathead defy normal prediction. Haven't you learned anything this past week? No computer is going to accurately predict what's going to happen in these many microclimates twelve hours in advance. That's an on-the-spot estimation."

Julia was shaking her head. "I'm always wrong and you're always right."

"Holy smokes, this is not a competition." Where had this come from? Becca was floored. "This is about stopping a powerful force of nature. It's about predicting what the fire will do and when so that we can safely fight it as long as we can."

Becca wasn't getting through. She could tell by Julia's poker-faced expression. And then Julia opened her mouth and confirmed it. "The computer said—"

"I don't give a flip what the computer said," Becca cut Julia off, accenting her words with a sharp slice of her hand through the air. "The computer's been wrong fifty percent of our days here. How many teams have you seen come in here with charred suits and eyebrows melted? Are you going to stake someone's death on your need to be right?" Becca was so angry her limbs trembled, causing the baby to get jumpy as well.

"I didn't want to remind you of your insubordination earlier," Becca continued, trying to calm down. Sirus had done a good job of embarrassing Julia, and Becca didn't want to rub it in when it was obvious Julia was taking it so hard, but the time for being the kind, nurturing boss had ended with Julia's foolish actions this morning. Her assistant would have to work her way back into Becca's good graces.

"Let's get something straight, Julia. I'm only filling in on this fire. It's my last field job. If you really want Sirus to hire you, you need to be a team player *and* you need to think outside the box." Becca drew as deep a breath as she could given the baby was crowding her lungs. "There was a time when I thought you were perfect for this job. Prove me right."

Becca picked up the satellite pictures and pretended to be more interested in them than in Julia. "Why don't you take the afternoon off, think about things and we'll start fresh tomorrow?"

"HOW WAS YOUR DAY?" Spider asked Becca that night, catching up to her outside the Fire Behavior tent. He'd thought about her all afternoon and evening. Maybe she was right. Maybe he was pushing for no other reason than to tie up loose ends. Now he greeted her as if she were…a good friend? He didn't have any female friends under the age of fifty who weren't married to one of his buddies and out of circulation.

"Long." Becca's blue eyes were huge in her pale face. Upon closer inspection, Spider could tell she was close to collapsing from fatigue.

"You ain't kidding. Have you eaten or rested? You look like hell."

"Thanks." She crinkled her forehead in that way she had of showing her displeasure. "I'm still mad at you for calling me delicate."

"You know what I meant." He took her arm and headed to the dining area. "Did you eat?"

"I had some fruit earlier, and then things got crazy. Where were you?"

"I spent the evening with the caterers. Sorry I missed your briefing." She'd noticed he was missing. That made him smile. "Did the briefing go well?"

"The same as usual, except a couple of guys tried to get me to extend my predictions past twelve hours."

Everything about her looked tired and drawn, from her sagging shoulders to the dull sheen in her eyes beneath the stitches on her temple. Spider knew little about pregnant women and pregnancy, except what he'd heard from his friends about their wives' pregnancies—growing a baby in their tummy wore them out. Becca looked ready to collapse.

"You didn't spill anything, did you? Like when you think the fire will cross the highway?"

"The only thing I spilled was on me." She tugged on her shirt to show him a red stain over her breast. "Strawberry jam from this morning." She stumbled.

Aiden swore as he steadied her. "You need a keeper." She scared him with how frail she seemed.

Becca drew on some hidden well of reserves, straightening—which only thrust her belly out more—and somehow managing to look tougher. Still tired, but tougher. The more he saw of her, the more he admired her, though he had no idea what to do with those feelings.

"I've been taking care of myself for a long time and doing pretty darn well," Becca stated firmly.

"And now you're taking care of two, and you're not doing so hot. You can't keep up this pace. I'm going to tell Sirus that you need to rest." Before fatigue sent Becca to the hospital.

"You'll do no such thing." She walked steadier now, as if drawing strength from her indignation. "I've got to be bulletproof if I want to get that position in Boise, Aiden, and, frankly, things aren't going as planned."

He chuckled, despite the concern she'd raised. "You'll be fine. You know, no one calls me Aiden but you." They were almost to the chow area now. Encased in evening shadows, it was nearly deserted.

"I'm not calling the father of my baby Spider," she said in a low voice.

There was something about her statement that filled Spider with pride. He was going to be a dad. At some point soon, he'd figure out how to be a dad and a free-wheeling bachelor.

"You sit. I'll bring you something." Aiden settled Becca on a bench. She was so tired, she didn't argue. Then he filled a plate with cold pasta, ham steaks, bread and fruit.

She didn't talk much while she ate. Mostly she smiled weakly and waved at people who passed by or stopped to place a bet with Spider.

"Why do they call you Spider?" she asked, pushing her plate away and propping her chin on her palm as she leaned on the table with droopy eyes, looking completely kissable.

He was starting to get used to the longing she aroused in him.

Still, Spider steeled himself to the fact that she was going to laugh at him when he told her about his name. "I watch a lot of horror films, mostly the bad ones because they're more amusing than scary, and mostly the ones with bugs that have been doused with radioactive waste and grow to be Gigantor-size, terror-inducing creatures." He held his hands in the air like claws.

She didn't laugh, perhaps because she was too tired, but Spider preferred to think that she liked him too much to hurt his feelings.

Becca's smile was as worn out as she was. "I suppose there are worse nicknames out there."

Spider nodded. It was true.

"Someday, when you feel your immortality, you'll drop out of the Hot Shots and drop your nickname."

"Never." He sat back in mock horror. That meant growing old.

With the same tired smile, she told him, "That's what I thought you'd say."

He shook a finger at her. "I am not predictable."

"Everybody's predictable once you get to know them." She pushed herself up, disentangling her legs from the picnic table. "You want to think of yourself as some bad-ass, but—"

"Did you just call me a bad-ass?" He hurried around the table to her side, but she shook his hand off her arm.

"—your grandmother would probably say she raised a gentleman."

"Let me walk you to your tent and you can tell me about what a gentleman I am." So they could talk a bit, so he could squelch this need to kiss her.

Who was he kidding? The longer they were together, the more he wanted her. Perhaps if he set his watch to beep at ten-minute intervals, he'd discover a safe exposure limit to Becca. Ten minutes? Five? Didn't matter now. He was already over the limit. He wanted her.

She didn't refuse him, but said, "I'm going to the showers first."

"Not a problem. I'll just walk you to your tent by way of the showers." They could talk while she waited in line. Talking was safe. He had questions only Becca could answer.

Because the fire never slept, sleep was a rare and precious commodity in the field. Spider was bone tired. Becca had to be surviving on willpower alone. She needed a distraction and he had just the topic.

"When did you discover you were pregnant?" he asked, falling into place beside her.

"A few weeks after I met you in Las Vegas." There was no hesitation in her answer. She delivered it in a matter-of-fact voice that probably discouraged most guys.

Good thing he wasn't most guys. "And how did you know it was mine?"

She shot him a venomous sideways look. "Is this an interrogation?"

"No, I'm just curious." His next question was even more touchy. "Did you ever...uhm, consider...you know, not going through with it?"

The expression on her face was incredulous. It was clear the thought of terminating the pregnancy hadn't crossed her mind. She slowed down as they neared the shower line, either because she was tired or to give them a few more minutes of privacy.

"Did you even try to find me?" he asked.

"It's not as if I needed to tell you. I'm *old enough* to make decisions on my own." She emphasized the words *old enough* ever so slightly, as if to remind him of their age differences.

Spider frowned. "I seem to remember something you said to me in Vegas."

Becca looked like she didn't want to know, yet she didn't

jump in and change the subject, making Spider suspect that she wasn't as indifferent to him as she tried to appear.

"When we walked out of the bar and I realized how tall you were…" Taller than him in her sexy high heels, although barefoot they stood about the same height. "You told me that no one was short in bed."

As far-fetched as it seemed given their time in Vegas, under the yellow lights NIFC had brought in and the orange glow from the fire in the distance, Becca seemed to be blushing.

"It doesn't matter how old you are or how old I am. We're having a baby together," Spider stated, trying to remember if she'd been hesitant or demure in Vegas. He hadn't thought so, but he'd had quite a few beers by the time she'd come his way.

Her temper flared. He could see it in her defensive stance, one hand over the baby, one on her hip, then she glanced around camp to see who might be watching, before lowering her voice. "There is no *we*. I don't want to talk about this." She hurried forward into line, perhaps thinking that he'd just follow her orders.

Not.

He was going to make sure she went straight to bed after this. She and the baby needed sleep. He stood right behind her in line. This close, he could see her curves. She may have filled out, but she'd filled out well. Becca had the ripest pair of breasts he'd seen in a long while. Reflexively, his hands clenched as if anxious to explore her more-than-generous curves.

He shoved his hands in his back pockets.

Despite her weight gain, she still had that proud bearing. And, unlike the long list of babes he'd known, she intrigued him after the act. She could hold her own with the big guns of IC, like Sirus, yet she cared about the men and women assigned to fight the fire. She was almost ferociously protective of their baby. And when he was near her, he felt both more alive and more at peace.

Drawn to Becca, unable to leave her alone, Spider leaned forward and spoke just above the chugging hum of the generators so that only she could hear him, not the five people in front of her. It was an intimate move, but the question less so.

"Why did you decide to become a Fire Behavior Analyst? I'd think a woman like you would be a CEO or running her own business." She certainly had the brains and willpower.

With stiff steps, Becca moved forward in silence.

At first, he thought she wasn't going to answer, but then she admitted, "My brother was a Hot Shot."

"So I heard."

She tossed him a questioning glance over her shoulder as if to assess what he knew.

"Someone said he died."

"He was my older brother." She faced forward again, adding softly, "My only brother."

"I'm sorry."

She sighed heavily. "He died in the Glen Allen fire of 1993. He and his buddy didn't realize how dangerous their assignment was—putting out spot fires on a southern canyon slope. The wind kicked up mid-afternoon and created a crown fire, then…" She half turned to him, dropping her voice. "From what I heard, the whole slope exploded into flame. I don't think they knew the extent of the danger until it was too late. There were no *what-if* scenarios back then, computer simulations weren't sophisticated and safety precautions not near as stringent."

"I'm sorry." Spider patted her back awkwardly. So that was

why she took her job so seriously. "We've come a long way since then."

She gazed up at the smoky night sky. "I think I can remember every NIFC meeting where I've fought for progress." She sighed and looked at him. "Not that the government doesn't want to keep firefighters safe. It's just they don't always want to spend the money necessary to develop the tools that increase the chances they'll live to a ripe old age. And there's still a long way to go."

Spider silently agreed. People were still dying with too frequent regularity on fire crews. Spider was reminded of his own ominous feelings about the Flathead fire.

"What do you think about this fire?" he wondered aloud. The topic had turned somber, but at least they were talking.

She shook her head, staring up at the orange outline of the ridges above them. "Do you want the IC team answer, or my own?"

"What do you think?"

"That you have no patience for politics." She smiled, but then her expression sobered and she lowered her voice. "Sometimes you have to fight fires with a toothpick and that's when mistakes start to occur. You've been in the meetings. It's no secret that we're not getting the support we need."

He nodded. "Thanks for being candid. I heard that you were one of the best behavior specialists around."

She made a little movement with her head, half acknowledgment, half discomfort. Becca knew she was good, but didn't seem to want praise.

"After working with you, I can vouch for that. Not all the support staff take such a personal interest in our safety." Some, like Julia and Carl, seemed more concerned with having their recommendations and predictions accepted than protecting firefighters. Becca not only had a good sense of what the fire would do, she made the conditions and risks of each fire zone clear, as well as calling out superintendents by name and telling them it was their responsibility to monitor the situation. That was smart on her part because it made the supes personally vested. If they didn't perform as she advised, they'd not only have to answer to the incident commander, but also to Becca and the rest of base camp who'd heard her give advice.

But the important revelation was that she was on a mission for her brother. This wasn't just a job, it was a calling. He understood now how important the promotion was to her. She'd probably really shake things up in Boise, but it didn't look like she'd get the chance.

With a sigh, Becca dug her thumbs into the small of her back and arched, the movement reminiscent of something they'd done in Vegas. Spider knew on some level that the action was innocent now. But...

Oh, Mama.

"No one told me that babies weighed so much," she said with a small smile.

Even though she was inches away, Spider resisted moving her hands aside and stroking her back to offer comfort.

"Did you attend the conference in Vegas?" he asked instead.

"I spoke the first day," she admitted, as if speaking at a conference in front of several hundred peers was no big deal, when Spider knew only the best of the best were chosen to speak. He was small potatoes in the scheme of things compared to her.

They'd met on the evening the conference had begun. Spider had hung out in that same bar the remaining nights of his trip in the hope they'd hook up again. "Did you leave early or something? I looked for you."

"You didn't know who I was."

"That didn't stop me from looking for you."

Spider was rewarded with a small smile, as if she were pleased he hadn't simply forgotten her.

"It would have been fun to wake up together," he added.

"Fun?" Everything about Becca stiffened.

He'd stuck his foot in it again. "I'm trying to say that I would have liked to get to know you better. I'd like to get to know you better now."

"I hear you don't do girlfriends," Becca said.

"So, you've asked around about me." Spider had little to be ashamed of. In fact, he was pleased she'd nosed around until he realized what that also meant. "And yet, you didn't tell me about our baby."

"My baby," she reiterated, lowering her voice. "And there was nothing you would have wanted me to tell."

Had she been put off by his reputation and then just dismissed him? "Don't believe everything you hear about me, Becca. If I listened to what people said, I'd think you were a cold, calculating woman." Who was she to judge him? She'd enjoyed their sex just as much as he had. Maybe he enjoyed sex more frequently than she did and with more women, but so what? "Instead I found one hot mama who intrigues me to no end, who still intrigues me, challenges me, and drives me nuts."

"Keep your voice down," Becca whispered, casting her gaze about to see if anyone had heard him.

Spider was pissed off. There was almost more adrenaline pumping through his veins than he knew what to do with. "Worried what people will think about you and me? Well, too damn bad. Listen, honey, pretty soon everyone's going to know about us and that baby of ours."

She gasped, then narrowed her eyes at him. "You promised not to say a word until later."

"And I won't say more until they make a decision about the job you want, but let me make one thing clear." He moved into her space, until her belly nearly touched his, until he thought he'd go crazy if he didn't kiss her again. He could see by the way her eyes darkened that she felt the same. "There's something between us and it's more than the baby."

Heaven help him. He had no idea what he meant by more.

CHAPTER ELEVEN

"YOU KNOCKED HER UP, didn't you?" Roadhouse asked, intercepting Aiden in the middle of camp. He'd seen Aiden and the Fire Behavior Analyst in the shower line. There was no other reason for Aiden to pay that much attention to a pregnant woman. He just wasn't the type, being too much like his old man.

"Do you have to be so crass?" Spider said gruffly, but didn't immediately send him away.

"Seeing as how you haven't gotten married first and then gotten her pregnant, I'm just calling them as I see 'em. What are you going to do about it?"

"Are you being nosy or are you going to give me unwanted advice, too?"

"Probably a bit of both," Roadhouse admitted with a smile. Aiden seemed off balance and open to his presence again. "She's not your usual type of woman, so I figure you'll need help."

Aiden snorted, but he didn't cuss him out or walk in the other direction, so Roadhouse continued. "A classy woman like that won't be bullied or coerced into marriage."

"Who said anything about marriage? You, of all people, have no concept of what marriage is."

"How else are you going to guarantee your name is on the birth certificate?"

Aiden stopped and stared at him. "Please don't tell me your name isn't on the birth certificate of your other kids."

Roadhouse shrugged. "Joan wasn't going to put me on that birth certificate. Can't say for certain about Ava. She didn't want much to do with me after she moved to the Southwest."

"Are you sure there aren't others?"

"Can't say for sure. Can you be sure you haven't fathered other kids?" There was so much Aiden didn't know about him, but the way his son uttered the question, as if he couldn't stomach being near his own father, hurt. Still, at this point, Roadhouse wouldn't lie. "Look, I told you why I couldn't see Joan anymore. Ava didn't want to see me either. I used to meet women and one thing led to another, if you know what I mean. Never saw them more than once or twice." Roadhouse sighed. "Kind of like your Fire Behavior Analyst, I'm betting."

Aiden took off again, his pace brisk. "It's not nearly the same."

"Ain't it?" Roadhouse's laugh was as bitter as his own memories. "She holds all the cards—the baby, being a mother, there being no relationship prior to the event. You didn't date her, did you?" At Aiden's silence, Roadhouse continued, "Thought not. You aren't going to have to worry about that baby at all. Not unless you really, really want to." Roadhouse held his breath, realizing he was pushing things, but needing to know whether Aiden planned to be involved with his grandchild—*his grandchild*—or not.

"I can't believe I'm listening to you," Aiden said, slowing down.

Roadhouse almost wanted to moan in relief, his knees ached so bad. Instead, he said, "You know there's just one thing that captures the attention of a smart, controlling woman like that."

"I bet you're going to tell me." Aiden glanced to the side as they walked, as if he weren't interested in the conversation.

"Make her hot for you. A woman like that doesn't date men like us. We scare them because we can make them feel things they don't feel right feeling. You know, they're a bit frigid on the outside, but once they thaw out, they're hot in bed."

"Do you believe half the stuff that comes out of your mouth?" With a look of disgust, Aiden stepped into the latrine, ending the discussion.

"It's a proven fact, my boy," Roadhouse called after him before sidling away to find his own bedroll.

Aiden would either understand that he had to marry the woman if he wanted a role in that baby's life or he wouldn't, in which case he'd know exactly how Roadhouse felt most days—like the world had passed him by.

"HAVE YOU SEEN HIM?" Victoria asked later that night as she and Chainsaw walked up the hill toward Spider's perch near the latrines.

"Who?" Spider asked. He was sitting in the dirt, elbows looped around his knees, keeping an eye on the shower trailer into which Becca had disappeared earlier.

"That old guy in Montana #5. You know, the one who walks funny, like he's in pain?" Victoria described Roadhouse.

Knowing Roadhouse was Spider's dad, Chainsaw exchanged a meaningful glance with Spider, who frowned and asked Victoria, "Why are you looking for this guy?"

"Hold the phone," Victoria held up her hands. "I don't want to run into him. He stares at me funny. I want to get in line for the showers, but not if he's around."

"He's not around." Spider had seen him go bed down with the rest of his crew a few minutes ago. He'd be glad when this fire was over and he wouldn't have to deal with Roadhouse trailing him every day. His old man seemed to be waiting for Spider around every corner, trying to make conversation. Didn't he realize that he had crushed Spider's belief that he cared for him, in the same way that his belief in Santa and the Easter Bunny had been shattered so long ago?

"Good." Victoria headed to the showers.

Chainsaw settled in the dirt next to Spider, smelling strongly of smoke. "What are you doing here?"

Spider didn't take his gaze from the shower trailer Becca had disappeared into, barely acknowledging his envy at Chainsaw's field assignment. "Waiting."

Chainsaw leaned forward, peered into Spider's face and sniffed, until Spider shoved him out of the way. "You haven't been drinking," Chainsaw noted.

"No, I haven't been drinking." Besides the fact that alcohol was a big no-no in camp, who had time to drink with so much to do? Just a few days after coming to base camp, Spider no longer considered them slackers. These guys—and gals—busted their humps making sure things went smoothly and safely for the firefighters.

"So, if you haven't been drinking…what's up?"

"I'm just waiting, that's all." For Becca to get out of the shower and walk back to her tent. For his chance to talk to her again and perhaps try—God, help him—his dad's advice. Maybe if they made love again, they'd come to some sort of middle ground where she didn't stubbornly shut him out of her life whenever he got too close.

Chainsaw looked from Spider to the shower trailer, then

snapped his fingers. "It's that blonde, right? The Fire Behavior Analyst's assistant."

"No." Julia wasn't worth his time. It was Becca he wanted.

"So, who is it?"

"Don't you have something else to do?"

"Yeah, I need to take a shower. But if you're going to be sitting here watching, I'll be too creeped out to go in the shower trailer." Chainsaw shrugged out of his backpack. "It's not like you to stalk a woman."

"I'm not stalking her. It's just…" Spider sighed and looked at his friend. "She drives me absolutely nuts. She's smart, gorgeous, a real looker, but—"

"Not into you, huh?"

Spider searched for a way to describe what he'd gotten himself into without giving away that Becca was the object of his vigil. "She is… She might be… One minute she is, and the next, she's the ice queen. She drives me crazy."

"Is this mental craziness or woody craziness?" Chainsaw asked.

Washing a hand over his face, Spider admitted, "Both. I like her. I want her. Then we argue and I think she's the most impossible woman on the planet. Then she'll give me a look, and I'm on fire."

"You do have it bad." Chainsaw slapped Spider on the shoulder a couple of times. "It's not like you to expend so much energy on a woman. What was it you said once?" He gazed up at the smoke-strewn starry sky. "Oh, yeah. Any woman that didn't nibble on the first hook you dangled wasn't worth the wait."

Those were the days. Things were simple. Either a woman wanted you or she didn't. But this was different. His kid was involved. And the compelling, complexity that was Becca. "That was when I had control of my life."

"Let me see if I can put my advice in terms even you'll understand." Chainsaw stood. "Don't control what you're feeling. It's like…it's like an orgasm. You just surrender to it. If you fight it, if you pull back, it feels good, but it's not enough, not near as satisfying as letting yourself experience the end result of all your foreplay."

"You're saying I should have sex with her?" Spider sighed with relief. That was what his dad had recommended, too. Maybe the old man wasn't crazy.

"Obviously, my use of metaphor was lost on you." Hefting his backpack, Chainsaw chuckled. "I'm saying you should just let yourself fall in love with the woman."

Spider sank back on his elbows. "I don't do relationships, and neither do you."

"Someday you will, buddy, and someday I will, too, for the right woman." Almost in slow motion, Chainsaw shook his head. He'd lost his heart to his high-school sweetheart and had hardly dated since. "Maybe you should try it this once. People change. They grow up. They get married and have babies, and forget the stupid things they did in their youth."

"Holy crap." His dad's advice was more appealing than Chainsaw's. Growing up was like…death.

Chainsaw squatted down, peering in Spider's face again. "Do any of my statements scare you?"

"Heck, yeah." Spider was the least likely to be picked out of a lineup as marriage material.

And then Chainsaw changed Spider's perspective with his usual insight. "And what if that woman walked out of your life tomorrow, and never looked back? How would you feel then?"

"Like I missed out on the best thing that's ever happened

to me," Spider answered without hesitation. "Whoa, where did that come from?"

"Your heart, buddy. It's about time you listened to it, don't you think?"

"BECCA, CAN YOU SPARE A MINUTE?" Spider stepped out of the shadows at the side of the tent where Becca slept, intercepting her on her return from the showers. "Can we go over to the chow area, and get a cup of coffee or something?"

"Can't it wait until morning?" Becca looked ready to check out, but beautiful with her face freshly scrubbed and her hair looking darker than usual in a wet braid hanging over her shoulder.

"No." When a man realized he was in love with a woman, he had to act on it immediately...before he lost his nerve. When she opened her mouth to refuse, Spider added, "I'm not going to press for custody or anything. I just really need to talk to you."

Becca must have seen something in his eyes to sway her, because after a moment, she nodded and led the way to the dining area.

When they were settled at a table—Spider with a steaming cup of coffee and Becca with a bottle of water—she prompted Spider. "You had something on your mind?"

"Yes. Yes, I did." He set his helmet on the table and ran his hand through his hair. He hadn't seen enough date movies to know how to tell her how he felt. Blurting out three words seemed nearly impossible, and, given their circumstances, even a bit premature. He'd known her just a few days. At the same time, it seemed as if he'd known her forever.

He'd sat next to her this time instead of across from her, with his thigh casually invading her space, so that he could feel her warmth. The silence stretched uncomfortably as he choked on any words that even came close to describing how he'd come to care for her.

"Hey, need any company, Becca?" Victoria called as she walked back from the showers with her hair in a towel.

Spider laid a hand on Becca's arm. "I really wanted to talk with you alone."

Becca waved Victoria away after a quick glance into Spider's eyes. "I'll be fine."

Grinning, Spider couldn't resist sending Victoria off with a zinger. "You go on, Victoria. Big day tomorrow. You'll need all your energy."

"You shouldn't talk to her like that," Becca warned.

"When I get back out in the field, her life is in my hands. If I talk to her like that here, she won't want to screw up around me," he said in earnest, because he didn't want Becca to think he was totally insensitive. "Your so-called sisterhood won't do her much good on the line."

"You're such a butt-head."

Spider drew back, laughing. "Years on the fire crews and that's the best you can come up with? Butt-head?"

"Let me sleep about ten or twenty hours, and I'll come up with something better."

Spider sobered, brushing her bangs back out of her eyes. *Tell her you love her, you idiot.* Instead, he said, "You're not getting enough rest."

Becca's eyes drifted closed. "I think I've finally hit my limit. I'm too tired to fight you."

"I find that hard to believe." They were sitting close enough to kiss. How Spider loved the way she kissed. It was the same way she did everything else—with wholehearted focus and energy. Only they were out in the open, where anyone could see them. Becca would have a major freak-out attack if he tried to kiss her out here.

"You make it harder when you're nice." Slowly, on a sigh, she revealed those fabulous blue eyes. "Can you say something mean?"

"No," he said gruffly. He couldn't find the words to say he loved her, but he sure as hell wasn't going to start a fight with her now.

"Ow." She rubbed a spot at the top of her rib cage. "The baby's kicking."

They stared at each other so long that Spider found it hard to resist her magnetic pull. He leaned closer. Maybe his dad was right and Chainsaw was wrong. "Would it be so bad—"

"No." Becca sighed, leaning into him as well. Then she straightened abruptly, as if the baby had kicked some sense back into her. "Yes. Oh, my God, we're out here in the open where anyone can see us."

She was going to leave him. He put his hand on her shoulder. "I wanted to talk."

He could feel Becca holding her breath. He should tell her how much he admired her strength, how much he enjoyed talking with her, how much he wanted to lie next to her and hold her in his arms. And he would, as soon as he got over his intimidation at being a younger man, a high-school graduate who was clueless when it came to love.

"You're worried about being a dad, aren't you?" Becca sneaked a quick glance at him. "I can tell you're worried."

No. He was becoming paralyzed with the realization that he loved her and couldn't do a thing about it.

"You'll be fine. Just trust your instincts," she said softly.

"What if my instincts are telling me that being a dad isn't enough?"

She did look at him then, with slender eyebrows raised. "Your instincts could be wrong."

He shook his head slowly. He wasn't wrong. She was the woman he'd waited for.

"You think you're having these feelings because I'm going to have a baby you had a hand in creating," she whispered.

He swore. "How can someone so smart be so stupid?"

Becca rose stiffly, moving in that careful way she had, less graceful now that she was upset.

Spider made no move to stop her. He wasn't able to put his feelings for her into words that would convince her. He should have known that nothing with Becca was simple, not even falling in love. "Becca?"

She stopped a few feet away from him, but didn't turn around. Maybe he'd find the courage to tell her what was so important that it couldn't wait until morning some other time. Tomorrow loomed as a better choice. For now, he had to know where he stood with her. "Would you say that our situation is hopeless?"

For a moment, she didn't answer and Spider thought she might turn around.

"Yes." The single word was drawn out with a sadness that seemed to propel Becca away from him.

"Nothing is hopeless. You know that, don't you?" He called softly after her, but she didn't look back.

TUESDAY MORNING, Becca entered the IC tent with Julia in tow for the morning's pre-briefing meeting. Julia was very reserved compared to the day before. Becca had to wonder if there was any hope of salvaging Julia's career—or her own. It was still dark outside, but Becca had already downloaded the weather report, satellite pictures and fire simulations. She could sense the fire was gathering its resources and even Carl had admitted that the weather was about to change. She was prepared to argue for a two-pronged defense on the southern ridge. Two lines, not one, because the fire would move south and west with the shifting winds.

"So we pull out our fire shelters…." Aiden was sitting on a desk, telling a story to the support staff, who all clustered about him as if he were a rock star.

Becca could relate. She was drawn to him as well, but she had more reason to resist, even though it felt good knowing he supported her belief that the fire would take the highway. Twice last night he'd told her that there was more between them than the baby. Guys like him, young and unfettered with responsibility, tended to get excited about things and then regain their sanity when the initial thrill passed. Aiden had to be confusing his excitement about the baby with his feelings—let's face it, it was a healthy dose of residual lust—for her.

The tent door swung open and Sirus strode in behind her. "Let's get to it people."

Becca stood next to the table, one hand supporting her lower belly, and began pointing out changes in the fire map since the night before.

"The fire front has expanded." Becca paused for the usual negative reaction, moans, groans and so on. Instead, people just nodded and waited for her to say more. Aiden's morale program seemed to be working.

"It's picking up steam even at night," Aiden noted. "How many acres would you say it's burned so far?"

"It's on pace of about six thousand acres a day, so maybe thirty-six thousand acres so far," Sirus said. He looked more relaxed this morning than previous mornings.

Someone whistled. Thirty-six thousand acres wasn't a record, but it was substantial.

"And they still won't be sending us more resources?" Aiden asked.

Sirus shook his head.

"The fire created vortex winds yesterday afternoon. It's working against us all the time as it advances through this intricate series of ridges. And all we're doing is containing it on the northern boundary." Becca pointed to the area northeast of camp. "As most of you know, according to locals, the winds have a history of shifting with dropping temperatures, and will soon work harder against us."

"If history repeats itself," Carl said.

"I'd prefer Becca's prediction to yours," Aiden muttered half under his breath.

Becca ignored Carl and nodded in Aiden's direction. "Assuming the wind shifts, we need to cut off the head of the fire, not just the southern tip, but the western side as well. Here…and here." She pointed to the key ridge. "It means risking letting the fire spread on the northern flank, but we'll be stopping its forward progress." She tapped the map with her pencil. "We can't delay any longer. By my estimation, this convergence of wind shift, terrain and fire will be more than our resources can handle if we let it get to this point." Becca tapped the ridge on the map again.

"If the winds shift as the fire reaches this point, even base camp won't be far enough back for a safe retreat," Julia added, with a careful look in Becca's direction.

Becca blinked in surprise, recovered, and gave her assistant a nod of approval.

"That's a fairly aggressive ground attack. Do we have the manpower for something like that?" someone asked. "I don't think we have the manpower for something like that."

"What's our team status, Pat?" Sirus asked.

"No new teams expected," Pat, the personnel officer, reported. "In addition to that Washington blaze, state parks are on fire in California. They always get precedence."

"Air tankers?" Sirus turned to Angus, their sole helicopter pilot.

Angus resettled a baseball cap on top of his long, stringy black locks and shook his head. "Just my bird." Which could dump water and the fire suppressant, slurry, but not in large enough quantities to make a difference.

The tent became silent.

"Have you thought of calling in volunteers to build lines ahead of the fire?" Spider asked.

"Originally, yes," Sirus said. "But then the fire got ugly."

Aiden set down his coffee cup. "It's still one nasty beast, but we've got plenty of room for them to build a break near the road as a last defense. We should shift some resources to build what we can at the ridge where Becca thinks we should make our last stand. What do you think, Bec?"

She nodded slowly. "It's a start. Not near enough to stop the fire if we get an alignment of forces though." Alignment of the right wind, slope and fuels would cause a deadly blowup they'd have no chance of stopping.

"What's plan B?" Sirus drummed his fingers on the table.

"Plan B?" Aiden pushed Carl out of the way, moving closer to Becca. "Shifting some crews instead of all of them. You need a plan C."

Consoling herself that they stood united, Becca resisted touching Aiden, although she longed to.

"Why the hell do we need a plan C? Don't you see the pattern here? The score is fire ten, us zip." Aiden referred to the number of days they'd been on the fire. "If the winds shift, the fire continues, and we're screwed. We have no defenses to the south."

"*If,*" Carl said quietly, not even giving Aiden the courtesy of looking him in the face. "Sure, a cold front is coming in, but I'm not convinced the winds will shift."

"That's a big if," Sirus said, shaking his head. "With no more manpower and no air support, we can't risk building so much real estate in front of the fire. And we can't use civvies that close to the fire."

"We've got to try. The risk increases if we don't change our tactics." Becca wasn't ready to give in. "Even if it's just a few crews, they could slow it down."

"Becca, as much as I want to support you, I can't switch strategies based only on some local Indian legend." Sirus sounded apologetic. "Every data point we have indicates the fire will advance to the north."

"Actually, I found some documentation of the wind shifting when the temperature drops in this area on the Internet," Julia said, making Becca smile and Sirus frown.

"You could change tactics if you believed your Fire Behavior Analyst," Aiden said in a low voice, giving Sirus a hard stare. "We're screwed if we don't do something."

"Spider." Sirus looked displeased.

"I won't let this deteriorate to one-liners." Becca held up her hands, pleased when Sirus and Aiden looked a bit repentant. "If you won't consider a dual defense, I strongly recommend protecting the road by building a line on the south side of this ridge. At the rate the fire is moving, if we move four crews from the northern to the southern flank we should be fine to the north and protected to the south."

The IC staff became uncomfortably quiet.

"When do you think the front will move in? Just give me your best guess," Aiden demanded of Carl, his patience long gone.

"Two days from now, maybe three," Carl said, looking flustered before admitting, "I can't say exactly when. It could stall or speed up at any time."

"Friday," someone murmured.

Angus swore. "I bet on Thursday."

"Three days," Aiden appealed to the group. "We've got three days to do this."

"It's too late to build that dual defense with limited man-power. Unless…" Becca glanced at Angus. There was still hope. "We drop slurry on the western and southern flanks of the fire. That would give the crews enough time to build something substantial without putting them at such risk." She turned to Sirus. "To be on the safe side, do you think we can get volunteers to build a line at the highway?" Normally, roads were considered a natural firebreak, but this highway was quite narrow, barely two lanes.

"I'll have our public liaison track down some volunteers for the highway." Sirus frowned. "But I'm not onboard with the dual defense. It's too risky."

"Why not?" Becca wouldn't let it go. "If the wind starts blowing to the south and the fire eats up the east side of that ridge, we'll lose the valley and the road."

"I said no. We could lose control of our northern line."

"You've got to be kidding. This is how you make decisions every day?" Aiden was beside himself. "You look at the facts and say screw them? This is so messed up. We've got *three days.*"

"Spider, just because something usually happens—like winds shifting when temperatures drop—doesn't mean it *will* happen. No offense, Becca," Sirus added.

Aiden slapped his palm on the map. "Look at the map and tell me Becca's not right."

Becca laid a hand on his arm, hoping Aiden would regain his composure, then let it drop when she saw Julia looking at her.

"Becca's predictions are solid, but our main fire strategy takes precedence over something we're not sure will even happen." Sirus was firm.

"Carl?" Aiden looked to the meteorologist.

"I can't help you on this," the meteorologist said.

"You mean you won't." Spider pounded the table with his fist. "That bites!"

"Are you willing to put your life on the line in support of Becca's theory?" Sirus asked Aiden.

"No!" Becca wanted Aiden to say the word so desperately that she said it out loud for him, even as Aiden said, "Yes."

Then he added, "If you're willing to compromise, I'm willing to lead three to four crews in building a southern defense."

It was dangerous, or at least it would be when the wind shifted. Everyone was looking at Becca, wondering why she didn't want Aiden to go, and at Aiden, wondering why he wanted to go.

"All right, Spider. Let's get you back out in the field," Sirus said.

Her heart sank. She didn't want him risking his life. Sometime during the last day or so, Becca had fallen in love with Aiden even though she'd tried so hard not to. Somehow, his determination, compassion and energy, as well as his triumph over a difficult childhood, had found a place in her heart that she'd kept guarded for years. But she couldn't let the feeling go further than this awareness, otherwise she'd be defenseless when Aiden realized that he'd confused physical attraction and excitement at becoming a father with deeper feelings for her.

They stared at each other. Becca wanted to tell him not to do it. If the winds shifted and they were too slow in their defense…A man couldn't outrun a fire that raged as fast as a speeding freight train.

"It's the right thing to do, Becca. I have to believe that. I have to believe in you." Aiden said this last in a gruff voice, his dark eyes determined. "I'll go."

CHAPTER TWELVE

"THANKS FOR NOTHING, Spider. Socrates pulled me off the crew and onto Incident Command," Golden said, catching up to the rest of the Silver Bend Hot Shots as they were filing into the chow line for a predawn breakfast. The fire was getting closer, so fire crews could bed down and eat in base camp before heading out for twelve to sixteen hours of work.

When his announcement rendered the others speechless, Golden filled them in, more than a trace of frustration in his voice. "Socrates thinks I'll be able to help here. He said something about your moral standards being too high."

"Sorry," Spider mumbled. But if he had to do it all again, he would still stand with Becca.

"No, I'm sorry. I should have known it couldn't be helped." Golden rubbed the back of his neck. "He's wanted me in IC for months. Your being here just postponed the inevitable."

"Hey, just don't go on any flyby inspections without your shelter," Logan advised. "The old man tends to forget he's in a fire zone when they drop him off somewhere to observe." About a year ago, Logan had been escorting Socrates and three others in IC when they'd been trapped by a blowup, barely escaping being roasted.

"The good news is that Spider will lead the team for the

rest of the fire," Golden announced, with a tight nod in Spider's direction, as he obviously tried to shake off his disappointment at being left back at base camp.

Spider exchanged a quick glance with Logan. They were equals and both would have been up for the job.

"I told Golden it was okay with me days ago when we first heard Socrates wanted Golden on IC," Logan admitted with a grin. "I thought it might be fun to watch you lead for a change."

Spider felt a surge of pride. He loved being in command. And to receive such an honor with the approval of his friends made it seem more special. Now if he could just stop the fire from sweeping across the highway, maybe he'd prove to Becca that he was more than a two-Sundays-a-month dad. Perhaps she'd be able to see that they had something worth exploring between them.

"It'll be one big party." Doc slapped Spider on the back as if they were about to pull something over on a substitute teacher.

With a shake of her head, Victoria moved ahead of them toward a table. The rest of the group followed.

Spider's bubble burst. He wasn't the same man he'd been even a few days ago. He was a man to be taken seriously. A man a son could be proud of.

"We'll miss you up there, Golden," Spider said as he reached across the table to shake Golden's hand.

"Not near as much as I'll miss you. A desk job." Golden shook his head. "It's the first sign of old age."

Spider had always thought that getting married and having kids was a sign of old age, but now he wasn't so sure.

"No," Spider said. "The first sign of old age is when you want the desk job."

"GOOD TO SEE YOU BACK OUT in the field." Roadhouse stopped in front of Aiden. "Water?"

Roadhouse had been assigned hydration duty. With a five-gallon water tank strapped to his back, Roadhouse was the water boy for three teams, filling their canteens and water bottles. It wasn't work he preferred, and it was hell on his knees, but it was good to have an excuse to talk to his son.

"Did it work?"

"What?" Aiden thrust out an open canteen.

Roadhouse inserted the spout and toggled the switch so that water flowed into his son's canteen. "My advice…about her." He finished filling it and handed it back.

"No."

"Oh." The letdown was incredibly abrupt. He'd hoped that helping his son would open the door for him to be a part of his life. Fire season was drawing to a close. Soon, he and Aiden would be going their separate ways. Aiden back to Silver Bend and Roadhouse to heaven knew where. Unless…

"Victoria mentioned you've been staring at her," Aiden said, interrupting Roadhouse's thoughts.

"Who?"

"Victoria. The Queen." Aiden gestured to the redheaded woman on his fire crew. "She says you give her funny looks. You aren't thinking of hitting on her, are you?"

Roadhouse squinted as he looked at the woman. "Her? She reminds me of someone, that's all."

"Not another lover." Aiden's expression turned to one of disgust.

"No. She's the spittin' image of Jeremiah Hackett."

Aiden took a swig of water, looking more curious than disgusted now. "Who?"

"Jeremiah Hackett. A Hot Shot. Old school. Way before your time."

Aiden hesitated, glancing over at the woman. "Did he ever serve on Silver Bend?"

"Yeah. Same as me for awhile."

"Is he alive?"

"Last I heard, but he could have been run over by a bus or something since then." Roadhouse wanted to smile. They were having a regular chat, like two civilized relatives.

"Would you recognize him if you saw a picture of him?"

Roadhouse paused. "He looks like her. What do I need a picture for?"

"Never mind." Aiden bent back to his task.

Roadhouse felt his chance slipping away. "Are you going to winter in Silver Bend again this year?" he blurted.

Aiden didn't turn around. "It's where I live."

"It's a nice town. Thought I might check it out this winter." Roadhouse tried to be casual, when in reality, so much hinged on Aiden's response.

Aiden's voice was flat and unwelcoming. "Why? What could possibly draw you there?"

"Well, I—"

Aiden wasn't through driving him away. "It's not as if you have family or anything in Silver Bend. I don't have family there."

"But—"

Turning slightly, Aiden lowered his voice. "Don't you dare say it. Family is about sacrifice and emotional support, two things you know nothing about."

It took Roadhouse a few seconds to say what he'd been

wanting to say to Aiden for years. "Give me a chance, son." He swallowed thickly. "I'd like the chance to do those things. I know I can never make up for your childhood but I'd like the opportunity to start fresh."

When Aiden didn't answer, Roadhouse walked away with a lump so large in his throat he could barely breathe. He didn't notice that Aiden had stopped working and was watching him walk away.

"YOU LOOK LIKE YOU COULD USE some company."

Becca glanced up from her turkey-casserole dinner to find an old firefighter standing on the other side of the picnic table with a plate of food. She didn't much feel like company, having been worrying about Aiden all day, but the older man's smile seemed genial enough, so she nodded. In her experience, most firefighters just wanted someone to listen to them, so she probably wouldn't be asked to provide much to the conversation.

It wasn't until he took his helmet off that she realized he was the firefighter that had been staring at Victoria the first day they'd met.

"Roadhouse." He offered his hand.

Not sure if she should stay or leave, Becca made sure his hand was clean before she shook it. "Rebecca Thomas."

"It's been a long fire season," he noted before taking a bite of his casserole. He also had two thin white-bread sandwiches stacked in front of him, along with a big pile of mustard potato salad, a cluster of grapes and a small package of cookies. Despite the amount of food on his plate, he was gaunt.

"Longer than most years," Becca agreed. "I work mostly in California. Are you Montana crew?"

"I picked up an open slot on a private crew in Montana a

couple of months ago, but I spent years working in the Southwest. The fire season is long there." There was something about his eyes that seemed familiar, a deep loneliness. "Makes the off time of winter go faster." He gave her a lopsided grin.

Before she could stop herself, Becca wondered what Aiden did during the winter. Was he like some of the younger Hot Shots who took on seasonal jobs at ski resorts during the cold months? Or did he just take the time off?

"I saw you talking to a friend of mine the other day," Roadhouse said, interrupting her musings.

The baby kicked her bladder, as if in warning.

"A guy named Aiden Rodas," he continued. "He's a good guy, don't you think?"

She'd been expecting him to say something about Victoria. She'd feared he'd say or do something weird. Caught off guard, she hesitated. "I…I barely know him."

"He's an assistant super on the Silver Bend Hot Shots."

Not knowing what to say, Becca took a bite of her casserole.

"I've known him since before he was a rookie," Roadhouse went on. "He's a good kid…." He gave her a strange look and corrected himself. "Er…man. He hangs around with a good group of guys. And he's reliable."

Something cold and uncomfortable gripped Becca's stomach. "You sound as if you're trying to convince me of something."

He picked up a fork. "Naw. I mean, maybe I am. I don't want you to get the wrong impression about him."

"Why?"

"Why what?" Roadhouse was trying to look innocent and not really succeeding. There was something about his eyes, shifting to the side beneath slim silver brows, that indicated he was uncomfortable with her question.

"Why are you so concerned that I have the right impression of him?" She was getting goose bumps now.

"Well, I...you know..."

"I'd like the truth, or you can take that plate and eat elsewhere," Becca stated coolly, even though her palms had started to sweat. When had she become such a heartless witch?

When she'd decided her baby needed protection. And if her reputation was ruined, she'd have a hard time working in fire, much less landing a management position with NIFC in Boise.

Roadhouse stared at her for what seemed like a full minute, then he looked over each shoulder as if concerned that someone might hear him, finally whispering to her, "I'm his father." He blew out a breath. "You don't know how long I've wanted to tell somebody that." Then he looked suggestively at Becca's tummy. As if he knew she carried his grandchild.

The cold knot in Becca's belly spread through her veins until her hands and face felt numb.

"Holy crap." Roadhouse jumped up and raced around the table. "Don't pass out on me now. Aiden would skin me alive."

"I'm fine," Becca protested, but Roadhouse had already encouraged her to turn sideways and bend over, crowding the baby, crowding her lungs. "I just need a drink of water."

"Humor me, missy, and count to ten."

"Then will you let me up?" Out of the corner of her eye, she could see them attracting attention. Her image as the woman who could keep up with any man was quickly being dismantled.

"Then we'll see if you have any color in your cheeks." He kept one hand pressed down between her shoulder blades, even as he knelt awkwardly next to her.

"I can't believe he told you about me. About the baby," Becca mumbled, eyeing him between sips of water when he finally let her up.

Roadhouse rubbed his gray-stubbled cheeks. "He didn't tell me anything. I just know my son, is all. I can't wait to see the little booger."

"He didn't tell me you were working this fire." Becca wondered if Aiden would have. Irrationally, she was upset that he hadn't.

"We're not exactly on good terms right now." Roadhouse's smile was rueful, as if the situation was more painful than he wanted to admit. "You know how it is sometimes between fathers and sons."

Having come from a loving family with open channels of communication, Becca didn't know, but she nodded numbly anyway.

"He's a good kid. He really is. You should see him out on the fire line. He just whips those men along. And when they get tired, he's the first to make a joke to lighten their spirits." Pride rang in his words.

Becca couldn't resist asking about Aiden's childhood, which he'd painted as being incredibly bleak.

"It wasn't all roses for the kid, I'm sorry to say. Some of that was my fault. He was..." Roadhouse looked up at the smoke-laced sky while he gathered his thoughts. "He was a handful, always moving, couldn't sit still in church to save his life. He rode his bike everywhere. And friends... man, he had a lot of friends. I couldn't keep up with them all." And then Roadhouse grinned, the expression as impish as Aiden's.

She couldn't help but smile at the love Roadhouse obviously had for his son. Becca could almost picture Aiden at age eight or ten—a huge grin on his little face, pedaling his bicycle past the other boys, charming the minister out of punishing him for being a wiggle-worm in church. That grin of his had probably saved Aiden's sorry butt many a time.

"And that kid was so determined. Once he set his mind to it, there was no stopping him."

"I can see that," Becca said, loosening up for the first time all day.

"WHY DON'T WE JUST COYOTE OUT? All this back and forth to base camp is cutting into my sleep time," Doc groused, voicing what many of them had to be thinking—if they went *coyote out,* as Hot Shots called camping out in the field, life would be better all around. At this point, the fire was so close to base camp that it made no sense to spend their time off in the field.

"You like hot food and showers, don't you?" Spider leaned forward so that Doc could hear him, which was dangerous considering they were in the back of a truck bouncing down the rutted fire road on the precipice of a mountain at a speed that made even Spider nervous.

"The days just seem really short is all." Doc shrugged.

Lately, Doc was too gung ho for Spider's taste, which was saying a lot, since Spider was usually the gung ho one.

Maybe Spider was getting old. Or maybe it was unexpected fear that he wouldn't live to see his kid's birthday. He couldn't pinpoint any one reason he'd become a nervous Nellie.

The truck came to an abrupt halt in the staging area of base camp, sending everyone slamming into everyone else's shoulders. Spider was crushed by Chainsaw, sending air whooshing out of his lungs. Several curses went up. With a dark look, Doc jumped out of the back of the truck and headed with purposeful strides to the truck driver—some pimply-faced teen who seemed more concerned with speed than safety.

Victoria hopped off the truck before Spider. She scanned what she could see of the camp before picking up her gear and heading to the small area of base camp the Silver Bend Hot Shots had claimed as their own. Spider bet she was looking for Becca.

Instead of cleaning up, Spider made for the mess area. It was late for dinner, but Becca was usually one of the last to eat.

Sure enough, he spotted her golden braid at the far end of the dining area. She was sitting with an old firefighter...

Correction. She was sitting with his father.

Spider's strides came quicker, almost a run. He had to dodge through people—couldn't they see he was in a hurry?—but they just weren't getting out of his way. He'd thought a lot about his old man these past few days, about his ability to forgive and trust. But what had his father done to earn any of that?

"What are you doing here?" Spider demanded when he reached their table, immediately suspicious of his father's motives.

Becca looked up at him with a frown. "We're eating."

"Not you." He tossed his head in Roadhouse's direction. "Him."

"I was just leaving," Roadhouse said, gathering his things.

"Good. Don't let me see you around her again," Spider warned. He had no idea what his father was up to, but he'd bet it was no good. Roadhouse had recommended he have sex with Becca, instead of telling her his feelings, for cripes sake. What kind of fatherly advice was that?

"Roadhouse, you don't have to go," Becca said, glaring at Spider.

"Yes, he does." Spider straddled the picnic bench next to Becca and sat, dumping his backpack on the ground.

"He does not."

"He's already gone," Spider pointed out, taking a carrot stick from her plate, but his hunger had disappeared, and his hands were filthy. He tossed the carrot under the picnic bench for the squirrel. "What did he want?"

She looked toward Roadhouse's retreating back.

"Did he…did he tell you—"

"That he's your father?" She turned to him then, her eyes full of compassion, but he wasn't certain who the emotion was directed to—himself or his dad. "Yes."

Spider swore and took a deep breath. "Hardly anybody knows that. I'd prefer to keep it that way."

"Why?"

Because he'd manipulate the situation, get Spider to care again and then disappear, leaving Spider with an empty spot in his heart he'd have no hope of filling. The realization had Spider slumping on the bench.

"Don't believe a word he said," Spider managed to say. "He's never been reliable, and he sure as hell was never the dad I needed him to be." He ignored the fact that his old man had been trying really hard this past fire season to be something in Spider's life—father or friend, he didn't know which.

Becca stood, her belly nearly in his face since he still sat on the bench. "So, I guess I should just forget the fact that he talked about you like he loved you and had been proud of you since the day you were born."

"He what?" No way had his dad bragged about him. But Spider didn't have time to figure out what Roadhouse had been up to because Becca was leaving.

"There you are, Becca," Victoria said, coming up behind

him. "I was hoping to have dinner with you, but I guess it's too late for that. Who did you have dinner with? I thought I saw you with *that guy*," Victoria said, dropping her voice. "But I knew that couldn't be right."

"In fact, I did have dinner with him. His name is *Roadhouse*." Pausing, Becca stared pointedly at Spider, as if she were waiting for him clarify to Victoria that Roadhouse was his father. When he kept quiet, she added, "He's very sweet."

Spider wondered what his father had said to Becca to make her defend him so.

"You can't be serious." Victoria was visibly upset. "He's so out there."

"He's not really. He's just lonely." Another meaningful look Spider's way from Becca, another pause.

He was getting the distinct feeling that she was disappointed with him. Hell, she was delivering her feelings as if she were holding up a sign that said Spider Needs to Give His Dad a Chance. Spider had a news flash for Becca. He was fresh out of chances when it came to his father.

"I have to go." Becca turned and walked away in that funny pregnant walk of hers that usually made him want to smile when he wasn't wanting to yell at her. At the moment, he didn't want to do either. He wanted to wrap her in his arms and have her tell him not to worry about a thing—not the baby, not them, not the fire, not his father.

Victoria watched Becca walk away, too. "You may as well give up on Becca. Your Peter Pan ways are all wrong for her."

"Someday, my Peter Pan ways are going to save your ass. Again," Spider snapped back, irritated that Victoria thought she knew Becca well enough to know what was good for her—and that he wasn't it.

ROADHOUSE TRIED NOT TO DWELL on Aiden's anger, tried not to be hurt by his continued determination to shut him out of his life. But it did hurt and he couldn't seem to get past it.

Without really thinking about it, he found an empty pad of paper in his hands and a chewed-on ballpoint pen. He started writing, *Dear Aiden...*

Twenty minutes later he heard his superintendent calling his team together for the nightly briefing. Jack-Ass was all about appearances. Every private crew member needed to appear interested and involved in fighting the fire. Sucking up to the Incident Command team was one way not to get sent home early. Knowing what you were doing and doing it well was another.

Roadhouse folded the letter and stuck it into a plain white envelope, then into his Ziploc bag of letters. He then tucked the whole thing into an outside pocket of his backpack as he jogged as quickly as his stiff legs would allow through the sleeping tents toward the Incident Command tent, dodging other fire-crew members, not even noticing when the bag of envelopes fell out of his pack.

"I DON'T UNDERSTAND why you'd talk to that guy." Victoria was waiting for Becca by the Fire Behavior tent after her pre-briefing. "You saw how crazy he was."

"I did see him that day," Becca said, moving to stand in the shade. "He wasn't acting crazy. He might have been tired and just happened to be looking in your direction when he vegged out."

Victoria vehemently shook her head. "He's been on other fires with us lately. He stares. No one else stares like he does."

"I don't know what to say." Becca liked Roadhouse. She'd

only seen him act odd that one day. And the fact that he was her baby's grandfather and trying to find a way back into Aiden's life ensured Roadhouse the benefit of the doubt, and a soft spot in her heart.

"He's like a stalker or something. I'm afraid for you. Say you're not going to see him again. Please."

"I can't do that." In the same way she couldn't refuse Aiden some form of contact with their baby, she didn't have the heart to shut out Roadhouse, not when he was so clearly excited about Aiden becoming a father. Becca's hand stroked over her belly.

"Be careful." Victoria gave up trying to convince her.

Becca watched Victoria walk away through the crowd, left with an unwelcome seed of doubt. Roadhouse was not a danger to her. She was sure of it. Becca turned to resume her walk to her tent and her path intersected with Aiden's as he barreled around a corner.

"Hey." He steadied her arms, but her heart was anything but steady at his touch. "I'm glad I caught you. I want to explain."

"Explain what?" Trying not to be obvious as she made sure no one was looking at them, Becca shrugged out of his hold.

"About Roadhouse." He looked pained.

"You don't need to explain anything." *But try,* her heart silently and irrationally begged.

"Maybe not." He shifted his stance, as if uncomfortable, not looking at her. "But I do need to apologize for what I said earlier and I thought you might like to go into town for an ice cream."

Ice cream. The smooth, cool treat was her idea of heaven. She wanted to, more than anything, but she had the evening briefing to give. "I can't."

"Maybe you'd like to think about it first." Aiden's smile was strained. "I asked Logan to cover for me."

"I bet you'd rather have a beer. Why don't you go into town and get a beer with your friends?"

"No." He washed a hand over his face, looking worn out. "As long as the ice-cream parlor is air conditioned and what I'm putting in my mouth is cold and refreshing, I don't care if it's beer, ice cream or pickles. You said it was going to cool off, but it's still hot."

Air conditioned. Becca almost fainted with longing. It had been weeks since she'd been anywhere climate controlled. Sure, it cooled off every night and became chilly, but with the fire closer, the air was hot and dry, and Becca's underthings were damp with sweat.

As if reading her mind, Aiden continued to taunt her. "Someone gave me directions to this ice-cream parlor. Apparently, it's as cold as an igloo inside." He flashed her a scrap of paper with scribbled lines. "Since my crew all came on one bus, I don't have any wheels. You'd be doing me a huge favor by driving me in your vehicle."

"That's a great idea, Becca," Sirus said as he walked by. "You need to get away. I'll have Julia give the evening briefing."

Becca's mouth fell open. Julia had been on her best behavior since her public humiliation, and Sirus was giving her a chance to take responsibility. The hope Becca had buried days ago for the Boise job peeked out in the form of a smile.

"See?" Aiden grinned. "You have permission. Besides, I hear we're actually going to make an attempt at the western line tomorrow, a whole day early. It's my last chance at air-conditioning and ice cream for awhile."

She shouldn't go, even if Sirus said it was okay. She should just hunt up the keys to her SUV and give them to him. But

Aiden was smiling at her and, irrationally, she'd missed him today. In the end, that and the promised treat of air-conditioning and ice cream was too much to turn down.

CHAPTER THIRTEEN

"BESIDES YOUR BROTHER, DID anyone else in your family go into fire?" Spider asked as he drove Becca out of camp with the air conditioner blasting. He'd insisted upon driving her old white Toyota Forerunner since she looked so tired and, surprisingly, she'd handed the keys over without much fuss.

Ecstatic just to be with Becca, he searched for something to talk about as he drove. Everyone liked to talk about their families, right?

"No."

Spider scanned the two-lane highway for traffic before he pulled out. Not that he needed to. At this late time of day with the sun beginning to fade, a car was rare this high up in the mountains.

Think of something to say, stupid.

He was never at a loss for words. And yet, they passed several miles of pine forest in silence. He couldn't even look at Becca for fear she'd realize how lacking he was in conversation skills. She had to think he was one conversationally challenged idiot. Correction. She'd label him a predictable, conversationally challenged idiot.

Think, think, think.

What had they talked about that night in Vegas? The merits of bottled versus tapped beer. The amount of money he'd lost gambling. Neither of which seemed like topics the Becca he knew today would be interested in. Or a good segue into what he really wanted to talk to her about—his love for her.

"Baseball," he blurted out suddenly. The word sent her limbs flying.

Criminy. She'd been asleep. She gazed over at him with sleepy eyes and just a tiny bit of drool on the corner of her mouth. She wiped it off self-consciously and settled deeper into the seat.

"You like the…Giants." Spider should have risked looking at her. Then he would have known she'd been asleep.

"The As," she murmured in a sleepy voice, barely audible above the SUV's engine. She'd been pushing herself too hard.

He slowed the truck and kept silent the rest of the way, letting Becca rest. Without conversation, his own eyes felt heavy from lack of sleep. Luckily, he'd reached a place where he had to pay attention and look for street signs to get them to the ice-cream place. The challenge kept him alert.

When he pulled in front of the Waltzing Bear Ice Cream Parlor a few minutes later, he put her SUV in park and let the air conditioner continue to blast them, taking advantage of Becca silent and approachable in sleep to study her.

It was hard to believe that his child grew in her belly. The need to place his hand over the baby was strong, but he didn't want to wake her just yet. The drive had only taken thirty minutes. That hardly seemed enough time to restore Becca's energy. He looked at his watch, calculating the amount of time it might take to eat an ice cream and drive back, calculating the hours of sleep that he'd be able to get when he collapsed in his sleeping bag later.

He'd felt especially rested when he'd slept with Becca in

Vegas. Perhaps that was because he knew on some level that he loved her.

He snorted. Yeah, and pigs could fly.

Still, it'd be nice to feel that way again—safe, loved, rested as she held him in her arms.

Only one thing stood in the way of him having that feeling again. Becca had no idea that he loved her. He was going to change that. He had momentum. She was here with him now, wasn't she? Sure, she was sleeping. And Spider had to admit he was a bit jealous of her sleeping. Once she was awake and he got the conversation rolling, she'd realize that taking a chance on him in Vegas was the best bet she'd ever made.

He blew out a heavy sigh, and her eyes flickered open.

And then she was straightening. "Tell me I didn't fall asleep."

He'd tell her almost anything she wanted to hear if she'd just let him into her life. "You didn't—"

She cried out and bucked against the seat belt. "Ow-ow-ow-ow!" Her foot was thrashing against the floor board.

"What's wrong? Is it the baby? Let's get you to the hospital." He jammed his foot on the brake and put the SUV in reverse.

Becca threw a hand on his shoulder, her leg still spasming. "No, I'm all right."

The tears in her eyes wouldn't let Spider believe her.

"It's just a leg cramp," she gasped out the words.

"A leg cramp?" He didn't want to say it, but he thought it anyway—if she was that sensitive to a leg cramp, how in the heck was she going to handle labor? She needed him more than she realized.

"Is this the place? I need to get out." Becca climbed gingerly out of the cab before Spider could put it back in park and help her down. She limped up onto the porch.

Cold air wrapped around Spider as he followed her inside. The ice-cream parlor was small, with a couple of wood booths lining each wall and a round, plastic, kid-sized picnic table in the center of the place. Eighties rock music was piped in through little speakers in the ceiling. There was only one other couple inside—teenagers—huddled against each other as if they were freezing. More than likely, they were burning up, what with their hands all over each other.

The teenager behind the counter waited for them expectantly, his green apron embroidered with a smiling bear wearing lederhosen.

"Banana split. Banana smoothy. Banana milk shake," Becca mumbled under her breath, as she looked at the menu.

"Do you like bananas?" he asked.

"The potassium in bananas is supposed to prevent leg cramps."

Feeling his calves cramping up, Spider said, "I'll have a banana shake."

The teenager looked at Becca expectantly.

"Oh, we're not together," Becca said. "Go ahead and ring his up."

"My treat," Spider said through gritted teeth. She was the most difficult woman. "Give her a banana split with extra bananas. And we'll both need a water before our order."

When Becca opened her mouth to argue, Spider held up his hand. "This was my idea."

"But—"

"I have more to give than my *sperm*." He cut her off, irritated that she couldn't even accept an ice cream from him, irritated further when the teenage couple looked up from their public grope session at his comment.

"Really?" Becca crossed her arms over her chest, which

looked a bit awkward considering her arms rested on her belly. "Like what?"

He took the ice waters and led Becca to a booth near the front door. As they seated themselves, Spider chose his words carefully.

"A shoulder to lean on, an ear to vent to, plus I'm full of advice, that's what. Drink your water." Dehydration was a problem for everyone on a fire, not just firefighters. In this heat, a pregnant woman could lose a lot of fluids.

Scowling, Becca took the water and drank deeply. So did he. Half their glasses were gone before either spoke again.

Spider shook his drink, making his ice rattle. "I'm pretty good at teaching things, like how to swing a baseball bat."

"I'm having a girl."

Somehow, Spider had always visualized having a boy. He studied her face for a minute, before saying, "You're bluffing."

"I could be having a girl," she conceded with a sideways smile.

He held up the keys to her truck, dangling the key chain in front of his face—a blue baby rattle. "Either way, they'd need to learn how to swing a baseball bat."

"It was the only color they had." Becca smiled as she explained her key chain choice, then shook her head. "That's not the kind of advice I need."

"Okay, so maybe you know about baseball. What about my other talents? I make great tamales, I can change a tire pretty quick, and I can dig a mean hole in the ground when it's time to plant flowers in the yard. I could go on." He could offer her everything he had to give.

She laughed. "You sound like you're applying for a housekeeping job."

"Maybe a roommate." When she quit laughing, he held up a hand. "Just thinking of you and all those late-night feedings."

"I'm going to breast-feed," she deadpanned, but her blush indicated she wasn't as cool as she tried to appear.

Trying not to grind his teeth, Spider took another drink of water, watching Becca, judging what he should try next. She looked so tired and he really wanted to make things easier for her, although how he expected to give her advice on raising kids when he knew nothing was beyond him. He knew about fires and keeping a team together. Of course!

"How was IC today? Julia give you any trouble? I could pick a fight with her if she keeps giving you grief," Spider joked.

"She's fine. No need to bring in your muscle to keep her in line." Becca relaxed back into the booth and smoothed her T-shirt over her belly. "It's the strangest thing. I really lost my temper before, and she became this model employee."

"So you told her off, did you? I wish I would have seen that." He smiled at her, proud that she'd finally drawn the line with Julia.

She took another drink of water, looking at him over the rim of her glass. "I don't think it was the telling off that did it as much as my explaining that I didn't want to work with Sirus permanently. Apparently, she thought we were competing for the same job."

"When will you hear about this new job? I'm starting to want to spread my news. I'd like you to meet my friends, too."

"Why do you want me to meet your friends? Don't you think they'll look at me and accuse me of robbing the cradle?" Becca eyed him warily. "Don't you care what other people think?"

"Hell, no. You think my friends are going to say I knocked up some old lady?" Spider couldn't look at Becca, because essentially, his friends had noticed their age difference. "Give yourself and them some credit. You've still got all your teeth. And my friends would accept you as the warm, intelligent woman that you are." That, at least, he was sure of.

Her cheeks were bright pink and she wouldn't look anywhere but at her hands, which were busy winding a paper straw wrapper around her forefinger, the straw discarded on the table. "You're talking about us as if we're a couple."

Spider was wondering when she'd notice. "What if I am? No one cares that there's a difference in our ages but you. I'm old enough to be the father of that child and your partner in life. That's all that matters to me." His voice carried through the ice-cream parlor.

The make-out teenagers grinned and gave him two thumbs up.

"You should care." Becca tore the straw wrapper in bits and tossed the shreds on the table. "People talk and stare, and opportunities are lost if you don't conform."

"Conform?" He tossed his hands in exasperation. "I'm the man who ran down the hill in his boxers, remember? And if I didn't think you'd hold it against me, I have plenty of other things in my past that would prove explicitly that I don't give a damn what other people think. It hasn't held me back in the slightest."

Becca almost started to smile, then she shifted on the bench and looked away. "We're in different places," she began.

"If you try to tell me I don't understand, you're just going to tick me off." He was already getting really frustrated. Much more of this and his dial would click over to red-hot irritation. "It's all in the way you carry it off. I tend to shrug and pretend I don't give a shit."

Becca shook her head. "You like to be in someone's face. You like to take risks. It's easy for you."

"You don't think making the decision to have that baby was a risk?" Spider reached across the table and covered her hand with his when her eyes widened in apparent surprise. "Confronting the IC team, bringing Julia in line. Hell, even giving her a second chance when she doesn't deserve it. It all tells me that you're more courageous than you think."

She appraised him in silence, clearly considering his words, before sighing and changing the subject with a weak smile. "Is it a good thing to say I believe you've made a fool of yourself repeatedly?"

"As long as we leave it at that." Spider laughed at himself, then sobered. He had an objective here. "Have you ever thought people were talking and staring at you because of your beauty? You're a beautiful woman, pregnant or not. And you'll be a beauty twenty years from now."

She blushed, realized he still covered her hand with his, and pulled away. "There you go being nice again."

"I like talking to you. I like being able to tell you things. I've been able to tell you things from the moment we met that I've never told others. Why can't you give us a chance?"

She took a sip of her water, looking at him over the rim. "Since you mentioned chances and risks, why won't you give your dad one?"

Aiden lowered his voice. "Whoa, my dad is off-limits. You have no idea what he's done…or what he hasn't done in the past."

"Why don't you tell me?"

"Bananas up!" The teenager called.

Grateful for the distraction, Spider went to get their ice cream.

"I don't know what to say about my dad," Spider said when he sat down. "There are a lot of things that I won't say."

How he'd been jealous of the other boys in Little League whose dads helped out at practice and sat in the bleachers at games. How he'd floundered through dating without anyone to talk to about girls, expectations and sex.

Becca gathered a bit of banana in her spoon, dipped it into whipped cream and fudge sauce, then slid it in her mouth, leaving a trail of chocolate on her lips. "Why don't you tell me what you're comfortable saying?"

Aiden was only barely able to keep from running his finger over her chocolate-coated lips. "So you can use it against me at a later date?" He stirred his shake with his straw, avoiding her probing gaze, refusing to take the bait.

"Forget I asked. You're right. It's none of my business." She concentrated on her treat.

She was ignoring him, leaving Spider strangely bereft. Maybe he could tell her some small bit of the truth about his father that wouldn't make him look too pathetic. Spider sucked on his milk shake and watched her eat her banana split, wondering what he was willing to tell her.

"My dad was pretty much a no show by the time I was five. He sent money every once in awhile, but my grandmother and I were on our own. And I knew it." Spider drew a deep breath. "He didn't care then. He doesn't care now."

"But he's come back into your life." Becca's blue eyes were searching for truths Spider had no intention of revealing.

"Hell, no. Our paths have crossed, that's all." Spider shifted, uncomfortable on the wooden seat. "I'll admit, sometimes I think my dad has changed, but Roadhouse has always been a slick talker. And really, why would my old man start to care now?"

Becca continued to inspect him as she took a bit of vanilla ice cream. "I don't think he ever stopped loving you."

"You met him once." Spider barely resisted laughing outright. "Don't be fooled. He wants money. It's not unusual for him to appear on my doorstep and want cash."

"Maybe it's different this time. You didn't hear him talk about you. Maybe —"

"You can't change my mind about him, Becca. I know he's good with the ladies. He just admitted this past year that I have a half sister and a half brother conceived while he was married to my mother."

Her eyes had widened at his tirade, but she seemed about to defend Roadhouse again, so he cut her off.

"He's got three kids by three different women—one he married, one was married to someone else at the time he got her pregnant, and one dumped him. I saw him maybe two, maybe three days a year. He could have come home during the off-season, but he didn't. He doesn't care about anyone but himself. Don't believe a word he says," Spider said.

"Are you always so harsh with people? Don't you believe in second chances?" She fell silent.

Spider scowled and managed to say, "I'm not harsh with you."

"You treat Victoria like crap." The way Becca said it, Spider could feel her disappointment as clearly as if she'd kicked him in the shins.

All this talk about his people skills was starting to get on his nerves. Was there a point to this discussion? There couldn't be. And...yet... "You think I'd treat our kid the same way I treat my dad or Victoria?"

She arched a brow—a subtle attack. His hopes sank. How could he believe in his parenting potential if Becca didn't?

"Victoria needs to be pushed," he reiterated, firmly hanging onto his temper. "And I have history with my dad that you obviously can't begin to understand. Why can't you put a little faith in me?"

She didn't answer him. Despite the frigid air-conditioning, her ice cream was melting. Becca put a drippy scoop in her mouth, some of which got caught on the corner of her lips. Unable to resist this time, Spider swiped at the chocolate with his finger and then sucked his finger clean.

In Becca's haste to put space between them, she bumped back against the wooden bench. Her reaction eased his anger, replacing it with a pleasant sensual awareness. He couldn't resist giving her a slow smile.

"Stop that," she warned him, keeping her back against the wall, but her eyes were locked with his.

"You can't pretend there's nothing between us, Bec."

"Hypothetical question. Your sixteen-year-old son starts rebelling. He stays out late at night. You don't like the friends he's hanging out with. And his girlfriend turns up pregnant. What are you going to do?" she asked.

"Besides blame you for raising him without me?" He tried to make a joke of it.

She frowned, clearly not amused.

Spider set his milk shake down. He wanted to be a part of his child's life, damn it, and a part of hers. "You think I'm going to treat my kid like dirt after the way my father was?"

"Maybe because I don't know you," she said slowly. "Do you really know what it is you want? It's not as if you have a job that will make it easy for you to be involved…once you have a child. Your whole life will change."

Her words cut deeper than he wanted them to.

They'd shared something real, created what he was coming to consider a life-changing miracle, and Becca was now pretending none of it involved him.

"And you? Why is it so important that you raise this baby on your own?"

"None of your —"

"I answered your questions." He cut her off. "Even the personal ones."

She closed her mouth on any arguments she might have voiced, so he answered for her. "You spend so much time watching out for others that life has passed you by, didn't it? And now you're going to do things your way, no compromises."

At her shocked expression, Spider couldn't keep from cursing. "Why is it that you don't think I pay attention when you speak? I absorb everything about you like a sponge— your sweet smell, the careful way you carry that baby, the way you try and make everyone come together through peaceful negotiation, and the way you keep everyone at arm's length." He blew out a breath. "You know, back in Vegas, you let me into more than just your body. You let me see a side of the real you, the one you keep trying to hide."

He locked his gaze with hers. "I know all the arguments you're going to make about our difference in age and that it's too soon, but I love you, and I want a whole lot more than court-sanctioned visitation. I want a church-sanctioned marriage."

He hadn't meant to say that. He couldn't believe he'd said that.

"It's pretty hard to argue when you've already laid out my objections," Becca said in a weak voice. Her gaze kept darting between him and her ice cream.

"Can I take your silence to mean you'll think about it?" Spider willed her to say yes.

Becca leaned back in the booth, pushing her arms behind the small of her back. "We'd just be complicating everything—our lives, our careers, the baby's life. I went into this thinking it would just be me and the baby."

"So now that you've been blessed with this kid, you figure why bother with a man? Even if it means you're missing out on loving somebody?"

Becca wouldn't look at him, but her gaze bounced around the room. He'd shaken her up. He just couldn't tell if it was in a good or a bad way.

She pushed her banana split into the middle of the table as if melted ice cream and a pool of whipped cream and fudge would stop him from coming near her or their baby. "I need to get back."

Becca wanted him, yet she couldn't put herself in what she perceived to be a vulnerable position. Spider wanted to punch something. "Fine. It's too cold in here anyway."

"YOU CAN SLEEP IF YOU WANT TO," Aiden offered as they started the drive back from the ice-cream parlor.

Becca stared out the window, wondering how she'd ever sleep again. Aiden wanted more than a role in her baby's life. He wanted to marry her! That was just too crazy. Forget that he made her feel sexier than a pregnant woman had a right to feel, or that she loved him. They were so wrong for each other. He was young and impetuous. She was seasoned—okay, older—and cautious. He was a playboy, full of energy, barely able to sit still. She was a homebody, content to relax in front of the TV after a long day at work. Together, they made no sense.

But he wanted to marry her…

An amazing calm threatened to settle over her, as if marriage were the answer to all her problems.

She had to snap out of it. When reality sank in after the baby was born, Aiden would quickly become bored with her, while she'd go through the agony of watching him pull away. She'd be left to pick up the pieces that he'd made of her life, plus have to deal with the legalities of divorce and custody agreements. He'd have a permanent say in her life and she'd be left with a broken heart, no credibility with NIFC and no job in Boise.

They passed pine trees with mesmerizing speed. The baby wiggled around in her belly, combining with the kaleidoscope of trees to make her feel dizzy. The air conditioner caressed her skin, sticky from a day of sitting in the stifling tent. Becca closed her eyes against it all—the baby, the exhaustion and Aiden. As she drifted off, she wished she could just follow her heart and let Aiden into her life.

In her dream, Aiden was supportive, he held her hand gently in his own and feathered kisses down the side of her face. He promised to be there forever and support her despite…

"…so scared and stubborn. It doesn't have to be this hard, Becca." Aiden's warm breath tickled down her cheek. Something firm yet comfortable pressed around her hand.

Becca's eyes flew open and met Aiden's.

"Oh." The word came out on a breathy sigh as Becca realized that Aiden held her hand, that Aiden had kissed her cheek, that she was too tired to fight him.

That she didn't want to fight him.

"I'm going to kiss you, Bec."

She stared at him, unable to move, unable to stop him because she wanted his touch. She wanted the feel of his body pressed against hers. She wanted what she shouldn't want— Aiden in her life.

His lips descended to hers with a soft touch. For a few moments she lost herself in this physical reunion. Reaching up, she pulled him closer, enjoying the feel of his solid chest against her own.

"Oh, Bec, I know we can work this out," Aiden whispered against the side of her mouth. Then he was kissing her again and Becca sank into a warm cocoon of desire: everything seemed destined for a happy ending.

"Woo-hoo! Take a look at this, Darrell. Somebody's going at it in that SUV." The crude male voice just outside her window sent Becca into rigid horror.

Hands that had been pulling Aiden closer now shoved him away.

Only he wouldn't move.

"Get back on your side," she whispered fiercely.

"Not until they're gone. If I move now, they'll see your face."

Becca ceased all efforts to push him away from her. He was still too close. She looked up into his eyes, mere inches from hers, demanding things she couldn't give. Then the reality of the situation hit and she shut her eyes, grateful the darkness would hide the blush that was heating her cheeks. How could she have kissed him? How could she want to kiss him again?

He chuckled, the low sound racing through her blood, fueling the almost unstoppable desire being near him sparked.

"Don't touch me," she warned, keeping her eyes shut tight and balling her fists to keep from touching him.

"I think we can safely say we like touching each other." His voice was soft and strained. "In fact, I'd like to talk about this baby while I'm laying…in bed with you."

She sensed he held back from saying something even more exciting, more intimate. Part of her longed to agree. And that's what scared her into launching herself from her seat and clumsily out of the SUV.

If she wasn't careful, she was going to let Aiden make a shambles of both their lives.

"YOU'RE GOING TO RUIN everything," Becca accused as she slammed the door of the Forerunner. She pointed her feet in the direction of her tent, praying that the people who'd seen them necking were gone and that no one else would spot them out here.

But Aiden wasn't far behind her. "What in the hell is that supposed to mean?"

"You think getting married will solve everything, when in fact, it just makes everything worse," she said over her shoulder, trembling, unable to stop. "I'm nothing like your father. If you say jump, I won't say how high."

"This isn't about my father, damn it. I don't want you to have anything more to do with him."

Becca could tell by his heavy footfalls that Aiden was almost upon her. She turned to face him. "See? You're trying to control me already."

"As if you don't try to control me?" He raised his voice. They were still in the parking lot, but Becca shushed him anyway. He ignored her. "You don't want anyone to see us together. You don't want anyone to know about Vegas. So now I'm the one not allowed to set any ground rules?"

"You only need ground rules in a relationship and we're not in one of those." She twisted the loose ends of her hair behind her ears with unsteady fingers.

"No, I'm just a good lay, is that it?"

That hurt. Becca couldn't blink back the tears fast enough. She brushed one away. It didn't matter that she wanted everything he had to offer. She doubted he realized what he was doing or what he wanted. He kept on attributing to her these golden qualities when she was incredibly flawed. She had to try and knock some sense into him by being heartless. Once he knew the truth, he'd never forgive her. It wasn't in his nature.

Struggling to keep her tears at bay, Becca pointed to her belly. "You don't want this. Not any of it. Not really. And I'm not asking anything of you." Her breath came in shallow gasps. There was only one way to get through to him. The truth.

"Do you want to know why I went to Vegas?" Becca forced herself to look at him. "I went to Vegas to get pregnant. You don't know how many guys I slept with to get this way. It could be your baby or a dozen other guys."

He was momentarily speechless.

"That's right. I went to Sin City and got laid. Again and again." She crossed her arms over her belly and dared him to contradict her lie.

It took him a moment, but he did. "You are so full of it. That would have worked on me a week ago, Becca, but I know you better now."

And she knew him better, too. Even in the dim light, she could see the hurt in his eyes, so she pressed on. "You're right. I woke up one morning and realized that life had passed me by. My work had become my life, but it was no longer enough."

With a shake of his head, Aiden reached for her. "Why can't you take a chance and let me in? I was serious about getting married. I lo—"

"Don't." Becca cut her hand between them. "There's more. I cruised the casinos and scoped out bars looking for someone to give me a baby. Someone alone. Someone a bit drunk." She swallowed back her tears.

"You're serious." He stepped back, clenching his fists. "No, I can't believe it. Not of you." He'd closed his eyes, but now they were open, and full of resolve. "You found me and we created something wonderful."

"Don't romanticize it. Can't you see? You live a nomadic life as a Hot Shot. We're a novelty now, but come spring, you'll be tired of diapers. You'll go off to a fire and wonder what you ever saw in me. Then on some hot summer day, a pretty girl will smile at you, and you'll do something you'll regret."

"You're rejecting me for my own good? I won't accept that." He looked away.

Becca crossed her arms over her belly. It wasn't just for his good, it was for her protection, too. "Think about it."

"I have thought about it. I want what's best for this little guy. I won't screw up his life like my dad did to me. I want him—or her—to know I love them, not guess or dream." He stepped toward her. "I'd want what's best for the mother of my kid, too. Besides, you're the last person on earth that would bore me. I won't repeat my father's mistakes." His expression hardened. "I won't cheat."

She backed up a step. "I'm not the woman you met in Las Vegas. I'm not sexy. I'm not brave, like you."

"I want the woman standing in front of me. I find you incredibly sexy, brave and intelligent. I want you to marry me."

"Aiden, this won't do our careers any good." It was hard to be strong. His words were wonderful to hear, yet she wished he'd kept silent. Marriage wasn't the answer.

"Who cares as long as we're together?"

"If people knew I'd slept with you…they'd talk. Opportunities would be lost."

"Like your job in Boise?" His expression turned cold.

"Yes." She was relieved he was finally understanding.

"Sometimes you have to think beyond the implications something has on your career, Bec." The shadows in the parking lot emphasized the disappointment in Aiden's eyes.

Becca hardened her resolve. "I'd expect you to say something irresponsible like that."

"And I'd hope that you'd be able to set aside work if that baby or someone you love needed you. People are important, not careers."

He made so much sense that Becca wanted to cry. She wanted a happily-ever-after with Aiden, but she couldn't believe what he felt for her was a real, lasting thing.

"Ow." The baby kicked her. Becca's hand went to her belly. As if knowing his baby was alert, Aiden moved closer.

"You've never let me touch the baby."

No. By touching the baby, he'd be touching her, starting fires she doubted she could control when she was so emotionally distraught.

"There's so much you've kept from me, Becca. Please, give me this one gift." He wanted to be a good dad, yet the only contact he could have with the baby right now was through her.

"May I?" he asked gesturing to her stomach with longing in his eyes that Becca could no longer resist.

She nodded mutely, realizing that she'd never shared her pride and joy with anyone else, not like this.

He placed his hand carefully on her tummy, so gently that he could barely feel a thing unless the baby hammered her. Becca put her hand on top of Aiden's, splaying his fingers so that he'd have a better chance of feeling something when the baby moved again.

His dark gaze locked onto hers and Becca couldn't help

but think that if he moved his thumb just a millimeter, it would brush against her breast.

Her breasts seemed to swell toward his hand, as if longing for his caress. One deep breath and there was no way he wouldn't be touching her.

The baby, of course, chose that moment to kick lower than the first time.

"Wow, was that him?" Aiden moved his hand lower. "That's one powerful kid."

Becca couldn't help but grin with pride. "This baby has spunk."

"Do it again." Aiden moved so that he was nearly straddling her belly.

Becca laughed, the baby kicked, and then she laughed some more at Aiden's wondrous expression. "I was going to say that this baby isn't a trained seal and doesn't perform on demand, but somebody was obviously listening to you."

"That's because I'm the boss. What I say goes. Do it again," he commanded.

Becca couldn't help laughing once more when the baby kicked and then kicked again, although the laughter died immediately when she realized her little one had gone back to kicking high and Aiden's hand was following the movement, heedless of the way the back of his hand was now against the lower side of her breast.

Her eyes were caught in his dark gaze and the memory of their time together flooded her senses. They'd made love three times in his hotel room overlooking the strip. Once he'd even moved her to tears because she'd felt closer to him than she had to anyone in years. And he'd been a fun-loving, sexy stranger then. A man she knew little about. A man whom she'd never expected to see again. A man with deep facets to his character that she was just beginning to discover, with painful emotional scars that she couldn't begin to heal, even though she longed to.

"What's going on here?" Aiden asked in a low gravelly voice that sent tingles over her skin.

"You're about to break the tension and say something mean." She'd had the excuse of wanting to get pregnant the last time she'd slept with him. She had no excuse now other than rampant hormones. She needed him to be the sane one. "Please."

Lucky her, there was no place in base camp where they could be alone. She'd move in a minute.

Thirty seconds… Ten…

"I find older, taller women a turn-on," he said.

Becca exhaled. "That wasn't mean." While they were standing there in the middle of the parking area with his right hand on her belly, she'd somehow managed to cling to his other hand. She wasn't sure anymore if she was just having a low-blood-sugar moment or if Aiden being so near was making her weak, but she needed his support.

He grinned at her, dangerously sexy. "It's mean when you realize I'm not going to do anything about it."

"Oh." A stab of disappointment.

He leaned closer, until his lips almost brushed her ear. "It's even meaner when I remind you how good I could make you feel with just a touch."

It wasn't a stab of disappointment, it was a sharp arc of desire. Becca was breathing deeply now. She remembered how his clever fingers had taken her into a combustible state.

"Someone might see us." Who was she kidding? People were still everywhere. Base camps never slept. People were probably watching the old, pregnant Fire Behavior Analyst holding hands with one of the young Silver Bend studs right now.

What would Julia say?

That she was robbing the cradle.

Right now, Becca didn't care. She was tired of being strong and pushing herself beyond her limits. If she was a quitter, she'd just curl into a ball in bed and give up.

Becca sighed. It was only worth quitting if she could give up in Aiden's arms. What he'd said about doing the right thing, about caring for his child, about placing more emphasis on those you love than your career, had melted Becca's defenses. His touch had brought them crumbling down.

Aiden led her away from the parking lot and the lights. And she let him. They walked through the rows of sleeping tents where the light was softer and there were more shadows. Becca was content not to talk, content just to enjoy the warmth of his hand encompassing hers. Tomorrow. She'd worry about the consequences tomorrow.

Aiden stopped in the shadow of one tent. He leaned forward and pressed his lips lightly to hers, eliciting a small whimper from her as he pulled back. She wanted more.

"If appearances are more important than what I can give you, I'll have to say good-night."

No! Aiden couldn't leave her like this. Becca was burning for him and he knew it.

CHAPTER FOURTEEN

MAYBE SPIDER'S OLD MAN was right. He'd certainly captured Becca's attention. She wasn't arguing with him, and she wasn't walking away. She was standing there looking at him with her lower lip in a slight pout.

"You get some rest. We'll talk more tomorrow when I get back from the field." Gently, he brushed her bangs off her forehead, careful of her stitches.

Still she didn't move.

Just to make Becca sweat a little more, and because he couldn't resist, Spider reached out and stroked his hand down her belly, back up and then alongside her plump breast.

Her breath seemed to catch in her throat, and then her arms wrapped around him, pulling him against her full stomach, pulling him farther until his chest was pillowed on her breasts, her mouth hot against his own.

Damn, the woman was sizzling.

All Spider could think of was what fun it would be to make love with Becca in her condition. He'd never done it with a pregnant woman before. It would almost be like doing it with props.

They were in the shadows, but anyone who walked close by could see them. Spider slipped his hand beneath her belly and touched her through her thin, stretchy shorts. It didn't take much.

Becca trembled, moaning into his mouth, sending his mind on a quick mental search of the camp for a place to drive her wild, a place where she could reciprocate.

"Who's out there?" A woman's voice, not Becca's.

From inside the tent.

Becca's tent.

The rasp of a zipper—not his—sent Becca stumbling to the ground with a dazed look.

Julia poked her head out of the tent flap. Her eyes landed on Spider first. "Oh, it's you," she purred, blinking puffy eyes.

Spider stepped forward to help Becca up off the ground.

"Becca?" She sounded incredulous. "And…and Spider?"

"Shh," Becca said, not looking at Spider at all. "Aiden was just helping me back through the dark and I fell. That's why I needed his help."

The assistant didn't look convinced, but Becca didn't seem to care. She moved over to the tent flap and zipped it all the way open.

"Aren't you going to thank me?" The question didn't come out as confidently as Spider would have liked. A minute ago they'd moved beyond Becca's hangups about their relationship and created something wild. She could just walk away from that as if he hadn't just rocked her world? No "we'll talk later?" No "see you soon?"

With obvious reluctance, Becca turned back to Spider, thrusting her hand in his direction. "Thank you."

He almost reacted too slowly. She almost pulled her hand back. But Spider gripped it before she got away and thrummed his fingers on her wrist.

"Anytime," he said, and for the first time in his life, he meant it.

"WHAT WERE YOU TWO DOING out there?" Julia demanded. "Was he making a move on you? I've heard he's a real player."

Oh, he was a player all right, only Becca had been the one about to play him. She'd been out of control. "He just walked me to the tent."

"What a pervert, making the moves on a pregnant woman." Julia sounded thoroughly disgusted.

"Julia!"

"I've heard some guys are turned on by that."

"Somehow I don't think Aiden is one of them." That was a lie. She'd felt his need for her when she'd pressed herself against him. She got warm just remembering how hard he'd been.

"You're probably right. He was probably just being a gentleman." She rolled over in her sleeping bag. "Someone with the laundry crew made it with him last summer. She said he barely gave her the time of day after they did the deed." Julia sighed. "She said he was most creative in bed though."

That was more information than Becca wanted. Despite herself, she was jealous of the woman on the laundry crew.

"He is a hottie," Julia said, yawning.

Hottie. That's the last word Becca needed to hear. She was already overheated just from pressing herself against him. And then he'd performed some yoga moves, somehow managing to reach around her tremendous belly and touch her there—in the middle of base camp.

She didn't just burn for him, she burned with embarrassment. And if Julia's reaction was any indication, Becca wouldn't do her career any good by allowing him to get that close again, much less accepting his marriage proposal. Tomorrow she'd put distance between them again.

But her body hummed in places it hadn't since Las Vegas, her heart ached with longing, and Becca had a hard time falling asleep.

"LET'S ASSEMBLE OVER HERE," Spider led his team to a spot in an area directly in Becca's path after her morning briefing. He wasn't going to step out of her life as easily as she'd like.

Of all Becca's protests and arguments last night, the one that Spider struggled with was her claim that she'd gone to Vegas to get pregnant. Becca wasn't the kind of woman to trap a man with a child. Besides, she could have met anyone in Vegas. Fate had directed her to him.

Becca had managed to avoid him at breakfast, and her gaze hadn't even skimmed over him during the morning briefing. But she'd have to walk right by him to get to the Fire Behavior tent now.

"Good morning," Spider called when he saw her a mere twenty feet away, his voice nearly cracking under the strain of wondering what this meeting would be like.

He loved a challenge, and the stakes between them were high and worth fighting for.

Becca hesitated, her smile fading when she realized he was talking to her. Not the best of signs. But she didn't turn around or veer off to the latrines.

Something spilled behind him with a jarring crash. The contents of Victoria's backpack scattered across the dirt. His already taut nerves tumbled over the edge of his control.

"What's the deal, Queenie? In need of some caffeine to wake up that brain of yours? It's a zipper, the same as on your pants."

The Queen's face was bright red. Then, to Spider's horror, she looked as if she might cry. He swore under his breath.

"You are such a butt-head." Becca thrust her belly into his

business. He'd wanted her attention, but not when he'd just acted exactly as she'd accused him last night. "It's an honest mistake. Why do you have to bully her all the time?"

He might have tried to react to Becca differently if the team hadn't all been staring at them, or if Becca hadn't just berated him as if she were his second-grade teacher, appalled that he'd eaten paste.

"Maybe I order her around because she needs it. She hasn't been able to think straight lately." Spider cast a dark glance at Victoria.

"Butt-head, butt-head, butt-head," Becca spouted. With her hands on her hips and her green T-shirt so tight across her abdomen he could see the outline of her belly button, he didn't want to take her seriously.

People around them slowed, turned to look, stopped talking. Spider didn't care.

Damn if Becca wasn't taunting him, just daring him to cross her. He bet she expected men to fall into a neat line with that glare of hers. Did she think he was a rookie? Gullible and wet behind the ears? Willing to defer to her just because she was a woman? Or worse, defer to her because she was *older* than him? He had ten years of experience under his belt. He sure wasn't the kind of man to be led around as if he were a schoolboy by a woman, especially this one. Anger raged in Spider's veins, barely contained by his need to play nice in Becca's sandbox.

The kid. Think of the kid. Or her kisses. Think of her kisses.

Spider tried, he really did, but she had pissed him off to the point where he found himself leaning into her until his nose was mere inches from hers. "The least you can do is think of something else to call me."

Several of the Silver Bend Hot Shots offered suggestions.

"Oh, please." Becca didn't break eye contact or back away. "Don't encourage him."

"Like you never do," Spider said, then dropped his voice suggestively lower. "You encouraged me last night."

Becca's eyes widened, then narrowed. "Don't you dare say more in front of them," she whispered.

"Dare what? Dare tell them about—"

Her clipboard and pen clattered to the ground as her palm clamped over his mouth and her other hand swatted away the hand he'd started to raise to point at her belly.

Someone in the crowd hooted.

Spider ignored them. He looked at Becca with what he hoped was a challenging expression—brows up—because she sure as hell challenged his patience, his sex drive and his sanity, not to mention the limits of his heart. Just to test her reaction, he let his tongue slip out to taste the salt on her palm.

What in the world are you going to do now, honey?

Her breath hitched. He had to give Becca credit. She was as unpredictable as a summer twister. He would have bet money that she'd slug him.

Her eyes darted to the right and she slowly lowered her hand from his mouth, wiping it on the side of her hip. Spider glanced over his shoulder and found Socrates watching them, along with most of the Incident Command team. Becca would accuse him of sabotaging her career, while Socrates would probably think he was harassing Becca.

Well, hell.

"You set me up," she accused in a deadly voice, bringing fully his attention back to her. "You waited for me here because you wanted to ruin my chances for that job. You think if you do, I'll have no excuse to turn you down. You set me up," she repeated.

He shrugged, although it was far from the truth. "What if I did?"

She bent down to pick up her clipboard and he knelt with her, retrieving her pen.

"You have the moral fiber of a snake, which is probably why I chose you in that bar in Las Vegas. I knew you wouldn't resist a freebie." She might have been whispering, but her words echoed in Spider's brain on full volume.

The world pitched off kilter as everything Spider believed to be true shattered. Becca hadn't been lying. The baby hadn't been an accident. Becca wasn't a saint who'd decided to raise his baby alone.

Spider blew out a frustrated breath, forcing himself to speak just as softly, with as much venom as she attributed to him. "So, it's true. You did go on a sperm-collecting expedition in Las Vegas. You really didn't care about me at all. I was just some lucky sap on a barstool."

"Yes." She lifted her chin. Becca stood on wobbly legs, brushing away his hands as he followed her up and tried to steady her when he should have been turning around and walking away. Hurt sparkled in her blue eyes. He ignored it and waited to hear what she'd say, hoping she'd take it all back so that his world would right itself.

It seemed the entire camp was silent, straining to hear what Becca said, although they'd been speaking so quietly their voices didn't carry more than a few feet.

"Never mind," he said. Becca was right. He was reading things where there was nothing. She didn't love him. Becca had taken what she'd wanted from him, only somewhere along the way, she'd snagged something she hadn't planned on taking.

His heart.

BECCA STORMED into the Fire Behavior tent, retrieved the printout with the latest weather updates and waddled at high speed right back outta there, fighting tears all the way to her SUV.

Aiden was right. Becca could think of better, more cutting names to call him. She even found herself mumbling a few as she stomped across the field that had become their parking lot to her dinged up SUV. The door opened with a creak and Becca somehow managed to climb up into the high cab to the seat Aiden had occupied last night, slamming the door behind her.

Why couldn't he have been patient? She'd seen the questions in Sirus's expression when they'd argued. The entire camp was probably talking about them now. At the end of the fire, Becca would be out of a job, her dream house unattainable, and Aiden would hate her forever.

Be careful what you wish for. For several seconds, Becca sat rigidly gripping the steering wheel in one hand and her reports in the other. Then, she let go of everything, crumpling across the bench seat and relinquishing the most pitiful wail.

Aiden would hate her forever.

Wasn't visitation going to be pleasant? Becca cried a little louder.

There was a knock on her driver's side window.

Becca's hands flew to her face. "Go away." Couldn't a hormonal pregnant woman get any privacy in this camp?

"Are you okay?"

Julia's voice. More than anything, Becca wanted to crawl back into bed, preferably her own bed in California several hundred miles away.

"Becca?" Julia didn't seem to take the hint that her boss was having a *private* breakdown. She obviously wanted to rub Becca's nose in her rather public fight with Aiden.

With a resigned sigh, Becca sat up. "I'm fine." *Hit me with your best shot.*

Julia opened the driver's side door. "I thought you might like some water." She handed Becca a bottle of water and then a tissue.

After a moment's hesitation, Becca took both. She blew her nose with the most unladylike sound, making her fight the tears all over again. Why couldn't she be more graceful? Then she tipped the water bottle back too far when she tried to take a drink and it spilled down the front of her T-shirt.

Becca closed her eyes. "I am such a klutz."

Julia shifted beside the old Forerunner, her boots scraping the ground. "I think you're tired and stressed out."

"And what would you know about it?" Becca demanded, suddenly angry that Julia had witnessed her breakdown, regretting the words as soon as they left her mouth, but unable to stop, or apologize, for them.

"Nothing," Julia admitted, taking a step back, then another. She shook her head and then she retreated, leaving Becca feeling even more of a failure.

NIFC was right.

Becca was a horrible manager.

"I apologize," Becca said to Julia when she returned to the Fire Behavior tent. "I shouldn't have snapped at you in the parking lot."

Julia sat hunched over a table covered with fire maps. She shrugged, wiped at one of her eyes but didn't say a word. Becca couldn't help but notice that her eyes were red again. Had Becca made her cry? She was a louse.

Sinking into her chair, Becca admitted, "You're right. I am tired and stressed out."

Julia nodded curtly, pursing her lips as if afraid of what she might say if she spoke.

"And I'm afraid I cried all over the daily weather report." Becca had crinkled it up pretty badly as well.

"Why don't you go lay down?" Julia said, sneaking a glance her way. "No one will mind if you get some extra rest."

Becca's back stiffened. "*Extra* rest?" That implied she needed more rest than anyone else. What would Sirus say if she went back to bed? He'd probably realize that she was trying not to burn herself out. He'd probably understand that she'd operate more efficiently with a little more sleep. He might even admire her for giving Julia some more responsibility.

Becca hung her head, actually contemplating it for several seconds. Becca's eyelids drifted down at the mere thought of more sleep. She was very tired. The baby elbowed her rib cage, jarring Becca awake.

The sound of trucks leaving and carrying crew up to the fire struck a chord. Aiden was probably on one of those trucks. So much for trying to insulate her heart from breaking. Becca wanted to curl up into a ball and cry.

If she did that, she'd be giving up. She may as well forget the job in Boise and hand over the baby to Aiden. There was no way she was doing that.

This baby is mine.

That management job hadn't been assigned yet.

Becca had plenty to do before getting some rest.

"THANKS FOR THE SHOW back at base camp," Logan said as they climbed a steep grade from the DP. It was barely eight o'clock, but the sun and the fire had already begun to warm the air around them. "For awhile there, I didn't know who was gonna come out on top—you or the Fire Behavior Analyst."

"It was the analyst," Doc said, his New Jersey accent grating on Spider's nerves.

"You're so clueless when it comes to women, Spider. That's what I like about you," Chainsaw observed, packing his namesake on his shoulder.

For once, Spider had nothing to say. The only other person who'd used him and disregarded his emotions to this extent was his father. Spider glanced up at the gray-brown, smoke-filled sky, wishing for a wiser head. Maybe then he'd insulate himself from the pain caused by people he loved.

"Yeah, why all the drama?" Doc asked from behind them. "I mean someone's already staked a claim on her."

Spider opened his mouth to tell Doc where he could stick his opinions, but before Spider could get out a word, he was ducking to avoid his buddy's chain-saw blade. "Watch it," Spider snarled as he stepped to the side of the trail.

"Sorry, dude. Need to readjust my load." Chainsaw swung his tool down on the other side of the track about two steps up from Spider.

Doc climbed past Spider with a grin Spider would have given anything to wipe off his face. Spider clenched his teeth. What did Doc know about problems? He was in med school, looking at a prosperous future that was far removed from the dirt and grime of the Hot Shot life. If Doc had a kid, it'd be born in a church-sanctioned marriage with a silver spoon in its mouth. Spider would never be enough man for Becca and her kid.

As Doc came even with Chainsaw, Spider's broad-shouldered friend shifted his foot into Doc's path. Doc stumbled and nearly fell on his face, protesting all the way.

"You can disrespect him." Chainsaw pointed at Spider. He was so much bulkier than Doc that Spider wasn't worried about the two fighting. "But you can't disrespect a woman like Becca, Doc."

"Yeah, where's your bedside manner, Doctor?" Spider snapped, glad the team's attention was focused on someone else.

Victoria sauntered past them all. "Children, behave."

Her label struck a raw nerve. Becca had implied more than once that Spider wasn't mature enough for their baby…or her. He'd been good enough for her that night in Vegas, hadn't he?

"I guess the pace is too slow if you all have time to chat like church ladies. Come on, hump it up the hill," Spider called out, pleased that Victoria had picked up her pace.

Spider and Chainsaw let the others hike on ahead of them.

"Thanks," Spider mumbled. Somehow, the big guy always knew when to step in.

Chainsaw rummaged in his pack until he found a slim beef stick wrapped in plastic. "So, what's the deal with the FBAN?" he asked with a much-too-casual look on his face.

"Becca? Nothing." Spider fiddled with a water bottle. "I just knocked her on her ass that one day and I…I feel sorry for her, that's all."

"Uh-huh." Chainsaw didn't look convinced. He chewed on his beef stick for a bit. "Can't say that I've ever seen you spend time with a woman you weren't sleeping with or trying to sleep with."

Spider didn't like the direction the conversation was taking. He forced himself to grin. "There's a first time for everything. I've matured."

"Apparently." With his beef stick hanging out of his mouth like a cigar, Chainsaw hefted the long saw onto his shoulders.

Then he gave Spider a sharp look. "Have you matured enough to be a daddy, 'cause I hear that kid doesn't have one."

"I…" *Lie. Grin. Put on a show like always.*

Only Spider didn't feel like playing the role of clown. Soon someone would be running around the world with Spider's blood flowing in his veins. He couldn't make a joke out of that.

"I got her pregnant," Spider admitted, amazed that the statement created such relief.

The beef stick dropped out of Chainsaw's mouth to the dirt.

"Yeah," Spider agreed. It was a solemn moment. He stared up at the sky, but could only see smoke.

"So she wants to get married?"

"No. She wants nothing to do with me."

Chainsaw kicked the beef stick beneath a bush. "That's…unexpected."

So much about Becca was. A sexy female on the prowl with the intent of getting pregnant? Sounded like a couple of the B movies in his DVD collection at home. Sounded like a femme fatale who'd snare him in her web. The question was, did it matter?

Chainsaw shifted around. "Look, maybe it's for the best."

But Spider was already shaking his head. "Unfortunately, I love her." Wasn't that a bitch? All the time he'd been hiking, he'd been wondering what to do, rather than hating her for using him. He was haunted by the way she always seemed to be alone. A few times he'd caught her looking off into the distance when she was walking about base camp. Could she have wanted a child to ease the loneliness in her life? Could he help fill that void?

Not that he was over the fact that she'd used him. Far from it. Next time he saw her, he was going to give her hell.

"Dude!" Comprehension dawned and Chainsaw slapped Spider on the back. "She's the shower girl." The big man sobered. "You're going to be a father."

"Yeah, I was thinking that I didn't want to be a Christmas card dad."

Chainsaw took off his helmet and rubbed his blond crew cut. "You know, your dad—"

"Won the World's Worst Dad Award annually. Yeah, I know." Spider took a swig from his water bottle. It was always painful to admit his past was less than rosy. "I'm the last guy anyone would expect to make a good father. But after the shock wore off, I couldn't imagine not being the kid's dad." The notion of fatherhood had been inexplicably growing on him. He'd have a chance to teach the little guy to shoot hoops and steal home, to drive in the snow and to shave. But the problem of Becca remained.

Chainsaw nodded slowly, then put his helmet back on. "Not that I speak from experience, but it seems like you need to be around more than a few months a year to be a good parent."

"That's bullshit. Look at Golden. He's got two kids. Two *great* kids," Spider amended, continuing doggedly. "And Logan. He's got four. I can do this." Better than his dad…he'd like to think.

"Both those guys have *wives,* Spider. They've got women who love them and are willing to make it work. Based on that display of yours this morning, it doesn't look like Becca's going to cooperate."

"She will if I marry her." It shouldn't matter how she'd found him. Heaven help him, he still wanted to marry her after all this. He loved her.

The look of disbelief on Chainsaw's face indicated that

was the farthest thing from his mind in terms of a solution. "You just said she wouldn't marry you."

"She's stubborn, but she'll come around." It took a brave woman to do what she'd done.

"Spider." The radio clipped to Spider's chest strap crackled to life.

"Spider, here."

Logan's voice came right back at him, irritation riddling the static. "Close ranks. The rest of the team is at the top of the ridge." Teams weren't supposed to get separated and here Spider had purposefully lagged behind with Chainsaw. A foolish mistake. If they'd been closer to the fire, anything could have happened while they'd stood there discussing Spider's private life like the church ladies he'd accused the rest of the team of being earlier.

"Maybe you should just try to get along with her," Chainsaw suggested. "You must have got along well enough…whenever…you know…" Chainsaw's cheeks reddened.

"I've told her how I feel. I've taken more abuse from her than I've taken from any woman, because once she realizes I'm for real, it'll all be worth it." Spider sighed. "You tell me what to try next."

"Flowers, candlelight and you…down on one knee."

CHAPTER FIFTEEN

AFTER LUNCH, SPIDER HACKED at a tree root as if it were the devil himself, because only the devil seemed to have the answers he needed to make things right with Becca. The afternoon sun combined with waves of heat from the front of the fire had sweat trickling down nearly every surface of his body. Rather than pace himself, Spider was using the physical work to channel some of his frustrations with Becca.

Somehow, he was going to prove his love was real.

"How about I finish that up for you," Logan said, gently guiding Spider away from the hand line they were scraping out of the mountainside. "Looks like you could use some water."

"I'd prefer vodka."

"Are you going to drink to forget?" Doc called as they walked away.

"Do you have a problem with me, Doc?" Spider snapped, stepping in his way.

The kid stared back at Spider in surprise.

Chainsaw stepped between the two. "Let's pick on someone your own size," he said to Spider.

"Now's not the time to have a meltdown," Logan warned, lowering his voice and pulling Spider farther away from the team.

"I'm not having a meltdown," Spider protested.

"You're just angry because you went through three rounds with that Fire Behavior Analyst and lost. That's no reason to take it out on the team," Chainsaw advised.

"Somebody hit me," Spider mumbled. He wouldn't throw the first punch, but he wouldn't mind brawling with someone. "She's got me so tied up in knots that I don't know what to do. There's so much more to her than there is to me. She's right, what can I bring to the party except the chromosome that helped create our kid? She can raise that baby with her eyes closed. I'll be AWOL, or when I'm there I'll be looking for the daddy handbook."

"You and the FBAN?" Logan grinned. "You're going to be a dad? That's awesome."

"It would be perfect if she married me and I knew the rules for being a dad."

"Hey. She'll come around." Logan held up a hand. "Being a father isn't about playing by the rules. Each kid is different and each kid is going to teach you how they want or need you to be."

"Women are the same way, dude," Chainsaw added.

"How would you know?" Spider challenged. "You lost your first love to another man." And he'd been saving himself ever since. They should have called him the Celibate Cleric, not Chainsaw.

To his credit, Chainsaw didn't pound one of his gigantic fists into Spider's face. Instead, he asked quietly, "Is this about being rejected by Becca or about being shut out as a dad?"

"It's about Becca. She's not the kind of woman who's going to deny me access to the baby just because she's rejected me." But it was Becca who would complete the joy of becoming a father. And all he'd done was stress her out by pressuring her to commit herself and the baby to him immediately, instead of waiting as she'd asked, or being patient enough to prove his love to her. No wonder she'd had a meltdown this morning.

"I misread her from the start," Spider admitted. "What can I say or do to make up for all this?" He'd probably cost her the Boise job.

"Your love," Victoria said, walking up from behind. "Sorry. I couldn't help but hear. Congratulations, by the way. But love—" She shrugged. "That's all any of us wants. When the fire season is over, she'll realize it, too."

Spider didn't want to wait.

"Much as I'd love to continue this Hallmark moment, we need to finish up." Logan gestured to the rest of the team, whose pace had slowed.

"I think this is yours," Victoria handed Spider a large Ziploc bag filled with letters. "I meant to give them to you this morning, but then everything fell out of my backpack and… Well, you know the rest."

"What is it?" Spider took off his gloves and opened the bag.

"I think they're letters from your dad. I read one and it was addressed to you. I didn't know he was your dad."

"Who?" Aiden knew he had some type of scowl on his face. His entire body felt sour and bitter.

"That old guy. I thought I saw him drop the bag in camp and then I couldn't find him." Her cheeks turned red. "I probably shouldn't have opened them at all, but I was curious. Besides, Becca gave him a chance."

"He's *not* my dad." Becca was a notorious softy who gave everyone a second chance. Would she give him one as well?

"Then the letters must be for someone else named Aiden."

Victoria reached out to take the bag back, but Spider had already withdrawn the letter on top.

Spider unfolded the paper. It was filled with lines of shaky scrawl.

Dear Aiden,

I know how hard it's been to have your dad on the past few fires with you. It's been equally hard on me. As my career winds down, I'm grateful that I was able to serve with you and see what a solid leader you've turned out to be.

If I could give you one bit of advice, it would be to beware of your pride. That emotion is like a wedge that creates distance between you and those you love. Pride stopped me from fighting for your mother. Pride stopped me from being a better father. I should have taken a job that would have allowed me to spend more time with you, but I wasn't willing to sacrifice something I enjoyed for the person who meant the most in life to me.

Please don't repeat my mistakes.

Love,
Dad

"He's *not* your dad?" Victoria asked.

Spider's throat tightened until he couldn't speak. It appeared his dad did indeed have regrets. He'd once told his dad that he needed to prove that he loved him. Spider had just been handed that proof.

"Yeah, yeah, he is," he admitted finally, tucking the letter back in the bag and stowing it carefully in his backpack. "I'll make sure this gets back to him."

Becca was challenging, obstinate and wouldn't let him put anything past her, but that's part of what made him love her. No one had ever been able to keep up with him. Hell, Becca made him struggle to keep up with her. He loved her, damn it. And as soon as he got off this mountain, he was going to drop down on one knee and ask her to marry him again.

"BECCA." JULIA'S VOICE CUT into Becca's consciousness mid-afternoon.

Despite her resolve, she'd come back to her tent mid-morning and collapsed, unable to go on without rest. Besides, Carl had been convinced that the weather would remain calm and that things would be quiet until the evening briefing. So, she'd come back to her cot and slept, the only relief from her heartache at finally making Aiden let her go.

Becca hadn't seen Sirus since the scene she and Aiden had created that morning. They may not have announced that Aiden was the father of her baby, but everyone in camp certainly knew that something was going on between them.

"Becca, are you in there?" Julia stuck her head in the door.

"Hang on a second." Becca sat up, swaying on her cot dizzily as the blood rushed away from her head. It took her almost thirty more seconds to be able to stand. "What is it?"

But Julia didn't have to answer. The tent door faced the north. Becca felt a cool wind blowing on her face. The winds had shifted early.

She hadn't fought hard enough for that second line of defense. And now there were teams of men and women up on the mountain in the fire's path. Becca's stomach roiled with fear.

"Aiden."

IT STARTED AS PRESSURE in Spider's ears. At first, he attributed it to the altitude. They'd hiked far up the mountain today and the air was pretty thin. The air was cooler, too, which was good when you were hacking away at the ground for hours at a time.

"Are you okay, Spider?" Doc asked. "We've still got a ways to go to meet up with that water-buffalo crew."

Spider continued to stand still. Something was wrong. There was an expectancy in the very air he was breathing. The smoke was thick up here such that it seemed like a foggy dusk—if fog were brown-gray. The slope they were working on was steep and densely wooded, limiting visibility even further.

"Hey." Chainsaw shook his shoulder. "You need to focus. We'll be back in base camp soon enough." Chainsaw assumed he'd been distracted by thoughts of Becca and the baby.

"Yeah, sure." Spider went back to work, swinging his Pulaski with skilled strokes, but his attention was on the brown-gray sky above them and, in spite of the heat, he shivered.

"The prediction was for no wind today," Sirus announced to the team in the IC tent, with a dark glance sent Carl's way. "We need to know what's going to happen next. Becca?"

"Give me a minute." Becca leaned over the latest fire map spread across the table, trying not to worry about Aiden, and failing, because his crew was directly in the path of the fire.

"Carl said there'd be no wind." Julia's eyes were streaming with tears.

Jackson Garrett charged into the tent. "Do you feel it?" He looked around with an almost palpable sense of urgency.

Nodding, Becca knew immediately what Jackson meant. He wasn't referring to the wind. The pressure was dropping. She could feel the pressure in her ears and in her belly.

Julia stood, sniffed and tried again. "But the computer—"

Becca hushed her. "If you need to go pull yourself together, please do so." Becca sank into the chair Julia had vacated. She needed to concentrate. She needed an extra pair of hands, but that wasn't likely when Julia was falling apart.

"I'm not crying," Julia said stubbornly, her cheeks still wet with tears. "I'm allergic to spruce or whatever is burning up there." She pointed in the general direction of the mountain accusingly. "My eyes haven't stopped running once since I've been here."

"I want immediate updates on the teams on that mountain," Sirus commanded their communications officer. "Where are they and how far are they from a safe retreat zone?"

"We've got three crews working too close to the southwestern flank of the fire," Jackson observed, looking at a map. "The winds are going to blow this beast straight down their throats."

"I agree," Becca said. "They're our number one priority, but there are also two other crews in danger."

"Let's pull them all out." Thank God, Sirus didn't hesitate.

Relieved, Becca turned her attention back to Julia. "Why didn't you go to the infirmary?"

"Because I wanted to work with you. I was willing to do anything to work with the legendary Rebecca Thomas." Julia blew her nose. "And then I couldn't do anything right until today when I adjusted the computer simulation to account for the change in temperature and wind direction, but it's too late to help us." She wiped at her eyes, then groaned in frustration. "Look at me. The wind is making me worse. My eyes are watering so bad that I can barely see the computer keyboard."

Becca didn't know what to say. Her opinion of Julia had been biased by the belief that she was averse to the outdoors when in fact she'd been suffering.

"Don't distract her, Julia," Sirus snapped. "Do what she says and take a break."

"No." Becca stared up into Julia's red, watery eyes. "I need her help."

Becca was rewarded with a hesitant smile from Julia. "What do you want me to do?"

"THIS ISN'T GOOD," Spider said, conferring with Chainsaw and Logan at the back of the fire-crew line. The wind whipped around them, first in one direction and then in another.

Small embers danced in the air. As they landed, the fire crew tried to smother them. But Spider could see there were too many.

The embers were getting bigger.

And the fickle, ever-changing wind made choosing a direction of escape a gamble.

"Doc, call IC," Spider commanded, pulling out his map. "Which location do you want to retreat to, Logan? The black meadow below us?" Which had been burned over two days ago. "Or that little rise to the east?" Which would only be good if the IC was sending them a helicopter. Considering this fire only had one helicopter, the chance of an air evacuation was slim unless they were in really deep trouble. And if they were in deep trouble, there was no way one chopper could airlift three teams to safety.

Spider was hoping they weren't going to need that helicopter.

"I'm betting on the black," Logan said slowly. "We've got two other teams out here. One other Hot Shot team and the Montana #5 private crew."

Spider's dad's team.

"There's too much static on the line. I'm getting nothing," Doc said. "Want me to run up to the ridge and see if the reception is any better over there?"

"No." Spider could almost feel the fire drawing itself up for one tremendous, fiery belch. They didn't have much time. Of all the days to be without Golden. "We've got to retreat. Now. Down to the blackened meadow."

Several of the men grumbled. One more hour and they'd be close to finishing. Retreating was like admitting defeat and they'd certainly done enough of that already on this fire.

"You heard what Spider said," Chainsaw bellowed, looking as if he'd willingly pound them into action. "Move your lazy butts down to the meadow."

Logan, Chainsaw and Spider stood while the rest of the team moved down the mountain, albeit slowly.

Spider turned his attention up the mountain, toward the fire. "I need you to take the team, Logan."

His forehead wrinkled. "Why?"

"Communications are for shit. I've got to warn the other crews." Spider scanned the slope above them, but didn't see a soul. To the northeast, the smoke seemed to be roiling into giant clouds that looked to be threatening rain. "That superintendent of Montana #5 is just looking for a chance to prove they're just as brave, or braver, than a DoF crew. He'll stay until the last possible moment and rely on his team's speed and mobility to escape."

Only not everyone on his team had speed and mobility. At least one guy was old and walked with slow, painful steps.

"Don't you think they already know it's time to back off?" Logan asked.

Spider thought about the stubborn leader of his dad's team, about the earnest way his father tried to help Spider despite being put down and rejected constantly. "I don't want to assume anything today. Do you?"

Logan slowly nodded and extended his hand. "Hurry down

there, man. I don't want to have to pull my suit out of the closet for you." For Spider's funeral.

"Don't bury me yet." He still had things to accomplish—a father to get to know, a child to raise, a woman to love.

"I'll go with you." Chainsaw took a step forward, but Spider held up a hand.

"The crew needs leaders right now. Without me or Golden, that's two less steady heads. You stay."

"DO YOU SEE THAT CLOUD forming here?" Carl said, pointing to the screen. "The fire's creating another thunderstorm. That's totally amazing."

"But will it bring rain, or lightning or both?" Julia asked, wiping at her eyes with a tissue while Carl looked at the screen, saying nothing.

"It doesn't matter," Becca said. "The fire will blow up before the first drop of rain hits the ground." Was Aiden paying attention to the conditions? He'd felt the pressure build during the first blowup.

Her stomach was wound up in such tight knots that she didn't think she'd be able to breath soon. It had become hard just to draw air.

"Those three teams still haven't called in," Jackson whispered to Sirus, but Becca heard him anyway.

"Which teams?" Sirus asked.

"Silver Bend…"

Becca didn't hear any more. Aiden was up on that mountain, at the heart of the approaching storm carrying a metal Pulaski—a miniature lightning rod as far as she was concerned, just a huge magnet waiting for a lightning strike. But there was a more imminent danger from the front of the fire.

Leaping quickly across the narrow ridges, it could take the men and women up there by surprise.

"The satellite won't be in position for another fifteen minutes to read the fire's progress," Carl said.

"Can we send the chopper?" Becca asked in a strangled voice.

"Angus isn't going to fly into a blowup in this weather, and I can't say as I blame him. It's a suicide mission." Jackson exchanged a look with Becca that was not at all encouraging. "But they're not a bunch of rookies, Becca. They'll realize there's trouble in time to head to the safe zone."

"What if they go to a pickup zone instead?" Julia asked.

Sensing her unease, Sirus put a hand on Becca's shoulder. "With the winds whipping around like this, they won't expect any air support."

In other words, they wouldn't expect a rescue.

"HEY," SPIDER YELLED as soon as he spotted men through the trees, hoping his voice would rise above the wind and reach the Montana crew. He'd already warned the second DoF crew to retreat.

Either they heard him or he'd come into their line of vision, because many of the crew looked up. The embers weren't as bad on this side of the ridge, but there were still embers in the air and crackling on the ground.

"We're falling back to the safe zone," Spider shouted as he ran up to the superintendent.

"At whose command?" the super asked, looking suspicious.

A couple of the veterans in the group kept hacking at the ground, including Spider's dad.

Spider forced himself to look casual. "Well, you can radio

in if you'd like, but the other two DoF crews have already fallen back."

The leader asked his radio man to make contact with base camp. Aiden knew it was futile. The smoke and clouds overhead were swirling, the air charged heavily with something bad on the way, and they were on the opposite side of the mountain range from base camp with no radio relay in between them.

"I guess we can fall back with you, but just remember, we were the last to go." The leader smiled triumphantly at Spider.

"What an ass," Spider mumbled to his dad when the old man came over to him.

"I've been trying to tell him for the past ten minutes that we should pull back, but I don't think he's ever seen anything like this," Roadhouse admitted half under his breath. "He doesn't know what we're in for."

Something changed. The wind became hotter. There was a roar in the distance, a fierce challenge to all who lay in the dragon's path.

"Run!" Spider shouted, hoping the team wouldn't put pride in the way of safety. He grabbed his father by the arm and together they stumbled down the path.

"LOOK AT THOSE WIND SPEEDS," Becca said, pointing to Carl's computer screen where several pieces of equipment Carl and Becca had installed in the fire's path were shuttling information like crazy.

"It's coming down the southwestern slope, isn't it?" Julia asked.

"Yes," Becca and Jackson said at the same time. The right slope, the right fuel, and the right wind were converging with potentially deadly consequences.

"Can we cut it off somewhere?" Sirus asked, the lines on his face deeper than Becca had ever seen them.

Becca and Julia pointed to the same place on the map at the same time. "Here."

Julia explained, wiping at her nose with a tissue. "At the bottom of the valley there's a river. The wind will channel it to the south, toward the highway, but it may not have enough force to scale the next ridge."

"It had better stall because that was the last ridge between the fire and the nearest town," Becca said.

"What about base camp?" Sirus asked.

"My simulation indicates it won't be threatened until to-morrow." Julia thrust a paper in Becca's direction.

After a quick perusal, Becca nodded at Sirus.

"If we can get some air support and dump a couple of loads of slurry…" Catching on, Jackson looked up at Sirus. "It's time to call in some favors."

Becca handed the printout back to Julia. "I always knew you had it in you."

Julia looked both pleased and saddened by Becca's com-pliment. "Sometimes it takes stubborn minds a bit more ef-fort to come around. I should have told you about my allergies. I'm sorry—"

"Don't apologize," Becca cut her off. "You've learned something and I've learned something." Not to be quick to judge. To communicate better.

It was unfortunate that Becca had learned how to manage too late.

IT ONLY TOOK THEM TEN MINUTES to make it to the safety zone. Days before the meadow had been burned over, the ground mere charred grass, but all the empty space seemed to be filled with the forty-odd DoF crew members already there. Fitting another twenty men and their shelters in was going to be a challenge.

"Move closer." Logan was shouting over the wind, trying to direct everyone to make room.

Faces—young and old—were pinched with fear. Men were sweating openly in the path of the ever-increasing hot wind. Explosions sounded on the mountain above them, trees being consumed in one fiery flame like a match. The roar of the fire grew louder, like a freight train, bearing down on them all.

Some were still tossing their packs aside, taking only water, wetting a bandana and covering their mouths in an attempt to cool the air they'd be taking into their lungs if the fire passed over them. Others had already deployed their shelters, fitting their feet in the bottom corners and hooking their gloved hands in the top corners, then flopping down with no grace onto the ash covered ground. The way some of the shelters were shaking and lifting in the wind, Aiden knew some firefighters were trying to dig a shallow hole in the ground for their faces to try and escape the poisonous gas the fire would bring.

The wind seemed to swirl around them, taunting with the promise of certain doom.

Spider began running around making sure his team members were deploying their shelters correctly. They all carried one in case of emergencies like this.

The roar of the fire intensified with another explosion—closer now.

O'Reilly, one of their rookies, was struggling with his folded shelter, as if the fireproof material were stuck together and unwilling to open. He shook it violently.

It opened.

And then blew away in the wind.

Before Spider could react, Victoria was standing next to O'Reilly, pressing her shelter into his hands.

"What are you doing?" Spider shouted, racing over.

"I'm giving him my shelter." Victoria's face was paler than usual as she knelt to help the nearly paralyzed rookie into his shelter. "He's got a wife and kid at home."

"WE'VE GOT REPORTS OF TEAMS in the safe zone deploying," the radio communications officer announced.

Aiden.

Jackson paced.

"Which teams?" Becca demanded with a crack in her voice. He couldn't leave her to raise their baby alone.

Julia was crying now, not just having an allergic reaction. She looked to Becca for support, and Becca held her hand tightly, repeating, "Which teams?"

"I don't know. It's all garbled. Listen for yourself." And then the communications officer unplugged his earphones and filled the tent with the static sound of radio traffic.

"It's coming…mountain…hear it."

"Where's my satellite feed, Carl?" Sirus was the calmest one in the tent.

Becca thought she might throw up. "Which teams?"

CHAPTER SIXTEEN

"VICTORIA, TAKE the goddamn shelter," Spider shouted.

She stood staunchly before him, her gloved hands limply at her sides, shaking her head. "There's no point."

"Take my shelter, Victoria, or so help me God, I will stuff you in it myself." The roar of the fire was deafening now. Spider glanced around the safe zone, looking for anything that would provide him with some level of protection. Maybe there'd be a miracle, as there had been last fall when Logan had found a coyote den.

Victoria raised her head, her expression sadly determined. "I will not take your shelter."

He grabbed her shoulder with one hand, being careful not to let go of the shelter in his other hand. "I will not stand by and let this happen."

"Get in the shelter with me."

Spider shook his head. "You know that doesn't work, there won't be enough oxygen. Take the shelter. That's an order. Every second you refuse is one more second I won't have to get away."

She shook her head. "I'll run downhill."

"You may be faster than me going up over a long distance, but I kick ass running downhill." And he'd have to if he wanted to live.

Becca...

He couldn't think about her now. Or the baby.

"There's no point," she repeated. "I have cancer." Victoria took a step back, her hands fisted. "I'm not taking your shelter."

Oh, God, it all made sense now. Victoria throwing up, her stamina decreasing, her concentration worthless. She'd been fighting cancer and hadn't let anyone know all these months. She'd tried to hang in there and he'd been an asshole, kicking her when she was down, just as Becca had said.

Spider lowered his head, clenching his jaw as he made his decision. He owed Victoria. "Look, nothing is hopeless. Not the way I see it." Unwilling to wait any longer, Spider thrust the shelter at Victoria and took off downhill.

"Damn you, Spider," Victoria called after him. "I'll tell her you love her."

"Aɪy-ow." Becca hadn't expected the sharp pain in her belly, couldn't believe that such a pain would rocket her out of her chair.

"Becca!" Julia helped ease her back down. "Are you okay?"

"I think so." She rubbed a hand over her stomach, which was tight as a band of steel. "Just a Braxton Hicks contraction."

"Teams deployed...pray...God." The static-filled voice descended over Becca like a cold shroud. How would she know if Aiden, Victoria and Roadhouse had deployed their shelters safely? How could she wait the additional ten minutes or longer wondering without going crazy?

Her belly tightened again, causing her to straighten in her seat. She'd never had the practice contractions hit her so intensely. This was painful. This was...

Labor.

"AIDEN...SPIDER...WAIT."

Spider skidded to a halt at the edge of the meadow, wasting too many precious seconds he couldn't spare for his dad to catch up to him.

"Deploy your shelter, Dad."

Roadhouse ran in a lopsided gait, as if his legs were hurting. The ridge behind him was ablaze with flames rising eighty feet toward the darkly clouded heavens, reminding Spider of what little time he had left.

"Take mine," Roadhouse shouted as he slapped his folded shelter into Spider's chest, not even pausing as he loped past him down the mountain.

"What the—"

"Becca and the baby need you," he called without looking back. And then his dad disappeared into the brush and down the mountain.

Foolish old man. What the hell was he thinking? He'd never outrun this beast.

Spider took a step after him, then paused.

A tree exploded quite near the edge of the meadow, sending a whole new wave of flame into the air and embers showering across the meadow. If Spider didn't deploy now, he'd die for sure. They'd both die.

The air seemed to slow around him, waiting, waiting for him to decide. Stay and brave the dragon or run after a father he'd only just learned really loved him? The air became heavier, pressing down on him, holding him captive until the decision was taken from him.

And what of Becca and the baby if he died?

With one last look down the ridge, Spider swore and sprang into action, pausing only to retrieve the bag of his dad's letters from his pack and stuffing them into his shirt.

With practiced, shaking hands, Spider shook out his dad's

shelter, fit the loops around his feet and hands, and flopped face-first onto the ground, his ears filling with the roar of the dragon's anger.

The hungry beast had arrived.

"I CAN'T BREATHE," Becca struggled to fill her lungs with air.

"Calm down, we'll save them," Sirus reassured her, not looking up from the computer screen where he hoped to see the latest satellite picture of the fire any moment.

Jackson spared her a quick glance, then did a double take and swore. "She's not having a panic attack, she's in labor."

Becca's stomach muscles contracted, sending her arching in her chair. Her face felt hot.

She couldn't be in labor. She still had about five weeks to go. She cast her gaze around, looking for someone to calm her down, someone to reassure her that everything was going to be all right, but Aiden wasn't there.

She'd fallen in love with Aiden and rejected him.

What had she done? He might die never knowing how she felt about him. And it was her fault he was out there.

Someone—Julia—encouraged her to breathe.

How foolish she'd been not to realize that Aiden was perfect for her. Her heart had known in Las Vegas that he was the only one for her. She'd just been too stupid to see it until now, until Aiden was in danger of dying and her heart was in danger of breaking.

"Don't let him die," Becca whispered half to herself even as Maxine, the medic, burst into the tent.

SPIDER HAD NEVER FELT like such a coward. He never would have taken the shelter if his father hadn't mentioned Becca and the baby.

He wanted to see the spark in Becca's blue eyes when they

argued, and her smile when he said something that pleased her. He wanted to hold his baby in his arms, just once.

Pressing the corners of his fire shelter down with his hands and feet, he could feel the heat wash over the meadow and the sixty-some-odd bodies crouched as he was beneath a thin layer of aluminum foil and fiberglass laminate.

The wind and fire challenged the edges of his shelter, trying to lift it off the ground, trying to roast him alive. Reflexively, he jerked the shelter back down. The fire roared on and on endlessly above him.

Firefighters didn't call shelters Shake 'n Bakes for nothing. The heat inside was severe and threatened to suck the oxygen away just as Spider needed it most.

To his left, screams erupted.

"Don't run!" he shouted before dissolving into a fit of coughing as he fought for air. He prayed that whoever had been burned hadn't been burned badly enough to lose their composure and jump up. Therein lay certain death.

And what of his father? Had he been able to outrun the dragon?

More screams. Spider couldn't distinguish the voices. For all he knew, it could have been his father.

The sour taste of vomit filled the back of his throat.

He'd let his father sacrifice his life so that Spider could live. He almost wished he wouldn't survive this vengeful firestorm. Because if he did survive, he'd have to live with the knowledge that he was a coward—every day, for the rest of his life.

UP-DOWN. UP-DOWN. UP-DOWN. Don't think. Just move.

His knees were two knots of pain. It was excruciating just lifting his legs, much less running on them on an uneven surface. Not that it would matter. The roar of the fire filled his ears with a near-deafening challenge.

Roadhouse wouldn't be able to outrun the dragon for long.

At least he'd go out on his own terms. Death would come swiftly, and with it the knowledge that he'd finally done right by his boy. Well, one of his boys, anyway.

Up-down. Up-down. Over a felled log. Losing his footing. Sliding on his butt. Somehow managing to pop back up to his feet without losing speed.

All the while, the fire bellowed hungrily behind him, daring him to stop and look back.

Roadhouse didn't want his last memory to be of a wall of flame sweeping down upon him. He kept running even when his knees hurt so badly they'd become numb with pain.

Up-down. Keep your mind off the knees and the fire. Think of something else. Make it to the other side of this little meadow.

Familiar smells—smoke, pine, bear scat.

Bear?

He entered the stand of pine trees at the bottom of the meadow and nearly ran into a humongous grizzly crossing his path.

Bear and man let out yowls of surprise barely heard over the roar of the fire nearly upon them.

Roadhouse veered to the right, stumbled over a small boulder and flew into the air, his momentum carrying him over an outcropping of rock.

"LOGAN," SPIDER SHOUTED upon emerging from his shelter. The charred remains of their backpacks littered the meadow. Smoke drifted up from the burned ground as if it were dust kicked up by a light wind. The wind itself had died down to a strong, bracing breeze.

Firefighters began lifting off their shelters and standing, looking relatively unscathed, other than the emotional scars they'd carry from this day forward of barely cheating death.

Others rolled their shelters off and called for help, having been burned by flames licking under their shelter.

Spider jogged back up the slope to reach the rest of his crew, calling again for his friends. "Logan! Victoria! Chainsaw!"

He saw Doc first, and then the rest of the Silver Bend crew came into view.

"Are you all right?" Spider asked Logan.

"Yeah. Doc, do a head count." Logan's blond hair was streaked with ash, but he was otherwise fine.

"But how…" Victoria asked, looking frail and beaten, as wilted as a flower on a one-hundred-and-ten-degree day.

Spider understood exactly what she felt, what she'd been through.

"Roadhouse gave me his shelter," Spider admitted. Now that he'd seen to his people, he turned, about to charge down the hill to find his father.

"Why did he do that?" Doc asked.

Because he loves me, Spider realized. And he'd never given his father a chance to share that love until it was too late.

"For that matter," Victoria asked, "why did you give me yours?"

"Because you're a fighter, and you don't deserve to go down without a fighting chance."

"Thanks." She hesitated, and then she hugged him awkwardly. "I guess Peter Pan saved my ass again."

"The name is Spider," he called as he took off, no longer able to put off the task before him.

It wasn't until Spider was at the edge of the blackened meadow and facing a smoldering slope that he realized Victoria had followed him. Bushes were still on fire and the tops of trees still burned, their trunks blackened but otherwise still intact.

"How could anyone survive this?" Victoria looked around them.

"If anyone could, it would be Roadhouse…my father," Spider added when the name seemed too awkward in light of what his dad had given up for him.

Spider stared at Victoria for a long moment. "Do you still have that picture of your dad? The one in front of the Silver Bend sign?"

"Yeah. I kept it in my pocket."

"My dad knows who he is. They were friends. That's why he kept looking at you. He saw me give up my shelter for you." Spider swallowed and stared down the slope, not wanting to venture through it for fear of what he'd find. "I don't know what kind of man your father is, but if he's anything like mine, he's worth finding."

Spider didn't wait for Victoria's reaction. He plunged into the smoldering forest to find his dad.

"DO WE HAVE AN UPDATE on the fire? Is it on rails or at a station?" Jackson asked, meaning was it still racing over acres or had it slowed.

"It's not stopping, if that's what you mean," Becca managed to answer, trying to bat Maxine and her blood-pressure cuff away. "Hopefully, it will move over quickly and dance through the canopy, leaving the bush on the ground dried or burnt but not torched."

"But you don't know," Jackson said. "We don't have the latest satellite feed."

Sirus was on the phone with someone from NIFC, negotiating an air tanker. Given the number of people at risk, Becca doubted they'd turn him down this time.

"We've got to get you to the hospital," Maxine reminded Becca.

Becca's belly swelled and tightened with another contraction. When she could speak again, she announced staunchly, "Not until I know they're okay up there."

"Becca, there's nothing we can do other than wait. If you go, you'll be in radio contact the same as we are here," Sirus said.

"But I won't be here." She wouldn't leave without knowing Aiden and the rest were okay.

"I'm downloading the satellite data," Carl announced.

"Is it live or on delay?" Becca demanded.

"It's live. A continuous update. Here we go, folks," Carl said, pushing his chair back a bit from the screen so that the others could see.

Becca struggled to sit up, but Maxine pushed her back down. "Easy, girl."

"Holy cow," Jackson said, looking a bit pale himself. "Look at the heat that beast is generating."

"Let me see," Becca insisted, brushing off Maxine's hand and rising. "Then I'll go."

The satellite picture showed a huge red cloud over the mountain above them—the body of the fire was probably racing through the crowns of the trees at speeds that could easily trap a man. In its wake was a wide orange tail—a second wave of flame that would destroy whatever was on the ground that the crown fire had missed. The tail traveled slower, but was just as deadly.

"Thirty minutes until we get our first air tanker." Sirus

joined them at the monitor. "See you at the hospital, Becca. That's an order."

Tears spilled over Becca's cheeks as she whispered, "Aiden, where are you?"

THE FIRE HAD BURNED through the tree tops at high speeds, leaving some areas untouched and some small, spot fires on the ground where bushes had caught fire. Not that anyone could have survived the heat of the crown fire without a shelter.

Spider picked his way down the hill, trying to estimate how far his father could have gotten before the fire would have overtaken him. He had to move slowly and look at everything twice—every charred bush, every blackened rock, every spot fire of more than a few feet in diameter—just in case it was his father burning.

The other firemen were staying up in the meadow awaiting pickup. Spider was alone, which was the way he wanted it when he found the remains.

The smell of charred flesh filled his lungs and Spider couldn't stop himself from gagging. Then he saw a smoking mound in a stand of trees. At first, Spider was convinced it was his father. But as he came closer, he realized it was too big, three times the size of a man. It was…a bear.

Aiden moved on, climbing to the top of an outcropping of rock. Even though rock wasn't combustible, it had taken in the heat of the fire. He could still feel it through the soles of his boots. He looked around, nearly jumping out of his skin when something moved under the ledge of rock.

A booted foot.

"Dad." Spider jumped down, his feet sinking a few inches in ash. He crouched low until he could see his father's body wedged within a fissure in the rock, expecting the worst.

That's when he heard the low moaning and realized his father's body was trembling, his shirt and pants singed.

His dad was alive. Barely.

Aiden reached toward his father, but was afraid to touch him for fear he'd cause him more pain.

Spider yanked his radio off its strap. "Doc, are you out there? I need a medic sixty feet south of the meadow. I'm going to need an evac ASAP." His voice was surprisingly calm, with no indication of the bile pressing at the back of this throat.

He'd done this to him. Spider had signed his dad's death warrant when he'd accepted his shelter. "Help's coming, Dad."

His dad didn't answer.

With a hand that trembled, Spider steadied himself against the rock. Through his glove, the heat was still uncomfortable. How had his father survived such heat? Spider was afraid to touch him, but he was worried that his father might be literally cooking inside the rock. Should he pull him out?

Torn, Spider put a hand on his father's leg.

"You hang in there, Dad."

His father continued to tremble, not uttering a sound.

"FIREFIGHTER DOWN! How soon until we can get a chopper out here?"

"Aiden!" Becca had been walking out the door of the IC tent when she heard his voice. She rushed back to the radio, flooded with relief.

"We're sending out a bird. Can you move the wounded to the meadow?" the communications operator asked.

"Negative, not without a stretcher. We can't make one. All Pulaskis and shovels were burned in the fire." Aiden sounded shaken.

Overcome with concern, Becca grabbed the mic. "Aiden? It's me, Becca. Are you all right?"

"Becca, put down that microphone," Sirus commanded.

Ignoring him, Becca pressed the talk button again. "Aiden, I want to take you up on your offer. Do you hear me? This baby is—"

"Becca, don't." Sirus cut her off, putting his hand gently over hers, loosening her hold on the button.

"For crying out loud," Maxine said. "She's in labor. Let her say her piece."

"I'm trying to tell Aiden that he was right." She fought back a sob and pushed the button again. "I want you to know that I love you."

The airwaves were silent. No one so much as breathed within the tent. The microphone cord was dangling at her feet, having come unplugged during her breakdown. Aiden hadn't heard her, but everyone in the IC tent had.

"Becca, give up the mic," Aiden ordered. "I've got a man down who needs medical attention immediately. He was out in the fire without a shelter."

Becca drew a shuddering breath. It was too late for them. She'd had her chance. She'd dealt with Aiden the same way she dealt with everything. She'd stuck to her plan, waiting for the right moment. Only with Aiden, the right moment had never come.

And now she'd lost him.

"Get her to the hospital, Jackson. I need the medics in the chopper," Sirus said.

Strong hands gripped her shoulders and turned Becca toward the door.

"Thank you." She handed the useless microphone back to the communications officer, completely aware that she had probably made the biggest fool of herself in forest-fighting history. "I'm ready to leave now."

"WHAT DO YOU THINK, Doc?" Aiden asked.

With Doc's blessing, they'd moved Spider's dad inch by slow inch out of the crevice he'd crawled into. His face and ankles were burned, and he was having trouble breathing, as if his lungs had filled with too much poisonous gas. His gloves were melted to his hands, but his helmet and fireproof clothing had protected the rest of his body.

Roadhouse's eyes were glazed over and the only sign that his body was alive was the shallow rise and fall of his chest and the trembling of his arms. Spider sat helplessly at his side.

"He's in shock." Doc exchanged a glance with Spider. "It's his body's way of protecting itself."

Spider knew it was also the body's last defense before death.

"Where's that chopper?" Spider searched the sky, seeing nothing more than thick smoke.

"They would have had to fly around the fire," Doc said quietly. "They know we've got a man down. They'll get here as soon as they can."

"Chainsaw's waiting in the meadow to lead them down. It's no use sending up a flare with all this smoke around," Victoria said, kneeling next to Spider. She'd come down with Doc. "He'll make it. He's a tough old man."

Looking down at his frail, unconscious father, Spider found it impossible to agree.

"YOU'RE NOT BREATHING," Jackson reminded Becca for the third time since they'd left base camp. They were driving Becca's SUV to the hospital. "I've had two kids. Breathing is an important part of the labor process."

"There's something…about a man I…barely know telling…me how to breathe…that's a little…hard to take," Becca said between gasps of air. "If I told you…to shut up…would you be offended?"

"You're just worried about the teams on the mountain," Jackson surmised. "And in pain. So feel free to lay into me as much as you want."

Instead, Becca grew silent. There'd been no word about the injured firefighter on the mountain. Becca didn't know who it was or how badly they were hurt. But she knew it was her fault. She should have been insistent about the fire lines. She should have lobbied for it earlier. Aiden and others had risked their lives to build a long, two-sided firebreak that was now just ash. The fire had traveled more than a mile in less than fifteen minutes. She'd known the front would do that. It was the Coyote fire all over again.

SPIDER SAT HELPLESSLY at his father's side through the bumpy helicopter ride to the hospital.

"Talk to him," Doc encouraged, yelling over the helicopter's whining blades. "He can hear you."

"Dad." Spider gulped and blinked back tears. "Dad, you made it. Jeez, you wily old coot, how'd you find your hidey-hole?"

Eyes closed, his dad didn't respond. His body's trembling had all but ceased when they'd popped an IV into his system before takeoff.

"Keep going." Doc rolled his hand. "You're doing great."

Spider felt as if he were going to choke, his throat was so tight. "I don't think I've ever seen you move as fast as you did today. Those knees were pumping. Of course, you were going downhill."

Nodding his head, Doc squeezed the IV bag.

"Apparently, there was a bear that wasn't as lucky as you. He was roasted." Spider cleared his throat. "Just a few feet away from you. Did you fight him for that crevice?"

"The hospital's still twenty minutes away," one of the paramedics said. "Keep talking."

For a moment, Spider panicked. What else could he possibly say that would keep his dad's spirits up? He'd missed twenty-five years of Spider's life. They had a lot of catching up to do. And Spider hoped they'd have lots of time to do it in.

And suddenly, he knew. "Dad, did I ever tell you about the time I played in the Little League World Series? I was an all-star shortstop...."

"MR. RODAS," the doctor said as he entered the Missoula hospital waiting room in green scrubs. He looked tired and worn out.

Spider feared for the worse. He stood on shaky legs, then sank back down into the chair when his legs gave out on him. Doc was immediately at his side.

"Your father's condition has stabilized. He's in critical condition, so he's not out of the woods yet, but I'm hopeful that we're over the worst of it."

Aiden breathed a sigh of relief, hanging his head in his hands and pressing his palms over his eyes. He would have remained weak with relief, except that he heard the doctor's footsteps retreating. Spider lifted his head. "When can I see him?"

The doctor took in the state Spider was in with a disdainful look. "There is a huge risk of infection with burns."

Spider looked down, realizing he was covered with dirt

and soot. Doc stepped forward. "Look, we've been out fighting a fire and could use a shower. I know there's probably an empty room around here somewhere where my friend can clean up. In the meantime, we'll run out and find him some clean clothes. But it would help if you'd find us that room."

With a nod, the doctor left.

"Thanks, Doc," Spider managed to say before the energy drained out of him completely. He propped his head in his hands and tried to pull himself together. His father was going to make it, after all. They'd been granted a second chance. Now he just had to figure out what to do with it.

"YOU'RE VERY LUCKY, Ms. Thomas," the maternity-ward doctor told Becca over an hour later. "We were able to stop the labor. We'll keep you here a few days, confined to bed, until we feel it's safe for you to deliver the baby."

Absently, Becca thanked the doctor. Tubes ran into her arm. A monitor was strapped across her belly. Other monitors were taped to her chest. Machines beeped and hummed at her bedside. The baby was fine, but Becca's heart was not. Where was Aiden? Had he continued to fight the fire after the wounded were airlifted out?

Becca lay in a room with three other beds. Behind thin curtains, two other women labored, their husbands or lovers encouraging them to breathe, telling them how proud they were of them, making jokes with the nurses.

Becca was alone.

Jackson had driven her down the mountain to the hospital in Missoula, and then had left her in the capable hands of the maternity-ward staff, promising to check on her later. He'd gone in search of information on the Flathead fire burn victim.

Becca supposed she should call her parents, but they'd just come and make a huge fuss over her. They certainly wouldn't provide her with the support she wanted.

Only Aiden could do that.

She was alone. From the moment she'd conceived the idea of having a baby, that's what she'd wanted.

Be careful what you wish for.

Becca turned her head away from the doorway and surrendered to the tears.

"THIS IS ONE HECK of a hard ward to find," Golden said when he entered the burn unit at the hospital. He nodded at Doc, who was reclining on a couch in the corner with one eye open.

"I wish I wasn't sitting here waiting." Spider folded the letter he'd been reading and returned it to the plastic bag in his lap. He'd like the chance to get to know the man who wrote those letters. That man who obviously loved his son.

Golden sank into a chair next to him.

The details all came spilling out. "He's got second-degree burns on his hands where his gloves melted, and a third-degree burn on his left cheek where it rested on the rock. The doctor thinks he'll recover ninety-percent use of his hands with a couple of surgeries and therapy…if he pulls through." God, let him pull through.

"Was he burned anywhere else?"

"His lungs may have been damaged by the hot gases he was breathing." Spider had never seen anyone burned this badly and live.

"But they think he'll pull through?"

"They don't know." Spider went cold just saying it. Life couldn't be so cruel as to bring he and his dad back together only to have him die like this.

Golden laid a hand on his shoulder. "I'll be around if you need me to sit here for awhile. I've got some experience sitting in hospitals." Jackson's son had been born premature and very weak. Golden had stayed many a long night with his son at the hospital.

"I won't be going anywhere," Spider said, flexing his fingers. "By rights, it should be me in that burn ward, not him." At the moment, Spider wasn't sure he had it in him to go back to fighting fires. Even the strength needed to fight for Becca seemed beyond him.

He'd let his father give him his shelter. What kind of man was he?

"How are you holding up?" Golden asked. "I heard it was pretty rough out there."

Swallowing thickly, Spider shrugged.

After a minute, Golden cleared his throat. "You know, I nearly quit the Hot Shots after I fought fires in Russia."

Spider's eyes widened. He hadn't known.

"When things break down out in the field, you tend to doubt your reasons for continuing. You tend to doubt yourself." Golden's face pinched up into a fierce expression. "Anyone who says they don't get scared once in awhile is either stupid or a liar."

The two men sat in a silence broken only by Doc's snores.

Finally, Spider admitted, "He gave up everything for me. I feel so…so…weak."

"It's no more than you did for Victoria, and no more than you'd do for your own child."

Spider was horrified to find himself blinking back tears.

"I'm going to give you the same advice I got back then, whether you want it or not." Golden looked down at his hands and began twisting his wedding ring. "It's the balance of love and fear that keeps you careful out on the fire. You can still enjoy the rush of the excitement, but those two things will bring you home safe."

"Thanks," Spider mumbled, slumping back into his chair. "That's timely advice."

"I've got more." Golden smiled this time. "You might want to at least visit Becca while you're here, especially after that radio message."

Spider must have looked confused because Golden explained, "She's in labor-and-delivery."

"She's having the baby? Alone?" Spider shot up out of his chair, the packet of letters falling to the floor. He wasn't ready to be a father. And she wasn't ready to be his wife. He stood up and began to pace. "She doesn't want to see me. Are you sure she's okay?"

"She went into labor when the barometric pressure dropped before the blowup. The doctors were hoping to stop the labor. So you really didn't hear her radio message?"

Spider didn't know what to do. He was torn between his dad and his love. When it came down to it, he knew where he had to be—with Becca and his child.

Then Golden's words sank in. "Wait a minute. What message?"

CHAPTER SEVENTEEN

BECCA AWOKE smelling flowers, which was odd because she was in the hospital, tucked away in a curtained corner of the labor-and-delivery ward.

"I thought you might need some cheering up," Sirus said when she opened her eyes, gesturing to the small planter with miniature pink roses on her narrow side table. He was sitting in the standard wood-and-vinyl chair next to her bed.

"Thank you." She struggled to sit up without tangling herself or unplugging any of her wires. "I'm sorry I lost it with the microphone. What's the word on the fire?"

"We're planning on containment tomorrow or the next day. With the air tankers in, I had Angus fly me with some of the other injured firefighters over here. Julia packed your things." He pointed to her duffel at the foot of her bed, smiling easily. About the only time she'd seen him with a smile so carefree was during the off-season.

"I'm so sorry, Sirus." The apology came spilling out.

"For what?"

"For not convincing you about the fire. I kept thinking we'd get more help to contain it."

"It worked out for the best. Most of our people were safe, and the blowup pushed NIFC to send reinforcements."

"Still—"

"You have no more worries about this fire, Becca. None. Forget about it and concentrate on having a healthy baby."

She wished she could, but Becca couldn't seem to think about much other than Aiden. "How's Aiden?"

The IC commander's smile disappeared. "He's fine." Then he cleared his throat. "People are talking about your radio message though."

"What? The cord came out. Aiden didn't hear a thing."

He smiled at the flowers. "Oh, I think most of it went through."

Which meant Aiden would know exactly what kind of fool she'd been. A change of subject was in order. "How did Julia do?"

"She did fine." Sirus patted her hand. "We dosed her up with allergy medicine and she stepped right into your shoes. You trained her well. Even Carl was asking her questions when I left."

"So, fire season is over." And with it went her job. Becca let her head fall back on the pillows. There was no going back now.

"Hey, I can read your mind. You want news about that job in Boise." Sirus cleared his throat again. "Well…" He paused, as if uncomfortable.

In that moment, Becca knew she'd lost the job. To Becca's horror, her nose burned and her eyes bubbled with tears. She blinked frantically. Crying in front of Sirus was the last thing she wanted to do.

"Are you decent?" Aiden asked, pulling the curtain aside and stepping in with a dozen pink roses. He looked great in a pair of black jeans and a plain black T-shirt that stretched across his chest. He frowned when he saw the other roses, making room for his larger vase on the table and pulling it back a bit from the bed. Although Becca tried to catch his eye, he wouldn't look at her.

Becca's spirits sank. He was here only for the baby.

Sirus stood and shook Aiden's hand. "Good to see you. How's Roadhouse doing? He's my next stop."

Becca hadn't known the injured man was Roadhouse. Now the tears did spill over her cheeks. She quickly wiped them away.

"He turned the corner this morning," Aiden explained. "They moved him out of intensive care. Visitation is restricted, but they'll tell him you came by if you check in at the nurse's station."

"I'll do that. Oh, and before I forget, we need to announce the winners of your pool." Sirus hesitated, and when next he spoke, his words were laced with a teasing note. "It's nice of you to visit Becca. I hadn't realized you'd grown that close."

For the first time since Aiden had come in, he met Becca's gaze. For once, Aiden remained silent, as if he were waiting for something. Becca knew what that something was. He was waiting for her to tell Sirus the truth.

This was it. The job or her man. When it came down to it, there was no choice.

"We're very close, Sirus," Becca began, taking a risk. If she wanted Aiden, she had to be more assertive. And if he humiliated her in the next few minutes with rejection, she'd fight for him, even if Sirus witnessed every mortifying moment. "In fact, as you may have heard me say, I love Aiden. We're having a baby together, and I hope he'll marry me soon."

Aiden bowed his head and closed his eyes as if he were giving thanks.

The startled expression on Sirus's face was priceless. He

was usually so unflappable. Nothing fazed him. "I…well… that's wonderful."

"Yes," Becca said softly, wishing her boss would go away. "It is."

"I don't know why I'm surprised after that announcement you made," Sirus added.

"I wish I would have heard it," Aiden said. "Or at least seen you fight Sirus for the microphone."

Becca covered her face with her hands, feeling her cheeks heat.

"Woman, you need a keeper." His smile was devilishly priceless. "And I'm just the man for the job."

"Have you made arrangements for your maternity leave?" Sirus asked. "Have you told anyone when you'd like to come back, if at all?"

Just then, Becca didn't care about work. She just wanted to hold Aiden close and kiss him until her lips went numb. "Sirus, you and I both know I'm not getting that job in Boise." Especially now that the truth was out about her younger man. A younger man she couldn't seem to keep her eyes off.

"True."

Despite the warmth in Aiden's dark eyes, hearing that she'd lost the job still hurt.

"But they are offering you another job."

At the startling news, Becca was finally able to pull her gaze away from Aiden. "What?"

"They're creating a new leadership training program at NIFC, complete with a simulated command tent where cross-functional teams practice fire management and decision making. They'd like you to join the team."

Becca shook her head. "I'm not a good manager, remember?"

"That's bull—"

Sirus cut Aiden off with a raised hand. "You've been recognized as one of the leading Fire Behavior Analysts we've got and they want you to create worst-case scenarios for the program to encourage creativity and out-of-the-box thinking."

"That's right up your alley, babe." Aiden beamed.

"But what about…" Becca hesitated before saying it out loud.

"She's worried about the older woman–younger man thing," Aiden clarified with a disapproving frown. "She thinks people care about that shit."

"They do," Becca protested. "Especially when it comes to promotion time."

Sirus shook his head. "That would be called discrimination. I'm not going to comment on whether or not it still happens, but remember, what goes on in your personal life is none of your boss's business." He glanced at Aiden and then at Becca, then cleared his throat again, clearly uncomfortable. "Which seems to be a good place for me to make my exit, besides, I've got a helicopter to catch."

"Please do," Aiden said, stepping around him.

"Aiden!"

"He understands." Aiden came to stand next to her even as Sirus left the room, but he didn't touch her.

"Oh." Becca wasn't sure what to say. They had so many obstacles to overcome. Yet, he was here, and she had to clear the air. "Aiden, I have to be honest. I went to Las Vegas to get pregnant, but I walked through dozens of casinos and tons of bars before I saw you, and then I knew the search was over."

"Why would you do that? Couldn't you find a local man? Or go to one of those sperm banks or something?" He shuddered. "When I think of what could have happened to you, I just cringe."

"Something special happened to me. I fell in love at first sight," Becca said, reaching for Aiden's hand. "It just took a bit longer for my head to go along with it."

"We're going to be married soon and forever. Don't you worry," Aiden said as if reading her mind. "I love you too much to let you talk me out of your life again."

Becca tugged on his hand, wanting him closer.

But he held back, grimacing. "Ahh, I'm getting ahead of myself again. I would have come to see you last night, but I wanted everything to be just right, and the store didn't open until ten." Aiden got down on one knee next to the bed. "Becca, love of my life, will you put me out of my misery and marry me?" He withdrew a small velvet box from his back pocket and opened it to reveal a simple gold band with a small pear-shaped diamond on it.

"Oh, my goodness. You're going to have to take that back. It's too expensive. We have a house to buy and college to save for." But it was lovely.

"We're not taking it back. This kid is going to college on a scholarship." He winked at her. "Now, not only do I have perfect timing and exquisite taste, but I also have my father's bum knees. Will you accept my proposal, please?"

"Yes! Yes! Now come here and let me show you how much I love you." Becca tugged on his hand again, but this time he took the ring and slid it onto her ring finger.

"It fits," she said in surprise.

"They said we can get it resized after the baby comes." Aiden tucked the ring box between the two flower containers. "I've figured out a way to show you how much I love you." He stood and leaned closer until his lips were almost touching her ear, then he whispered his idea.

"Perfect," Becca said, drawing him down to lie on the narrow bed next to her. "Now kiss me, tell me how things went on the fire, and lie to me when you say you'll never be in that much danger again."

EPILOGUE

"SPIDER, I'D LIKE TO MAKE IT home in one piece," Logan warned from the back seat of Spider's pickup.

"We're going to a fire in Arizona. It'll only take a couple of days to contain. The first fire of the season is never that long," Spider mimicked Logan. That's what Logan had told him ten days ago when they'd left, assuring him that he'd return in plenty of time for this important day. Spider slowed down to take a corner, but didn't slow down enough, sending everything in the truck, including the passengers, listing to one side.

"Spider!" Chainsaw, Golden and Logan all yelled in protest.

"Sheesh, all right. We're at the city limits anyway." Spider let off the gas as he saw his destination up on the right—the Painted Pony restaurant in Silver Bend, Idaho, the place where his Hot Shot team met before they left for a fire and when they came home from a fire.

"Tell me again what this ceremony is for?" Golden asked.

"So that Becca can say, without a doubt, that I'm the father of Charlotte." She'd given birth to a beautiful baby girl with Spider's dark hair and eyes in early October. They'd had a Christmas wedding at a small church down the road, complete with Becca's family and a reception at the Painted Pony.

He pulled into the parking lot of the Painted Pony, and his friends all piled out before he barely had the truck in park. It took them less than a minute to greet their families with huge hugs and boisterous kisses.

Pausing for a moment after shutting the truck door, Spider filled his lungs with the clean mountain air and looked at the Painted Pony's namesake—a life-size plastic horse posed on the wooden porch. Inside, his wife and daughter waited for him. A change in his life awaited him.

And he was ready for it.

When he entered the restaurant, the buzz in the room seemed to stop. Then Becca was threading her way through the crowd, looking better than a wife was supposed to look in a red sheath dress and killer red pumps that made her two inches taller than him. A lesser man would have been intimidated. Spider loved it, loved her and loved the precious chubby baby she carried.

"You're late. You were supposed to be home days ago." With the baby propped on one hip, Becca hugged him fiercely with her free arm. "I can't believe I let you go out to a fire without me."

"You look good enough to eat." He rubbed his cheek against hers. Even though she hadn't lost all of the pregnancy pounds— a fact she continued to complain about—Spider loved her curves. "Promise me dessert later?" He gently brushed her bangs out of her eyes so that he could see the thin scar that had brought them back together. He pressed his lips against it briefly.

Little Charlotte bounced in her mother's arms and flung her upper body in Spider's direction.

"Come to daddy, Charley." He took her into his arms and had to close his eyes against the powerful surge of joy that Charley caused when she flopped herself against his chest and nestled her head in the crook of his neck. "You are a heart-breaker, pumpkin. You're gonna drive the boys in town crazy."

"She's only six months old," Becca chastised him. "Don't go giving her ideas." She leaned closer so that she could see Charlotte's chubby cheeks. "You want to be a rocket scientist, don't you?"

Spider could feel Charley's smile against his neck. She'd been born all smiles and energy. Spider challenged anyone to disagree that Charley hadn't been smiling moments after her birth. The kid knew what life was all about.

Other fire families were finishing up their reunions and moving toward the bar where Sirus's wife, Mary, the owner of the Pony, had set up a podium. Sirus stood behind the podium looking suitably solemn for the occasion. Surprisingly, he'd been the big winner in the Flathead fire betting pool.

Next to him sat Spider's dad, beaming at the crowd despite the bandages on his hands. His cheek was still pink where they'd grafted new skin. He had one more surgery to go before he'd tackle physical therapy. He was living in Spider's old apartment above the barbershop. Spider's family lived a few miles down the road in a two-story clapboard house with a wraparound porch.

When Becca's offer on the house near Boise had fallen through, they'd decided to settle in Silver Bend. Currently, Becca was working part-time from home, and was getting ready to work two days a week in Boise at her new job.

"Hey, Spider."

"Spider, way to go."

"Good to see you, Spider."

The greetings went on as Spider passed through the crowd carrying Charley, his fingers entwined with Becca's. He halted in front of the podium and turned to Becca.

"I'm sorry. I'm still in my fire gear." His Nomex green pants and yellow shirt. He was supposed to wear a suit for the ceremony, but he hadn't gotten home in time to change. At least he'd been able to shower before he'd gotten on the plane in Phoenix.

"You look fine," Becca reassured him, outclassing him in her come hither outfit.

Charley blew bubbles against his neck and started chanting, "Da-da-da-da."

"But we spent so much money on the suit and you really wanted me to wear it."

"Oh, you'll wear it for me later, won't you?" Becca raised her brows, demanding a promise.

The air whooshed out of his lungs. She could still do that to him. Sometimes he thought she was too much woman for him. Every once in awhile, she still got prickly about the age issue, but it really didn't matter to him, and she'd finally seemed to understand that when she'd told Sirus she was going to marry him.

"Hey, son," his dad greeted him.

Spider knelt next to his father's chair. "How're you feeling, Dad?"

"Better every day." Smiling big, the old man leaned forward and caught Charley's eye.

"People want to get home," Sirus said. "We need to get started."

"Okay." Spider stood up. Now that the time had come, Spider felt a bit at odds. In the scheme of things, this was huge, and yet…not.

"Let's get to it people," Sirus addressed the crowd, which immediately had the noise level dropping down to silence. "We are gathered here today to share in the ceremony of the

Rodas family. For many years, we've known this man as Spider, both on the fire and off."

Sirus cleared his throat. "Today, I stand before you to announce that from this day forward, if we are not on a fire, that you should call this man Aiden Rodas. And to make this decree somewhat legal and somewhat binding, you are invited to view Charlotte Ruby Rodas's birth certificate, which lists Aiden Rodas as her father, not Spider."

With a glance in Becca's direction, Sirus continued with a smile. "Those of you who fail to comply, will have to deal with Mrs. Becca Rodas."

"And me," his dad piped in, holding up one bandaged hand like a boxing glove.

Aiden turned his head to look at Becca. She'd told him once that she wouldn't call her child's father Spider. He'd gone to Becca in the hospital with roses and shown her how much he loved her by offering to shed his Hot Shot nickname, the name he'd come to refer to himself by over the years.

"Drinks are on Aiden," Sirus called out.

The crowd whooped it up and moved toward the bar or the tables of food on the far side of the restaurant.

"Da-da-da," Charley cooed in his arms.

Becca squeezed his hand and kissed his cheek. "Thank you, Aiden. You couldn't have given me a more perfect trio of gifts—our daughter, your name and your love."

Aiden grinned. In the embrace of his family, he'd finally found the balance between fear and courage, humor and seriousness, friend and lover, father and son. There was a lot of life he had yet to live, but with a family like his there wasn't much more to yearn for… Except—

"You know, Bec, maybe being an only child wasn't such a good thing."

This time, Becca kissed him properly, leaving them both a bit breathless, ending the kiss by murmuring against his lips, "I have complete faith in you, Aiden. You always seem to know what I need."

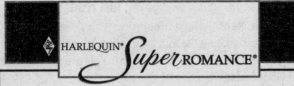

HARLEQUIN *Super*ROMANCE

THE WINTER ROAD

**Some say life has passed Emily Moore by.
They're wrong.
She is just waiting for her moment....**

Her moment arrives when she discovers her friend
Daniel is missing and a stranger—supposedly Daniel's
nephew—is living in his house. Emily has no reason not
to believe him, but odd things are starting to occur.
There are break-ins along Creek Road and no news from
Daniel. Then there's the fact that his "nephew" seems
more interested in Emily than in the family history
he's supposed to be researching.

**Welcome to Three Creeks,
an ordinary little Prairie town where
extraordinary things are about to happen.**

In
THE WINTER ROAD
(Harlequin Superromance #1304),
Caron Todd creates evocative and compelling characters
who could be your over-the-fence neighbors.
You'll really want to get to know them.

Available October 2005.

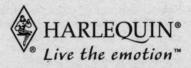

HARLEQUIN®
Live the emotion™

THE OPERATIVES

To save a friend. To protect a child. To end an evil.
Most of us could not bring ourselves to do the
unthinkable—even if it was for the greater good.
The Operatives do whatever it takes.
Because of them, we don't have to.

Sometimes the most dangerous people you know
are the only ones you can trust.

THE OPERATIVES—
an exciting new series by Kay David,
author of *The Guardians*.
Coming soon from Harlequin Superromance
and Signature Select Saga.

NOT WITHOUT HER SON
(Harlequin Superromance #1303), available October 2005.

NOT WITHOUT THE TRUTH
(Harlequin Superromance #1321), available January 2006.

NOT WITHOUT CAUSE
(Harlequin Superromance #1339), available April 2006.

Also,

NOT WITHOUT PROOF
(Signature Select Saga), available July 2005.

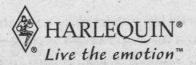

HARLEQUIN®
Live the emotion™

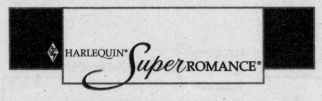

COMING NEXT MONTH

HSRCNM0905